Prologue

Kingsclere, 1077

It had been quite an innocent action, in truth, the attempt of one child to comfort another, for her heartbroken sobs at the loss of her treasure quite unsettled his composure.

What began as a childish challenge— "I dare you to walk out on that log that sticks out into the middle of the brook, for I vow you are too affrighted to try, being but a damsel, after all"—had ended in her falling into the cold water, though not before she had reached the end successfully and was turning to walk back. He had had to rescue her because her kirtle snagged on a submerged branch, so both had ended up drenched and shivering in the cool April wind.

Muddy, and leaving a dripping trail, they had sought refuge in a small room off the front of the barn where extra tack and blankets were kept for the mighty destriers and sleek palfreys of Kingsclere. They were making use of those same blankets to dry their chilled bodies when Aldyth discovered the loss of her beloved green hair ribbon and set up a wail.

Of course, Aldyth had many adornments for her chestnut tresses, but the one lost was the selfsame one that Ranulf had brought her from his trip to London, saying that he had been compelled to purchase it because it matched the jade green hue of her eyes. Now it was swept away by the spring-swollen force of the brook, and she was quite devastatedly sure she would never have anything as lovely again. In addition, her mother would probably beat her for muddying her new forest green gunna and kirtle. The hem of the outer garment also had a long, jagged rent.

All these upsetting thoughts added to her distress until Ranulf simply had had to pull her close and soothe her. Her cool, clammy skin touched his, for they had stripped, the better to huddle up in the blankets and warm themselves before facing her mother's wrath.

Completely unaware in the carnal sense of the feel of her childish breasts against his bare boyish chest, the boy shut his eyes and murmured endearments to her, some in Norman French, some in English. The clean fragrant scent of her hair blended in his nose with the stable aromas of horse, hay and leather—not an unpleasing mixture for a lad of seven, about to leave home to be fostered in the household of the Conqueror himself.

Aldyth had quieted under Ranulf's ministrations, having heard him pledge her more such ribbons of the same color, but then piped up, "But, Ranulf, the next time you will be in London is when you leave to join the court of the king! And then you'll not return until you are a man!" She began to sob afresh.

"Aldyth," he began, sighing into her ear, "I'll be permitted visits occasionally—it's not *banishment,* you know. And if the gift is more important than the giver," he added, holding her away a little so that she could see he was teasing, "I could always pay a courier to bring it . . ."

"Ranulf!" she squealed, embarrassed that she had sounded like a greedy brat in front of the friend that she adored. "I'll show you which is more important!" She flung herself fervently against him, pressing her mouth to his, just as she had seen the dairy maid do to the shepherd.

Aldyth's body had not yet begun to hear the far-off echoes of adolescence and the passionate nature that would be hers, but she did feel a precocious delight in the strength of his sturdy hairless chest against her and the enthusiasm with which he returned her kiss as he pulled her slight form closer.

"Oh, Ranulf, I will miss you so much..."

"And you, too, Aldyth... I didn't know how much until this moment. Wait for me, Aldyth."

Then suddenly, as childish promises were being exchanged, they were blinded as the door from the barn was opened, tentatively at first and then slammed against the adjoining wall to the extent its rusty hinges would allow as the two were seen. Ranulf found himself seized by the shoulder and pulled out into the sunshine near the barn's entrance by Lord Étienne himself, who paused as he recognized the shivering, blinking girl as the daughter of his trusted castellan, Nyle of Sherborne.

With a roar he boxed his son's ears, shouting, "Foolish puppy! Is *this* how you think to prepare for knighthood? By dishonoring the daughter of my vassal?"

"Nay, my lord," spoke up the boy, praying that his voice wouldn't quaver and the tears that threatened would not spill over. Rarely had he had reason to fear his sire, for the Earl of Kingsclere ruled his children with a firm but loving hand. He saw that Lord Étienne had misread the situation and hastened to add, "I was but comforting Aldyth. We fell into the brook and got wet, and she lost her ribbon—"

"And *that* required stripping down until you were as God made you?" Lord Étienne gave a mirthless laugh. "God's blood, I am not so gullible as that! I tumbled many a wench, lad, until I met your mother...'' At the mention of Lady Nichola his voice softened. "But I suggest you wait a few seasons and let one of the many willing serving wenches about the court initiate you! The daughter of Sir Nyle is not for your pawing, hear me, cockerel?''

Then, remembering Aldyth's presence just inside the tack room door, he called softly to her, "We are going. Put your clothes back on and go to your chamber for dry garments.''

Swathed in the blanket, she came to the door, where she could face him. "But, Lord Étienne, Ranulf has given you the right of it—he meant no harm. Please don't punish him or tell my mother and father!''

The earl stood firm. "Don't worry, Aldyth. You will not be blamed. The fault is with my son, who needs to learn the meaning of treating a maid with honor. Go now,'' he said, gesturing in dismissal, and she shut the door as Ranulf was dragged off to a more stringent penance.

"I had hoped to keep him by us until Michaelmas,'' said Lady Nichola that night as Lord Étienne held her close in their great bed. She had every mother's reluctance to release her firstborn son to the joys and responsibilities of manhood, though she knew it was inevitable. That was the way of noble houses. They did not rear their own sons, lest the sons grow too soft under their mothers' watchful eyes.

Once Ranulf left the keep at Kingsclere to join William's court, he would set his foot on the road to manhood, leaving, she feared, his need for the love of a mother forever. But not for the world would she have turned him aside from that road, for a boy kept at home was forever an object of derision and not worthy of knighthood.

"Yes, I know, *m'amie*,'' answered Lord Étienne. He was sensitive to her feelings and knew of the struggle within her to let go of her son and did not disparage her fears. "But you must see he is ready—today's event has proved that, if nothing else."

Lady Nichola could not repress a chuckle. "I'm afraid Sir Nyle would have been ready to come after your heir if he had been told. He idolizes his daughter, you know, as if he cannot believe that he and Mercia between them could have made such a lovely creature."

Lord Étienne smiled in the half-light shed by the embers in the brazier, picturing Sir Nyle's and Mercia's sturdy Saxon faces and the chestnut-haired beauty who had been born two years after Ranulf. The castellan and his family were visiting now from Sherborne, as Sir Nyle needed to consult with his lord about that keep's need for more adequate defenses.

He reached to pull the hangings of the bed closed around them. "I'll warrant Mercia did not hold the wench blameless when she saw the muddy dress, though to her sire, Aldyth can do no wrong. She's probably no more able to sit down than our Ranulf." Then, feeling they had discussed the children enough, he reached for his wife.

Two mornings later, Ranulf, accompanied by his father, mounted his palfrey manfully and set out for London, unaware that from the tower window Aldyth watched with tears coursing down her wan cheeks.

Chapter One

Sherborne, 1088

"The earl's son is back, I hear," Helwise the cook informed Goda the laundress as both drew water from the well in the bailey of Sherborne Castle.

"Young Ranulf back at Kingsclere? Has he left the court, then?"

"Nay. O' course not," the cook scoffed. "He's just here for a visit. And it's *Lord* Ranulf now," she added importantly. "Knighted by King William himself, he was. The first William, that is, not the new one—and the new one's gifted him with his own manor near Winchester."

But Goda was not interested in who reigned in far-off Winchester and London. They were all Norman, so what made the difference? She started to walk away, but Helwise was not about to lose her audience so easily.

"I just happened to be in the hall when Sir Nyle and his daughter were breaking their fasts, and Kingsclere's steward arrived with the letter. Sir Nyle had it read aloud— though you could have guessed the message if ye were deaf from Lady Aldyth's face," Helwise concluded with a snort.

"What d'ye mean?"

The remarks carried on the clear morning air to the stable door, where Aldyth was about to step back out into the sunlight after paying a visit to Robin, her palfrey. Hearing her name, she moved into the shadows, curious as to what Helwise would say.

"You'd have thought Saint Michael 'imself was coming for a fortnight," Helwise said.

"Humph," the other sniffed. "If you ask me, *that* wench has been allowed to run wild a little too long."

"Indeed!" Helwise agreed, warming to her subject. "Just imagine, a young woman of eighteen and not married yet! She should be a wife with a babe or two by now if her father had not allowed her to think overmuch of herself."

"It's Sir Nyle's fault, really. He's spoiled the wench ever since her mother died."

"Well, he's done her no favor if she thinks she will wed a young Norman who'll be an earl one day—he can look higher than an English castellan's daughter for a bride!"

"Aye, he'll know just what to do with her, and marriage won't be included," the laundress opined darkly.

"She's ripe for that sort o' trouble, all right," the cook said. "He'll ruin her and break 'er heart, and then a good English lad won't even look at her."

Both women *tsk-tsked* and strolled off in the direction of the hall, leaving the subject of their gossip fuming in the shadows, her fists clenched in the effort it took to keep herself from bursting out into the sunlight and denouncing them for the nasty cows they were.

The nerve of them, saying she was spoilt and willful and implying she was not good enough to be Sir Ranulf's wife. *They'd* see when he galloped into the bailey on his mighty destrier and begged her father for her hand in marriage. They'd be forced to eat their words as they cooked and laundered their way to exhaustion preparing for her wedding.

Ah, the wedding. Aldyth leaned back against the barn door. Her tensed features relaxed into a dreamy smile as she pictured herself standing in the church porch with Ranulf as they pledged themselves as man and wife. She would be dressed in green, naturally, the jade green that he loved because it matched her eyes. She would wear her light brown tresses loose and shining, crowned by a wreath of flowers woven with a jade green ribbon.

She had not seen Ranulf of Kingsclere since the Christmas four years ago when he had come home rather than crossed the Channel to spend the holiday in Rouen with William's court. He had been a well-favored youth then, handsome enough to turn any maid's head with his merry dark eyes, straight patrician nose and laughing mouth. Already he had been nearly as tall as his sire, and those of an age to remember remarked that Ranulf's thatch of unruly raven hair was the same inky black as Earl Étienne's had been before a score of years had sprinkled it with gray.

He'd not had much time for her then, being far too intent on impressing his royal visitor, Prince Henry, with the glories of Kingsclere Castle and showing off what a sophisticated fellow he was to an amused Earl Étienne and Lady Nichola, his parents. But she had forgiven him all the hurts he had so carelessly inflicted on her by his neglect when, flushed with mulled wine, he had caught her under the mistletoe hanging in the entrance to the hall and had kissed her with an expertise that left her breathless. He had sent her off afterward with a wink that she knew meant, *Be patient. Someday you'll be mine and I'll not stop at kisses*.

Ranulf would have only grown more handsome in the intervening years. He'd be like every damsel's dream hero standing next to her, lean-hipped and broad-shouldered, his brown eyes gleaming as he admired her. He'd smile as he remembered the time she'd gone wading in the brook on a dare from him and lost the green ribbon he'd given her, and he had comforted her in Kingsclere's barn. She'd paid for those childish caresses by a birching that had kept her standing for a week....

She grinned, remembering. It was this expression Sir Nyle surprised on her face as he rounded the corner and came into the barn.

"What mischief have you been plotting with Robin, then?" her father asked, his own features relaxing as he looked into the green eyes nearly on a level with his own. "I've learned to beware that look over the years!"

"Why, nothing, Father," she said, full of innocence as she peered at him through her lashes. Seeing that he was still skeptical, she turned the full force of her considerable charm on him. "I was just thinking of the last time Ranulf and I went . . . uh, swimming."

He couldn't resist her. When he looked at her, his heart melted with amazement that she was his daughter. Oh, he had no doubts as to her paternity. His own light brown hair was echoed in the chestnut hue of her thick, straight tresses, several strands of which had escaped the braid beneath the snowy *couvre-chef*. Like him and Mercia, she was tall, but where Mercia had been statuesque, Aldyth was slender and willowy. Her mother had contributed that proud, determined chin, but from which of her sturdy English parents had she gained that milky, sun-kissed complexion, that lush, wide mouth and even, pearly teeth or those startling green eyes? It was enough to make a man wonder why he had been so blessed, when girls born to kings were often as ugly as the wattle-and-daub dwellings from which Sir Nyle had sprung.

He knew he should have been more firm with her in the years since her mother had died giving birth to her younger

brother, Warin, when Aldyth had been eight. Sir Nyle had
sent her to Kingsclere so that she could grow up under Lady
Nichola's care while he learned to live again without Mercia.
Her stay at his liege lord's castle had lasted until Aldyth was
thirteen and home on a visit. She had seen the shambles his
hall had become without a chatelaine's care and refused to
leave again.

She ran his household with a firm hand, having learned
all the skills of a chatelaine from the earl's wife. The hall,
which had become little more than a drafty barn housing the
castellan's men-at-arms, hounds and frowsy serving
wenches, had been swept clean of accumulated debris.
Those who desired to go on serving Sir Nyle learned that his
daughter could not be ignored and had better be obeyed.
Men-at-arms wore clean tunics and learned to confine their
drinking and wenching to off-duty hours. Serving wenches
who combined harlotry with their more regular duties were
apt, if they refused to mend their ways, to find themselves
put out beyond the palisade to ply their trade however they
could. Soap was again required at Sherborne, for Aldyth
refused to tolerate servants who went all winter without
bathing. Rushes were regularly changed on the floors, and
tapestries, which Aldyth wove, covered the newly whitewashed walls.

Having set her father's hall in order, Aldyth answered to
no one, not even Sir Nyle. She did as she pleased. And it did
not please her to marry.

A handful of suitable young men, English freedmen who
had managed to gain small holdings even under the Norman
reign, had applied to Sir Nyle for the hand of his beautiful
though willful daughter. She had politely refused them all,
and the astonishing thing was that Sir Nyle had allowed her
to do so. He knew he shouldn't, for girls were expected to
marry as they were told, but he admitted to himself that he

couldn't bear to impose on his beloved daughter a choice that was not to her liking. He told himself that he was selfish, that the real reason was that he just didn't want to see the hall fall into disarray again, a problem that could readily be remedied if he would just bestir himself to remarry.

He suspected she was waiting for Ranulf, his liege lord's son. He feared that she was doomed to disappointment on that score, for if rumors could be trusted, Ranulf seemed to have outgrown the childish affection he and Aldyth had shared.

Ah, well. Aldyth would have to learn for herself, he thought, still gazing at the winsome young woman.

"Did you...*want* something, Father?" Aldyth inquired, an amused gleam lighting her leaf green eyes. He'd swear she could read his mind sometimes, just as Mercia had been able to.

"I? Uh...yes. I've come to ask you what you'd think of paying a visit to Kingsclere? We could see your brothers, and we should pay our respects to our liege's son. He'll have all the news from London."

"Oh!" The sudden radiance of her face was startling and, to her father, alarming. "I...I'd love to see Warin and find out how he likes his duties as a page, and Godric, too. And of course it would be interesting to hear about the new king. I hear he is called Rufus because of his ruddy complexion," she said, looking down, her voice carefully casual.

Sir Nyle was not deceived, but he responded mildly that he was sure Lord Ranulf would be able to tell them all about the successor to the Conqueror, who by all reports was a very different man from his father.

They departed on the short journey from Sherborne to Kingsclere after the midday meal the next day.

The October air was crisp, and the sun revealed the oaks, yew and ash in their full gold and crimson glory. Squirrels leaped from bough to bough, collecting their fall supply of acorns before the coming cold days kept them snugly dozing in their nests. The action of one particularly rambunctious rodent sent a shower of multicolored leaves on the small mounted party, causing Aldyth to laugh.

They came upon few people as they rode through the forest. The only indication that any humans lived there was the occasional charcoal burner's hovel they glimpsed through the thick undergrowth. Aldyth did not doubt that their passage was marked by other, less honest denizens of the wooded area, but she knew the presence of their mounted, armed escort discouraged would-be robbers.

They came into rolling farmland as they journeyed farther, and glimpsed serfs in the fields bringing in the harvest. Taking advantage of the last few days of mild weather, many of the men were bare to the waist, their backs glistening with sweat as they toiled. They had been hard at work since the dawn and would labor till the sun set, with only a brief respite at midday to eat their cheese and drink their small beer. They eyed the traveling party at the edge of their fields curiously; one bold youth even hazarded a wave as he spied the comely young woman on her bay palfrey. After a glance to assure herself that Sir Nyle's attention was elsewhere, she waved back.

Father and daughter had been appreciating the autumn scenery for many minutes when Aldyth broke the silence. "I wonder if I'll even recognize Warin—he will have grown so much since he went to serve at Kingsclere. I suppose he's conquered his homesickness by now."

"Aye, and doubtless he'd not appreciate it if you were to remind him he ever longed to come home," Sir Nyle said with a chuckle. "He did have a rough time of it at first,

Lord Étienne told me, being the only English lad among the pages with all the rest of them Normans determined to make him feel he was but an upstart. Our Warin soon showed them, though, that good English blood is nothing to be sneered at." Sir Nyle smiled as he remembered reports of youthful Norman noses bloodied—with Earl Étienne's blessing—until his son was an accepted member of the Kingsclere household.

"I wonder how we'll find Godric?" Aldyth mused. Godric was Aldyth's elder brother, born in the same year as Ranulf. He had long since graduated the duties of page and served as squire to the earl.

"I hope so. He was such a sullen lad when I saw him last. And I'll be damned if I understand why he resents them so much, when he's known nothing else."

"Why indeed, since *you* came to terms with them, Father, after Senlac."

"But he's come in contact with many English who are still resentful of the Norman invasion—you must remember, daughter, I've been more fortunate than many of my countrymen by having Earl Étienne as my liege lord and friend. I have risen to castellan, while most of them were demoted to serf status. So I suppose Godric sees me as being a traitor to true Englishmen."

"If he thinks the English will ever be what they were before Hastings, he's a fool," Aldyth said with spirit. Privately she planned to have a talk with her elder brother if the opportunity presented itself. Godric should know how his rebellious attitude was worrying their father. There was nothing she could do about it now, however, so she might as well enjoy the ride and plan what she was going to wear when she saw Ranulf and what she would say to him, the man she loved.

* * *

The object of her thoughts was nowhere in evidence as they rode into the bailey at Kingsclere and were ushered into the solar, where Earl Étienne and Countess Nichola greeted them warmly. It was more than an hour until supper, but Lady Nichola assured them she was having heated water brought up for them to wash and meanwhile they must warm themselves with a cup of mulled wine. Aldyth and her father accepted the spiced beverage gratefully, for the sky had grown cloudy and the temperature colder during the last portion of their journey.

Though she had looked for Ranulf, Aldyth was glad she would have a chance to wash the scent of horse and the stains of travel away before she saw him. She would wear the jade green gown with some matching ribbons she had bought from a peddler twined through her hair to remind him of their disastrous dunking in the brook...

"I—I'm sorry, Lady Nichola. I fear I was not attending..." Aldyth stammered, realizing belatedly that the countess had been addressing her.

"I was saying what a beautiful young woman you've become, Aldyth," Lady Nichola repeated gently, unperturbed.

"And how can it be that you remain unmarried, as pretty as you are?" Earl Étienne joined in. "I would think the young cubs around Sherborne would be flocking into the hall, suing for your hand."

Aldyth blushed to the roots of her hair and looked down in confusion while her father spoke up. "Aye, that they do, my lord. She could have her pick of the shire. I'm afraid my Aldyth is entirely too choosy, though I'll not deny I've enjoyed having her at home to keep me company."

"Fie, my lord, you've embarrassed the girl," Lady Nichola chided her husband. "I have sent for Warin, and no doubt you will see Godric at supper," she said, turning back to her guests. "I knew you would be eager to— Ah, here he is!" She turned to the entranceway as a lad with the same brown hair as Aldyth bounded through it, then remembered his manners and bowed with all the grace of a French courtier.

"That's better," Earl Étienne said, approving the bow, while Aldyth marveled to see that Warin lacked but an inch till he was as tall as she. He was all long legs and arms, reminding her of a colt, and his cheeks remained smooth. His voice, when he spoke, showed an adolescent boy's tendency to leap from bass to treble, but the courteous greeting he murmured in Norman French was flawless.

"You have made good progress, son," approved Sir Nyle in the same tongue, then held out his arms, speaking in English. "Enough of that, now! Come greet your sister and me!"

After a nervous glance to make sure he had his lord's permission to abandon his newfound dignity temporarily, Warin leaped to comply, becoming just another boy reunited with his family. Excitedly he told them of his progress at tilting at the quintain, that dangerous game in which a horseman gallops at target, knowing that if he does not hit the target just right with his lance, a whirling, cloth-wrapped paddle will swing around from behind to buffet him from his saddle.

"I have become very good with my bow, too, Father," he added. "I can hit the bull's-eye at a hundred paces. And, Aldyth, wait till you see my puppy! He's a brachet, out of one of my lord's prized hunting bitches! His name is Roland, for the hero of the romance! And I can show you my lord's hawks—Lord Étienne says I'm the only page quiet enough to go into his mews!"

"You are not demonstrating that virtue now!" teased the earl.

Warin made a visible effort to calm himself. "I've saved the best news for last, though."

"Oh? And what is that?" his sister asked, smiling at his barely contained excitement.

"When Lord Ranulf goes back to court, I am to go, too! As his page!"

"I'm proud of you, son," Sir Nyle said, patting his son's shoulder. "You've done well."

"Your father and sister are no doubt tired from their journey," Lord Étienne interposed, "and will want to bathe before supper. Why don't you escort them to their chambers, then return to the hall to help set up for the meal? I'm sure some of this will keep until then."

Sir Nyle rose to go, but Aldyth had to know the answer to the question that had been tormenting her since their arrival. "My lord, will R—*Lord* Ranulf be present at supper? I . . . that is, *we* wanted to congratulate him upon his being granted a barony and hear all about the coronation of the new king." She was aware that she was blushing afresh as she said the name of her childhood sweetheart.

Aldyth was puzzled at the veiled look that shot from the earl to his countess before he replied to her question. "Yes, he'll be there."

Aldyth noticed the curtness of the earl's answer. She dared an uncertain glance at Lady Nichola, who seemed a little at a loss for words.

"I'm afraid you will find Ranulf slightly, uh, *changed* now that he lives at court," the countess said, her words uncharacteristically vague. "He's become quite the courtier, I suppose you'd say."

"That's not what I'd call him," growled Earl Étienne at her side. But at a look from his wife, he fell quiet again, leaving Aldyth to ponder the countess's troubled eyes.

Chapter Two

Though the steaming water in the big wooden tub tempted her to linger, Aldyth hurried through her bath and into the green gown that she knew became her well. She was eager to return to the hall below. Perhaps she would encounter Ranulf there before the supper horn blew and they would have time for conversation. Perhaps he would even ask her to sit by him!

Once in the great hall, however, the only familiar face was her father's. Sir Nyle was a simple man who had not taken long with his ablutions, either. Seeing her, he motioned Aldyth to the high table where he waited. Since there were no guests of higher rank, Aldyth and her father would have the honor of sitting to the right of the Earl and Countess of Kingsclere.

Below the dais, all the lesser folk were finding their places at the intersecting trestle tables laid with trenchers. The hall was filled with the babble of conversation as those who served the castle greeted one another, only to fall respectfully silent as the earl, his countess and their daughters, Adele and Agathe, made their way to their places at the center of the dais.

Kingsclere's priest said a sonorous grace, and then, at a nod from the earl, the servers began bringing around platters of roast meats, loaves of bread and bowls of stewed vegetables and baked apples. The buzz of conversation began again as the loaves were broken and the platters of food were passed down the tables.

Godric appeared in front of the high table, kneeling gracefully in front of the earl and his lady with his platter of roast venison. As squire, it was his duty to serve his liege lord. He would eat only after they were finished. He smiled when he saw his father and sister and promised to meet with them later.

"He looks well," Aldyth commented to her father. Godric had grown. His shoulder muscles strained the livery tunic of blue and crimson. His flaxen hair, though longer than a Norman youth's, was nevertheless clean and well brushed. A pale mustache that Aldyth had not seen before graced his upper lip, accenting a face that was colored by much time spent outdoors.

"Aye. Perhaps he is over his youthful rebelliousness. And see—there's Warin!" Sir Nyle said, and pointed while Aldyth looked down the table to where her younger brother was struggling to pour wine from a huge flagon without leaving any crimson stains on the spotless linen. He paused to bestow a cheerful grin on his sister, which Aldyth returned, her heart swelling with pride over her two handsome brothers.

But where was Ranulf? The place to the left of the earl and countess was still empty. Surely he didn't intend to miss the meal.

Aldyth was determined she would not betray her feelings a second time by asking about Ranulf. The delicious meal, however, went almost untasted and their hosts' courteous talk only half-heard as she watched the arched entranceway for any late arrivals.

Just as the second course was being served, a huge bear-like man with a black patch over one eye entered the hall and surveyed the lower tables for a seat. He must surely be the tallest man I've ever seen, thought Aldyth. She wondered briefly if he had lost the sight of the one eye in battle. A shaggy reddish beard matched the unruly thatch of crinkly hair that grew on his head, further contributing to the man's resemblance to a bear.

His immense size, plus Godric's arrival before them with a platter of capon, prevented Aldyth at first from seeing the man who stood behind the giant. When she looked up again, however, the big man had sat down, and she saw the figure making his way to the dais.

The man moved languidly, his gait drawing attention to a pair of scarlet leather shoes with ridiculous toes that curled up stiffly like rams' horns. He paused, reaching up an elegant, long-fingered hand to smooth shoulder-length curled black hair, then his thumb and forefinger stroked his small beard and mustaches.

His dark eyes roamed the tables with a bored indifference as he strolled the length of the hall. He was clothed in a black velvet tunic emblazoned with the silver unicorn that was the Kingsclere emblem.

Who was he? Aldyth wondered with a shudder of distaste as he reached the dais, then she was conscious of the earl stiffening as a wave of musky scent swept over them.

"I pray your forgiveness for my lateness, Father," the man drawled. "I just *couldn't* seem to pick which ring to wear." As if to illustrate his plight, a large ruby winked obscenely on his hand as he gestured.

A vein bulged dangerously in the earl's forehead as he answered, his voice a growl, "We have *guests*, Ranulf. Perhaps you would like to make your greetings to them and

beg their pardon for your rudeness before you seat yourself."

This coxcomb of a knight was *Ranulf?* The youth whose
virile charm she had always remembered with a certain
warmth and a quickening of her pulse? Aldyth felt the blood
drain from her face as she heard him drawl a greeting to her
father and then move to stand in front of her place.

Her eyes met his as he raised the hand she had left lying
on the linen cloth to his lips.

"Lady Aldyth, well met. It has been a long time," he
said. Within the dark depths of his eyes danced amusement
at her discomfiture. "You have grown into a beautiful
damoiselle, but then, you always were a comely maiden,
even when soaking wet."

"I th-thank you, m-my lord," she stammered at last. For
the life of her, she could think of nothing to say to this
transformed creature, and she knew he knew it.

Mercifully, he cut short the embarrassing moment. "Go
on with your meal, Aldyth. We will have time to talk later,"
he said, going around the table to seat himself at his father's left. As soon as he had heaped his plate with a selection of delicacies offered by Godric, he engaged the priest
on his other side in conversation.

Aldyth, whose mind was still whirling in confusion, felt
Lady Nichola's eyes upon her. "I fear you find our son
much changed, my dear," the countess whispered. "I, too,
was rather startled when he arrived from London dressed in
that mode, but he assures me 'tis merely the fashion at
William Rufus's court."

"All the young nobles go about . . . like that?" Aldyth
asked in disbelief.

"They do if they have no self-respect," Lord Étienne
growled, not troubling to lower his voice as his wife had
done. "Bah! The Conqueror must be rolling about in his

grave if he **is** aware that men appear dressed almost as women now, in flowing garments with trailing sleeves, silly shoes and scented, curled hair nigh long as a woman's!''

His words attracted his son's attention. Pausing with his eating dagger poised above his plate, Ranulf said mildly, "Surely each new reign will set new fashions, Father. Mayhap your sire looked askance at the shaven napes that were popular in *your* youth."

Lord Étienne's face grew flushed with anger. "My father was dead long before our duke became King of England, but that is beside the point. No one ever had cause to suspect my manhood from my style of dress!" He ignored the gentle, restraining hand that his wife laid upon his shoulder.

It was an insult that was clearly heard, for the entire hall had hushed at the heated words thrown by the earl at his heir. Aldyth watched as Ranulf's face paled, but he only raised a languid hand to cover a yawn. Then he said in an infuriatingly lazy drawl, "Father, please. You'll shock the guests."

Lord Étienne ignored his wife's entreating look. "As if *you* have not already done so? And by what right does your precious Rufus have the crown anyway? He isn't the eldest son of the Conqueror!"

"He's not *my* precious anything," Ranulf said. "But he *is* the Conqueror's choice as his successor. Would you give the throne to reckless Robert, who can't even rule his own duchy?"

"At least he has proved he's a man by siring a bastard or two. From what I hear, I doubt if Rufus is capable! And to look at you—" his angry eyes took in the long beringed fingers and his son's shoulder-length hair "—no one would guess you were capable, either. Perhaps your younger brother Richard will eventually be my heir—if he does not take after you."

Now he had gone too far. In the absolute silence that had
descended upon the diners, Ranulf rose, his chair scraping
across the stone floor of the dais. Gone was the languid la-
ziness. His hand went to where his sword would have been.
"Be careful, my lord. Other ears might call your opinions
about the king treasonous. And as for my abilities, well, I
asked if I might bring my leman so that my bed here would
be as warm as she keeps it at court, but you refused, lest my
mistress's presence here distress my lady mother. The sight
of Vivienne and the love children she had borne me would
have put the lie to your fears, though, my lord father." With
those parting words he stalked from the hall, head held high,
two spots of color on his angular cheekbones.

"That Norman trollop? Under the same roof as your
mother? I think not!" his father roared after him, but his
son did not slacken his pace.

For the rest of the meal, Aldyth kept her eyes glued to the
table. No one knew what to say.

Pleading a headache—which was the truth—Aldyth excused herself before the sweet wafers were passed and sought
the refuge of her chamber. She couldn't stand any longer the
sight of Lady Nichola's pale, strained face.

She paced back and forth in the small chamber, but the
images of Ranulf, with his long, curled hair and ridiculous
shoes, still rose up to mock her. He had boasted of a mistress who had not only shared his bed but given him children.

How could she have been so wrong about a man? She felt
like such a fool, having loved Ranulf ever since she was a
little girl. Oh, she knew well enough that men hardly ever
came to their marriage beds inexperienced virgins like the
virtuous damsels they expected to wed. Men had needs,
needs they satisfied with a certain kind of woman before
they married or when they were away from their wives for

long periods of time. It was called a sin by the Church, and those who indulged in it confessed their sins eventually, did penance and resolved to do better. They did not boast of their mistresses and bastards in front of their mothers and the gentlewomen they would marry!

She would never think of him again, she vowed. But she knew even as the thought was formed she would not keep such a vow. She had loved him from childhood, and she loved him still. The kind, thoughtful, affectionate boy he had been was still buried within the man he had become. And he *had* seemed pleased to see her and to talk with her later. Might that not mean he still cared for her as he had years ago?

She still loved him. And if there was a chance he still loved her, was it not her duty to use that love to bring Ranulf back to the right path? Once he knew the love of a good woman, of a lady who was suitable to marry the heir to an earldom, he would surely not need a mistress. Aldyth expected him to support his children, of course. They were innocent. If he wanted to bring them into her household, she would accept them gladly, for they were of his blood.

Tomorrow she would seek him out, she decided, and make sure he knew that she remembered the love they had for each other once, and that she loved him still.

A soft knock sounded at the entrance of her room, startling her from her pacing. For a moment she just stared stupidly at the door, wondering who it could be and if she could possibly send the person away without showing her tear-stained face. Most especially, she could not face her father tonight.

The knock sounded again. Whoever it was would have to be answered. Aldyth hoped it was a tirewoman sent by the countess to attend her. She looked forward to having the back of her *bliaut* unlaced so she could undress and go to bed. However, it was Godric rather than a servant who stood at the threshold, bearing a tray with a flagon of wine and two carved wooden cups.

"May I come in? I thought you could use a bit more wine to help you sleep," her elder brother said.

She motioned him inside, taking a deep breath and hoping the tears no longer showed where they had trickled down her cheeks. "I'm glad you came, Godric. I had wanted to talk with you, but I was too tired to stay in the hall any longer," she lied.

"You mean you were upset by the spectacle that Norman lordling made of himself," Godric said shrewdly.

She nodded, helpless to prevent the flood of tears that cascaded down her cheeks again. Sobbing, she crumpled, and Godric gathered her into a brotherly embrace, stroking her hair and murmuring to her in soothing English as if she were a little girl. "Hush now, sister. I know you hurt because you loved him, but surely you see that must be in the past now."

She drew back and stared at him. "You—you knew?" She thought she had kept her heart's secrets well hidden.

"Yes, I knew," Godric said with a small smile. "Your heart was in your eyes tonight, sister. But never fear, it shall remain our secret. Ranulf is not for you, Aldyth, nor should any of the foreign invaders be considered a fit mate for a good English girl. Choose an Englishman, Aldyth—there are even a few that the damned Normans haven't totally dispossessed, but it matters not if he is poor. It will not be long until we English rise again and drive the Norman nithings right into the sea!"

The passion in his words distracted her from her sadness. "Godric, I thought you had learned the error of your ways! Surely you don't think England can return to the days of King Harold. Brother, the Normans have been here all our lives.''

''Bah! One generation! There are still good Englishmen who would drive them back to where they belong and slaughter the ones who won't go. They didn't kill all the patriots on Senlac field. What I've learned, Aldyth, is to pretend, to fool the Normans who are the masters for now—until the time is right.''

She stared at him in the flickering light of the fat tallow candle, chilled. Suddenly he seemed more like a stranger to her than a dear brother. Surely the tall youth with the zealot's gleam in his eye couldn't be the same towheaded lad who had patiently taught her to play cat's cradle and who had played at soldiers with Lord Étienne's sons?

''Be careful, Godric. I think you underestimate the hold the Normans have on England. I don't think we can go back to bygone days.'' She raised a hand when she saw he was eager to debate the subject. ''I'm sorry, brother, but my head is aching terribly. I think I am just fatigued from the journey, but would you mind summoning my tirewoman for me? I'd like to get undressed and get some rest.''

Godric took the hint. ''We can visit longer on the morrow, when you're feeling better, sister. Good night.'' He left after kissing her softly on the forehead.

She would have been surprised to know that Ranulf also paced his chamber, but he was not alone.

''By God's toenails, Urse, I don't know if I can carry on this masquerade,'' he muttered to the bearlike man who sat thoughtfully watching him wear a path in the rushes on the floor. ''I even sicken myself. I'm not sure if any loyalty is worth what is being asked of me.''

There was no sign of a languid courtier's stroll as he prowled the length and breadth of his chamber; instead, his catlike grace put the other man in mind of a caged leopard. A very *male* leopard.

"Surely tonight is the most difficult time you'll have," Urse offered hopefully. "Now that the change in you has been revealed, so to speak, you just have to maintain the pretense. You were *most* convincing, you know. Rufus would have been proud to call you one of his inner circle."

Ranulf shuddered. "Jésu forfend! My lord father must be cursing the seed that created me, and I couldn't even look my mother in the eye. She's probably on her knees at her prie-dieu even now, asking heaven to show me the error of my wicked ways so that she might have legitimate grandchildren to dandle on her knee."

"No doubt, but bad as that is, I suspect the real curse of your distress is the damsel Aldyth."

Ranulf spun on his heel, striking the whitewashed wall with his closed fist. "Damn you, you Breton scoundrel, you're entirely too clever. Yes, it was the sight of Aldyth's shocked face that hurt most of all—and the way she refused to look at me after that first disbelieving glance. Who'd ever have guessed that she'd still be unwed, and worse luck, that she'd be here this even? I'd assumed she'd forgotten me years ago and married some Englishman while I was off fighting the French in the Vexin for the old Conqueror. I pictured her a contented wife with a babe or two! I've never forgotten her, you know."

Urse snorted skeptically.

"I'm neither a monk nor a saint," Ranulf retorted. "Just a man, despite what my sire thinks. And no matter what sort of female I have had dalliances with, it was her face I saw, with those eyes of jade and that river of silky brown hair. Aldyth of Sherborne." His voice was bleak as he said the name. "*Eh bien,* she'll not want me now. I saw how she looked as I bragged of Vivienne and her babes! If only I could tell her—''

''Are you sure you must carry on this masquerade even at home?'' Urse interrupted. ''Surely you can let your father and mother in on the secret?''

''Nay, I'm depending on their shocked reaction to make this disguise that much more convincing. I'm sure none of them would be able to act as outraged if they knew it was but a pretense. Father frequently has guests at Kingsclere, important lords whose eyes see much, and servants talk, you know. I knew it was going to be difficult, gulling my parents like this. I just hadn't counted on having to live a lie before Aldyth, too. 'Twas obvious I am no longer her hero of chivalry.''

''Ah, I think you're giving up too easily,'' Urse said with a chuckle. ''I think if you talk sweetly to the maiden, she will still purr for you.''

''I'm not looking for a cat,'' Ranulf snapped. ''Aldyth is a lady, the daughter of my father's castellan and not for toying with.''

Urse shrugged. ''Then wed her. She will keep your secrets, I'd wager.''

''Nay,'' said Ranulf, beginning to pace again. ''It's a dangerous, deep game I'm playing. Love is a luxury I cannot afford to distract myself with right now. I do not know what I will be called on to do or where I will be asked to go on my lord's behalf. Nor would I expose Aldyth to the reprisals that might come her way if the king discovers the game.''

''Mayhap you won't have to play the game for long,'' Urse pointed out thoughtfully. ''Rufus is as much addicted to the pleasures of war as to his vices. Much can happen to shorten a warrior king's life, you know. Meanwhile, by acting as if you are one of Rufus's languid courtiers, you will be trusted by the King, and so you will be able to keep your true lord informed of happenings at the royal court. He will therefore be in a position to act quickly—and I think he will make it worth your while.''

''Mayhap,'' agreed Ranulf. ''But Aldyth must be lost to me. I doubt my lord can recompense me for that.''

Chapter Three

Ranulf tossed and turned all night long, pondering Urse's words. *Must I carry on the masquerade even at home? Surely I could be myself at home, with my parents? And Lady Aldyth would keep my secrets.* It became an echoing refrain, throbbing in time with the headache that pulsed dully in his temples: *Tell them, tell them, tell them . . .*

It was a very seductive thought. What a relief it would be to take his father and mother aside and assure them that what they were seeing was just a pose, one that could be abandoned as soon as Rufus was no longer on the throne. His mother's brow would magically lose its troubled furrow, and his father would stop snarling and pacing like an enraged lion whenever his heir was in the room.

Which was precisely why he couldn't tell them. His father would try to carry on the pretense that he was enraged and disgusted at the debauchee his son had become. Oh, he would make an effort, whenever they were in company, to criticize him on some point of his clothing. But the smoldering glare would be gone from the dark eyes so like Ranulf's, and he would again seek out his son's company as before. They would be seen walking companionably around the bailey or on the parapet, and like as not, Lord Étienne's arm would be affectionately around his son's shoulders.

Even if only servants' sharp eyes spotted them behaving as a normal father and son, servants talked—to other servants or to their masters, the very lords Ranulf was seeking to fool. No, he couldn't tell his father, or even his mother, for Lady Nichola would want to relieve her husband's worry over his errant son.

His mind turned to Aldyth. The sight of her had been like waking to a remembered dream. Ranulf sighed in the darkness, amazed that he had ever let the distance between them, the glamor of serving at court and the excitement of fighting in France, allow him to forget even for a little while how much he loved Aldyth. She had been a skinny, freckle-faced brat when she had dogged his footsteps and won his heart. Now Aldyth of Sherborne was a breathtakingly beautiful woman, with hair of burnished chestnut, eyes as green as jade and a lissome body curved in all the right places. A woman he could not have.

He ground his teeth in frustration that went far beyond his body's needs. Those could be satisfied easily enough. Many of the serving wenches at Kingsclere had made it clear they would welcome the earl's son in their bed. But all of these were a poor substitute for Aldyth. By the rood, if he could possess her— His blood ran hot at the thought of it, of being able to come to her and drop this disguise for a few hours in the haven of her arms. But it could not be, as he had explained to Urse this even. He dared not let himself be distracted from his purpose, even to love Aldyth. They could both end up paying too high a price for their passion.

It was dawn when Aldyth wakened from the deep sleep into which she had finally fallen. She hadn't missed mass, had she? She had wanted to be sure to pray for heaven's blessing on her plans! Hurriedly, she jumped out of bed and splashed some ice-cold water onto her face.

Sleep had not come easily to her, either. Her brain could not stop racing thither and yon, imagining the things she would say when—and if—she found Ranulf alone. She must be sweet and winsome, a maiden worthy to be his wife but with womanly wiles enough to compete with and surpass those of his Norman mistress. She wondered what she looked like, this Vivienne. Was she willowy and fair or petite and buxom, a lush, midnight-tressed armful? Aldyth, forgetting the pride she had always felt in her shining, thick chestnut hair, felt like a homely sparrow with ugly, drab plumage. Surely she did not have the attributes needed to lure such a man from such a woman! But she must, she must! She would pray, involving the Lord's aid in the campaign.

Even the hot posset offered by the tirewoman had not quickly brought the oblivion she craved, the freedom from the crushing disappointment she felt when she thought of the man Ranulf had become.

Lying awake, she had mentally reviewed the garments she had brought with her and decided which would make the most of her best features, her hair and her eyes. Now she pulled these, a *chainse* of fine linen dyed with saffron and a *bliaut* of russet wool with long trailing sleeves, from her iron-bound traveling chest and donned them hurriedly in the chill air. Aldyth combed the tangles from her hair and divided it into two braids. On her head she placed a little *couvre-chef* or veil, making sure her braids were pulled forward so they would show. Perhaps she could contrive to make sure the veil came loose if he embraced her? She wished she dared come to him with her hair unbound, but that was a harlot's trick, and one she would leave to Vivienne—until the night she, Aldyth, came to Ranulf in their marriage bed.

Attracted by the noise from the bailey, she gazed out her arrow-loop window at the bustling activity three stories below. A pair of servants coming from the castle kitchen carried platters of browned loaves, whose freshly baked aroma reached her even at her lofty height. A smith shod a restive horse tethered outside his shop, while from the armorer's shed came the clang of metal on steel. In the far corner of the bailey, a bell tolled, calling the castle folk to mass in the small stone church.

Good! She hadn't missed the service! Full of purpose, she hastened to attend. It was always a treat to hear the melodious Latin chanting of Kingsclere's priest compared to the monotonous droning of the unlettered English priest at Sherborne, but now she had a special need of God's blessing.

By the time she had descended the winding stone stairway and crossed the bailey, the service had begun, so she slipped in unobtrusively at the back. Her father and her brothers stood closer to the front, but she wanted to be alone with her thoughts awhile longer. Perhaps in this holy place, God would allow her to understand why this awful change had taken place in Ranulf.

He did not attend the mass, Aldyth noted without surprise. Naturally one so steeped in sin would not bestir himself to leave a warm bed for the comfort of the sacraments. In fact, he was probably as irreligious as William Rufus was reputed to be.

Ranulf did not appear in the hall to break his fast, either. Aldyth ate her bread and drank the watered wine hurriedly and murmured something vague to her father about spending time with Lady Nichola. Then she left the hall.

Wrapping her cloak about her, she began her search. He wasn't in the tiltyard, nor was he at the armorer's. The falconer, tending Lord Étienne's birds in the mews, said he hadn't seen Lord Ranulf. Pulling her cloak more closely about her, she ascended to the wall walk, but no Ranulf prowled the parapets.

Might he have gone late to pray in the chapel? Knowing the likelihood of that was slim, she nevertheless peeked in, but no one knelt in front of the flickering candles on the altar.

Was it possible he was still lying abed, hours after dawn? It wouldn't surprise her if sloth was one of his many sins, but she couldn't very well seek him out in his bedchamber—*could she?* Nay, what if he was not alone?

An hour later, she had but one place left to search. She had left the stables for last, unable to imagine the elegant Ranulf risking the soiling of his outlandish shoes in such a place.

That was where he was, however. She found him in a box stall with her brother Warin, bending over and peering at a gray palfrey's hock.

Warin saw her first. "Aldyth! Have you come to see my pony? And my puppy? And the barn cat has had kittens—come and see!"

Ranulf was startled to see her, and more startled still when he realized from the distracted way she replied to her younger brother's enthusiastic questions that she had come to find him rather than her brother. He had thought, after last night, that she would have avoided him like a leper.

He had been about to ruffle the lad's hair affectionately, for he really liked the young English boy, quite apart from the fact that he was Aldyth's brother. Just in time, however, he remembered his pose. Gesturing exaggeratedly with his hand, he affected a peevish tone. "Good morrow, Aldyth. I just came out to check my palfrey. Warin, see that you tell the groom there's *mud* still splattered behind his ear—the horse's that is—I don't care if the man is muddy!"

His tone implied that a spot of mud on his horse was among the worst of tragedies. "And by the by, the seneschal is looking for you. He sounded *disturbed*. What a sour-looking man!" he said, wrinkling his nose.

"Yes, my lord." After eyeing both his sister and Lord Ranulf, Warin excused himself. His retreating footsteps echoed in counterpoint to the steady munching of the horses .s they enjoyed their morning hay.

Ranulf drank in the sight of Aldyth. "Good morrow, .. dy Aldyth. You look *enchanting* to these poor eyes! A vision of autumnal loveliness in russet and gold, *ma chère*." He knew his compliments were fulsome, but he had to keep up the pose.

Latching the stall shut behind him, Ranulf watched as her eyes took in the scarlet cloak fastened on his right shoulder by an elaborate jeweled brooch, then wandered down to his feet. Again this morning he wore shoes with extravagant curled toes; this pair, however, was gold with a tooled design.

"Thank you, my lord," she replied warily at last, "but I daresay I look like a serf compared to your splendor." Aldyth gestured to the trailing, gold-banded sleeves of his tunic.

"Oh, *this?*" He made an elegant gesture that took in his entire ensemble. "His grace the king clothes his *pages* better," he said wryly. "These are fit to wear out here in the country, but never, *never* at court."

Her eyes widened and she bit her lip as if trying to think of something to say. He saw her hands, which had been nearly hidden in the long trailing sleeves, clutch each other.

"You had something to say, Aldyth? You do not like the cut of my tunic? Or is it my shoes?" he added as her eyes dropped away from his intent gaze.

"Your t-tunic? Your shoes? Nay, my lord, 'tis none of those things."

He came closer. "What then, Aldyth? Surely 'tis not difficult for one old friend to talk to another? Did you come to tell me I've sunk beneath reproach in your eyes?" He might as well give her an opening, he reasoned, so she could tell him how he disgusted her and be done with it.

"Nay, my lord. I...I've come to tell you how happy I am to see you again...and..."

"And?"

"And...forgive me for sounding so...bold, Ranulf, but I thought you should know...the love I felt for you as a young girl—the love which I believe was mutual—I still feel that love for you, Ranulf."

He stared at her, totally astonished. He had expected her to say anything but this. Had his father—or more likely—his gentle mother—put her up to this? Were they so desperate to redeem their fallen angel of a son that they would use this innocent girl?

Aldyth's eyes were enormous in her suddenly pale, upturned face. She trembled, but she returned his gaze steadfastly.

"Aldyth, sweetheart...you take me by surprise! I—"

"If you do not still cherish any feelings for me, my lord, I will understand," she interrupted him. "I...I just wanted you to know, e-especially after last night."

She was willing to tell him she loved him after he had done everything he knew to destroy her image of him as a hero straight from chivalry? After he had played the debauched courtier and boasted of having a mistress who had given him two bastards?

"Weren't you listening last night, sweeting? My father accused me of being everything but a Christian!"

"But I know *you*, Ranulf," she said, taking a step forward. "Your garments and your hair may look outlandish to your father, but I know you are a good man, with a kind heart. A man may... do certain things before he is wed, because he is a man, but I believe we would be good together..."

Ah, so that was it! Aldyth was offering herself as the good woman who could save him from himself, who could ransom his soul from the abyss. He would have to disabuse her of that notion, he realized. For her own good, Aldyth must believe it was too late, that he had already fallen over the edge and was far beyond her saving.

But he would have one kiss first, before he broke her heart.

"Sweeting..." he breathed, cupping her chin in his hand and lowering his head to claim the kiss that would have to last him for the rest of his life.

She smelled of lilies. Her lips were warm and soft, and sweeter than any mead ever distilled. He brushed them with his lips once, a kiss as tender as one they might have exchanged as children, then with more pressure, caressing her mouth with his.

Aldyth kissed like the untouched maiden she was, but with an innocent enthusiasm, sighing with obvious delight. She was so fragile, so sweet... he wanted the kiss to go on forever. He longed to go down on one knee right now and beg her to wed him. But he could not.

He raised his head, and when he opened his eyes, she was gazing at him rapturously.

"Ranulf—you *do* remember! You *do* still love me!"

He must not put it off any longer. He gave her a lazy smile. "Who would *not* love lips like those, my pet? I would have more of them..." His hands framed her cheeks as his mouth covered hers hungrily, the pressure of his lips forcing her mouth open so his tongue could ravish hers. She did not resist but trustingly allowed the kiss to deepen. He could feel her heart—the heart he must break—racing like a doe bounding through a wood.

His hands left her face and descended to her shoulders, pulling her more closely against him as his lips rained kisses on her cheeks and her neck. He felt her hands steal round his neck, one of them stroking through his long hair. He did not feign his shiver.

"Ah, my lovely one, your mouth tastes of honey," he murmured against her throat as she arched her neck backward to receive more of his kisses. Her breath came as raggedly as his own.

Ranulf's hand strayed as if by accident down her throat and past her collarbone, cupping her firm young breast, kneading it as his mouth plundered hers once more. He mentally braced himself, sure she would begin to struggle now, certain she must become frightened and beg him to stop at any moment. She did not, even when his thumb grazed her nipple and began to circle it. He felt it grow pebble-hard.

Clearly her ideal of saving his soul made her willing to go on, to brave the danger of arousing a man who was known to satisfy his carnal appetites as casually as he would eat an apple. He was amazed not only that she hadn't pulled away but that she had aroused him so quickly. Not all the courtesans at court, with their tricks and wiles, could have made him this hard, this ready. He wanted her. The tightening in his groin had already accelerated into an aching need.

It was not that he had been long without a woman. He had bedded a complaisant serving wench at an alehouse only the night before he had arrived at Kingsclere. It was, he realized with heart-wrenching certainty, because the girl within his arms was Aldyth, whom he had never really stopped loving. But because he did love her, he thought with the tiny corner of his brain that remained cool and clear, he would not leave her with any romantic illusions about him.

His other hand had been caressing her back, reveling in the supple curve of her spine beneath the fine wool, but now he dropped both hands to her buttocks, splaying his fingers and pressing her against the evidence of his desire for her.

"Aldyth," he breathed, "feel how much I want you...."
He backed her the remaining few inches against the outside wall of the stall and thrust himself against her once, twice, three times, ignoring his palfrey's disturbed snorting.

There. She had begun to be afraid now. Aldyth angled her hips away from his, seeking to avoid him, but she had nowhere to go. She placed a hand against his chest, pushing softly but unmistakably at him.

"Ranulf, no, I..." Her eyes were glazed with newly awakened passion, her face flushed.

He must be sure she saw him the way he wanted her to see him. "You're right, sweeting. Not like this. Let us find an empty stall somewhere, where we can lie down and take our pleasure." Inwardly he cringed, knowing he would never have chosen her first experience to be in the barn, even on the newest, freshest hay, where they could be discovered at any moment.

She pushed harder, staring up at him in the shadows. "No, my dear lord. You misunderstand. I would wait until our wedding night and come a maiden to our marriage bed."

Now he must do it, he realized with a sickening lurch in his stomach. He must deliver the *coup de grâce*.

"*Marriage?*" he drawled, shrugging back into the persona of the debauched young noble as if it were a cloak. "Who spoke of marriage?"

"Wh-why, I thought..." she began hesitantly.

"You thought I was looking to *wed* you? Surely you jest!" He laughed, the sound ringing cruelly in his own ears. "I do not look to marry. Why should I? Nay, Aldyth, 'twas my mistake, evidently. I thought *you* wanted to give yourself to me, to be initiated in the joys of love by one who knows what he is doing!" He let his voice drop and become lazily caressing again. "Surely you'll reconsider, my pretty vixen?" He reached out and twisted a lock of chestnut hair around his finger. "I swear by Saint Venus, love, I'd make it sweet for you. Once tried, I promise you you'd want more. If you learn quickly enough, well, I might even take you back to court with me as my leman!"

Ranulf saw the tears well up and cursed the day he was born.

"What of Vivienne, my lord? Surely she would mind sharing you."

He shrugged as if it need not matter.

"You thought I would go in a stall with you and let you do as you wished?" she asked, her slender frame rigid with shock.

He shrugged. "It wouldn't have been so unpleasant for you, my lovely Aldyth—especially after the first time. But if you're determined to find a proper bed, why not follow me in a few moments and steal up to my bedchamber? No one will be about at this time of day—"

"Is there no end to your arrogance, you conceited Norman magpie?" she cried. "You think you can have any woman if you mix the honeyed words aright?"

He stared at her, regret mixed with relief that she was finally angry enough to hate him. Now to set the seal on her anger.

"I rather thought I was the realistic one, *ma chère.* After all, however much my father disapproves of me currently, I *am* the heir to his earldom. You are but the daughter of a

English castellan. When I eventually marry, as I suppose I must someday, I can look considerably higher, you know. And I was offering you quite a favor, as well. You're very sweet, Aldyth, but you kiss like a timid virgin. One night with me and we could remedy that, if you care to reconsider.''

She slapped him then, the sound ringing through the quiet stable. ''Do you see what I think of your kind offer, you— you braying Norman ass?''

Aldyth would have run from the stable, but just then a figure appeared in the doorway and, seeing them, came forward.

It was Godric, and though Ranulf did not think he had seen their embrace or heard the heated words that followed, he was studying his sister's pale, tearful face and did not miss the disarray of her hair.

''Excuse me, Sir Ranulf.'' He bowed respectfully but the blue eyes that he trained on Ranulf were cold as shards of ice.

Chapter Four

Later, Ranulf thanked God for Godric's unexpected appearance, for if Aldyth's elder brother had not come, he thought he might very well have stopped Aldyth from going and confessed the whole ruse to her.

"Aldyth? My lord? Is...aught amiss?" Godric asked, his eyes narrowing as they shifted from his obviously distressed sister to Ranulf.

By the rood, it was fortunate that the youth wore no sword, for it looked as if Godric would like naught better than to run him through.

"Nay...n-nothing," Aldyth stammered. "I pray you would excuse me, my lord," she added, then dashed past Godric and out of the stable.

"My lord?" Godric persisted.

Ranulf knew he must assume the demeanor of the languid courtier immediately if his disguise was to be maintained. He didn't trust Godric any farther than he could throw him. The youth may have gulled Lord Étienne into believing he was reformed, but Ranulf knew Godric still hated anyone and anything Norman, and he was clever enough to figure out what had happened from his sister's appearance. He would have to watch his back with this English cockerel, Ranulf thought with regret.

"Yes, my good fellow?" he drawled, brazening it out and watching the young man's lip curl with ill-concealed disgust.

Godric evidently decided to be content with Aldyth's departure. "I . . . uh, that is, my lord, I was told you were displeased with the care of your mount. I came to tell you I would be correcting it immediately."

Ranulf stared him down, his gaze as chill as Godric's. Warin had obviously encountered Godric on the way back into the hall and had told him Aldyth was alone in the stables with Ranulf.

"How *very* good of you, but such diligence is *quite* unnecessary, I do assure you," he said with an elegant gesturing hand. "Thank you, but I'm sure my lord father has other tasks more suited to his personal squire." He nodded dismissively.

Godric bowed. "Very well, then, my lord. As Lord Étienne has indicated he has no need of me for a while, I will spend some time with my sister." He stared at something near Ranulf's foot, then leaned over and picked it up. It was Aldyth's sheer scrap of a veil, which had come off during their passionate embrace, Ranulf realized with dismay.

The youth gave Ranulf a look eloquent with warning, then turned on his heel and left.

"That filth! What did he do to upset you so, Aldyth?" Godric growled when he found Aldyth in her chamber, crying her eyes out. "Did he—I swear on our mother's grave, I'll run him through if he's despoiled you."

"Nay, of course not," she said quickly, frightened at the livid fury on her brother's face. "He merely told me a very sad story . . . about someone we both knew who had died."

"Don't play me for a fool, Aldyth," Godric snapped. "Your lips did not get bruised and swollen listening to a sad story—and here is your veil, which I found at Lord Ranulf's so elegant feet!''

''All right, Godric,'' she said with a sigh, accepting the wrinkled veil, which still had a wisp of straw clinging to it, ''but calm down. He flirted with me and kissed me...and then he, well, he just forgot himself. He meant nothing by it, Godric. Wooing a maiden is as natural to a handsome young lord as breathing, don't you see? But I slapped his face and made it very clear I was not to be toyed with.'' She studied Godric to see if her truth altering had worked.

It had, at least partially. Godric made a visible effort to slow his breathing. ''Thank the saints. I would have killed him for your honor's sake, never doubt me, Aldyth. Wasn't last night's exhibition enough to teach you to stay well clear of that demon? Now that you understand, don't ever let him get you alone again! I might not come along at such a fortunate time on another occasion, and I don't put anything past that scoundrel, even rape of a vassal's daughter.''

She didn't believe she had ever been in danger of Ranulf ravishing her—why should he? He could have any woman he wanted. But, she reminded herself sadly, she had also thought she had known Ranulf's truest self.

''Yes, brother,'' she said, suppressing the urge to argue against Godric's authoritarian tone. ''Do not worry. I shall never let that snake within striking distance again.''

Her brother sighed. ''I'm sorry, Aldyth. Perhaps you think I usurp our father's role. I merely would not see you hurt.'' He held out his arms and she went into them, steeling herself not to weep again, as much as she wanted to. She could only hope Godric believed the danger was over so that he would not do something foolish, like pick a quarrel with his liege lord's heir. If that happened, Lord Étienne might very well remember they were only English, after all, and cast her father, who was no longer a young man, Godric and her upon the road.

Suddenly she longed for the peace of Sherborne. At home she would not have to worry about such things. It was clearly best that she forget Ranulf, and the sooner she left Kingsclere, where she was likely to meet him in any corridor, the easier that would be.

The next day, Aldyth was pondering how to persuade her father to take her home, when the midday meal was interrupted by a messenger. The man, still dusty from his ride, brought the rolled vellum with its dangling ribbons and heavy wax seals to Ranulf.

There was a hush at the high table as Ranulf broke the seals and studied the brief message. Aldyth noted with a perverse stab of pride that he did not hand the letter to the priest sitting next to him to read it to him; unlike many Norman nobles, Ranulf was educated, as were his siblings.

"It's from the royal court, which lies at Winchester now," he said. "I'm commanded back to his grace the king's presence as soon as may be."

"Oh no, Ranulf," sighed the countess with a mother's regret. "You've only just arrived! What could be so important that you must leave tomorrow?"

"My lady mother, I fear I must leave within the hour," Ranulf corrected gently. "There's probably nothing more pressing than Rufus's desire for all his favorite hunting companions to be present. But I am his to command, you know."

"Indeed," the earl snorted, the one-word comment speaking volumes.

Ranulf favored his father with a mildly indignant look. "Royal favor is nothing to be sneezed at, my lord father," he protested with another of the studied gestures that made his father visibly stiffen. "Mother, Father, I pray you would excuse me. Mayhap a longer visit next time. Sir Nyle, Aldyth, my apologies for shortening your time with Warin. Warin, make your farewells—then make haste to pack your things, boy."

Warin was clearly thrilled rather than disappointed to be departing with Lord Ranulf sooner than he had expected, but he suffered through his sister's kiss with good grace. While he was being embraced by Sir Nyle, however, he noticed Aldyth's eyes were on Ranulf.

Ranulf gestured for the enormous Breton who was his squire to join him. Aldyth watched as he kissed his mother, bowed stiffly to his father and departed the hall with a few economical, yet supremely graceful motions. He did not look in her direction. She could not look away, though, however much the sight of him made her heart ache. Perhaps she would never see him again, so these last seconds were important—she must remember his image, if only to remind herself of the kind of man never to trust!

It was a simple matter for Aldyth to persuade her father to return home. After all, Ranulf had left, and paying their respects to their liege lord's heir had been the reason for the journey to begin with.

"Wouldn't you like to stay a fortnight or so longer, daughter? I would come and escort you back," her father offered.

She knew he was surprised at her eagerness to leave. Normally she loved her visits to Kingsclere and spent the time chatting with the lovely countess and romping with the twins, Adele and Agathe, whom she had tended as babes.

"Nay, Father. It's been pleasant, but I have much to do at Sherborne. There are apples to put up, herbs to dry, and I need to plan which of the livestock to slaughter for the winter meat...."

On the following morning, after they had bidden the earl and his lady a fond farewell and set their mounts on the road back to Sherborne, Aldyth broached the matter that had lain heavily on her mind ever since the day before.

"Father, I have decided I do not wish to marry."

Sir Nyle nearly dropped his reins. "Not wish to marry? What means this, Aldyth? Can it be you have discovered a religious vocation? I never thought to see you a nun rather than a wife and mother, but if 'tis your sincere desire..."

The thought was so ridiculous she laughed. "Nay, father, of course not! Can you picture me a meek and holy nun, praying all day and half the night and following some abbess's orders? 'Tis just that I have decided that—that the wedded life does not sound agreeable, either. I wish to just continue as we have been, Father. I will be your chatelaine, and you need never fear growing old without me at your side, helping you whenever you need it."

"I thank you very much, daughter, but I am not yet in my dotage!" Sir Nyle snapped, then sighed heavily. "And my still-nimble brain reminds me that what you have just proposed, though motivated no doubt by filial love, is out of the question. As much as I would keep you by my side forever, child, I know I cannot. I have already done so too long or you would not have gotten such an idea in your pretty head."

"Father, but I—"

She saw his mouth tighten. "Aldyth, however we would wish it were otherwise, there are only two places for women in this life—the convent or the marriage bed. It's time you chose one or the other."

Her mind spun in confused circles. "But why, Father, why?" *Why* was he speaking so now, when he had never before urged her to marry? She had been turning the pleasant young lads who would court her away from Sherborne ever since she had returned from living at Kingsclere!

Sir Nyle sighed again and wiped his brow. He clucked to his horse and motioned for both of them to ride a little ahead of their escort. "I merely realized I've been soft with you for too long, Aldyth. You ought to have been a young wife with babes of your own by now. Yes, and you would have been, too, but your father was too selfish to see it."

Aldyth put out a hand to her father's wrist. "You've been talking to Godric, haven't you?" She should have foreseen that her brother's worry would lead him to talk to their father. Godric was so worried she would fall afoul of Ranulf or some Norman lordling like him that he had felt bound to interfere. If only she could have reassured him that she preferred to marry no one, to continue keeping house for their father.

A new thought struck her. Had he told their father how he had found Ranulf and her in the stable? She did not want there to be bad blood between her father and the man who might well be his overlord someday, if Sir Nyle lived longer than Lord Étienne.

Sir Nyle waved a hand. "Now, Godric didn't say anything I hadn't been thinking. 'Tis just that I am growing older, daughter—my bones remind me of it every morning. I will not always be around to protect you—"

The thought cut her to the heart. "Father, you're not *ill*, are you? Have you been hiding something from me?"

"Nay, Aldyth, be calm. I am as hale as a man of my years could hope to be, but I do not deceive myself I shall live forever. I—"

"But you will be here for many years, please God," she said quickly, "and then, like as not, Godric will be castellan at Sherborne. I can keep house for him, as well," she said, aware of the desperation in her voice. *If* Godric minds his temper, she thought, and learns to accept reality, he will be castellan at Sherborne someday. If not...

Sir Nyle's voice was becoming exasperated. "Godric will marry someday, in the fullness of time. And he will bring his bride home to Sherborne, and she will expect to be mistress there. A keep cannot have two chatelaines, Aldyth, you know that."

Another woman mistress of Sherborne? Aldyth bristled at the thought, forgetting that only days ago she had dreamed of the day she would wed Ranulf and become the lady of his castle, leaving her beloved home behind.

"In the past you have turned away several young men who would have made good husbands for you. Some of them are still unwed. I want you to reconsider them, daughter," Sir Nyle continued, chewing on a hunk of the excellent cheese the countess had sent along. "There are plenty of young knights, as well, who would wed you in a trice."

"Normans, all of them," she retorted with asperity, "and only too glad to point out what a favor they were doing a humble English castellan, even as they used the dowry the earl was kind enough to give. Nay, Father, Godric is right. The English should keep to their own kind."

"Would your feelings have anything to do with the change in young Lord Ranulf?" her father asked, eyeing her keenly.

She looked away, lest her father see her wince. "'Twas but a girlish fancy, and calf love on his part, if anything. I'm ready to put away childish things, Father."

He looked relieved. "Well then, what about young Harold?"

Her father certainly meant to get down to business without further delay, she thought, startled anew. "Too fat," she said.

"Yes, now that you mention it, I thought so too, though he has a kind nature. What think you of Ailwin of Eastham Farm?"

"That pimply fellow who drinks overmuch? Father, he couldn't even ride from his land to our keep without a skin of wine on his saddle. I think he was far more enamored of our cellar than of me!"

"Osbert Osbertsson, then? He has a huge holding between Sherborne and Odiham."

"And six children from his late wife, whom he killed with bearing them in six years. *And* he has a shrewish mother living there. She'd make my life wearisome, if I survived Osbert's demands."

"Aldyth—" her father began in a warning tone.

"Father, each one you've suggested is worse than the last! I'd rather live out my life in a convent than wed anyone like those men!"

"Nay, daughter, do not fret. We'll find someone suitable," he said placatingly. Then he snapped his fingers. "I near forgot—what about Turold of Swanlea Farm?"

"Turold . . ." Aldyth repeated as a face came to her mind of the youth who had been a frequent visitor only this summer. Turold was a year or two older than she, a fair-headed young farmer with guileless blue eyes and a perpetually sunny expression. He was perhaps two inches taller than she, stocky rather than lean, but well muscled and not paunchy.

"Turold of Swanlea? I liked him well enough," she heard herself say. "Perhaps if I spent more time with him . . . if he hasn't already taken a wife, of course. Give me a day or two to put the hall to rights, then perhaps we could invite him to dine with us."

Sir Nyle, smiling again, reached out a hand and stroked his daughter's cheek. "That's the spirit, Aldyth. I won't demand you wed anyone you cannot like. Just give the lad a chance to charm you, that's all I ask.''

Turold of Swanlea. It was good that, physically, he was as different as possible from Ranulf, so that when she looked at him she would not be reminded of the Norman knight's lithe physique, dark features or intense expression. He was English, so he would speak to her in that tongue, not French—even the words he used when they went to bed would be different, she thought wryly.

All at once she thought of something. ''Father, will you have to ask the earl's permission if I wish to marry Turold?''

Sir Nyle's piercing eyes bored into her again. ''Of course. He is my overlord. Any betrothal I contract for you is subject to his approval, and I will owe him a fee. And of course he and Countess Nichola would want to come to your wedding, no matter whom you marry. You're practically a daughter to them.''

Ranulf would be bound to hear of her marriage when she wrote to tell Warin. Which did she hope for—that Ranulf's parents would tell their son afterward of her wedding, and how radiantly happy she had looked, or that he would learn of her plans in time to stop the marriage?

Was she foolish enough to think he would try to prevent her from marrying Turold? And then what? Would he be cured of his wicked ways and marry her himself?

Don't be a silly moonling, Aldyth! she scolded herself as she rode along, with Sherborne still leagues away. *Ah, if only my heart could work in tandem with my brain.*

Chapter Five

After Aldyth had been home a week, laboring feverishly to make the hall presentable and get the servants started on the seasonal tasks, she told her father she was ready. An invitation was conveyed to Swanlea, summoning a very surprised Turold to dine with them.

He came dressed in his best Norman-style robe. Aldyth could see at a glance that his usual smile was, if it was possible, broader, as though he understood the significance of the invitation.

Aldyth herself had dressed with more than the usual care, as befitted a young woman whose father was about to offer her in marriage to an eligible landholder. She chose neither the green *bliaut* nor the russet. Though she knew they were her best, she had worn them for Ranulf with such hope. Perhaps she would never be able to bear looking at them again. In the end she chose a *bliaut* of soft royal blue wool that complemented her gleaming chestnut tresses, which she wore loose, confined only by a thin gold fillet. The soft draping of the fabric and the narrow gilded girdle accentuated her tiny waist and lushly curving bosom.

Sir Nyle had arranged that the two should share a trencher during dinner, so that Aldyth could get to know the young freeholder better. He wanted her to be sure of her choice, he told his daughter before Turold's arrival. There would be time enough later to take Turold aside and conduct the dowry negotiations necessary before a marriage contract was finalized.

When Aldyth had first greeted Turold in the bailey, his greeting had been genial and courteous but restrained under Sir Nyle's watchful eye. Now, as he offered her a delicate portion of the venison in pepper sauce, he allowed his eyes to meet hers.

"Lady Aldyth, I must confess my astonishment at receiving this invitation. I thought... that is to say, I was under the impression this summer that you did not look upon my suit with favor."

Aldyth lowered her eyes as if the slicing of the meat required all her concentration. She couldn't meet those innocent blue eyes and lie. "I... reconsidered, Turold. I found I had been, uh, overhasty in dismissing you. Can you forgive me?" *And can you forgive me for the lie, sweet Jésu?*

"Then... you *are* willing to be my wife?" Turold's face beamed with joy in the torchlight. Forgetting the restraint still considered proper between a couple before the betrothal ceremony had been conducted, he grasped her hand in a transport of delight. Her pearl-hilted eating dagger *thunked* as it fell among the rushes at her feet.

As if in a dream, Aldyth saw herself nod, unable to find her voice to confirm her words. Turold must have taken this for maidenly shyness, for he only seemed more pleased.

Sir Nyle, on the other side of Turold, smiled approvingly. It was done, his expression said. His precious daughter's future was assured.

"Tomorrow is Sunday, sweetheart," Turold told her. "We can have the betrothal ceremony before the mass, so that the priest can begin to call the banns!"

The folk at the lower tables became merrily noisy, pleased at the prospect of a wedding for Sir Nyle's daughter. Most had grown to respect and even admire the independent, forthright Aldyth, but they liked a holiday even more. They would fill their bellies to the bursting point at the wedding feast. With the bride ale that would be flowing freely, they'd toast the return of a more free-and-easy life at Sherborne.

Only one became more sour as the celebrating escalated—Maud, Aldyth's tirewoman and the daughter of Helwise the cook. She sat in the shadows at the far end of one of the trestle tables, watching with growing fury as Sir Nyle's daughter claimed the man she thought of as her own.

She and the young farmer now sitting at the high table had begun walking out together during the past summer, soon after Aldyth had discouraged his earlier attentions. Turold had never made her any promises whenever they met in the wooded glen between Sherborne and Swanlea Farm, but that hadn't kept Maud from assuming someday they'd wed. As she walked back to the keep in a rosy haze after their trysts, it had always seemed to Maud that the handsome Turold was meant for her. Surely that was why he sought her out so often for their impassioned sessions of lovemaking. He was only waiting for the harvest to be over, when he would not be so busy, she told herself. Then his mother had been very ill for a time, and surely one could not expect him to suggest a wedding during that time, though he managed to keep his trysts with her just as frequently. Now that the weather had turned cold, they met in a deserted charcoal burner's hut.

Turold's mother had recovered and still he said nothing about making an honest woman of Maud. She worried ofttimes that he would get her with child, though she faithfully drank the foul brew that Helwise promised would

prevent such a disaster. She had refused to tell even her
mother the identity of her lover.

And now Turold had been accepted by Aldyth of
Sherborne, and Maud faced the wreck of her dreams. It
would be the knight's daughter and not she who would rule
Turold's hall and bear his babes, it seemed.

Well, that remained to be proven. She had not talked to
Turold yet. He was merely dazzled by the idea of marrying
a knight's daughter, she told herself. It did not occur to
Maud to be angry with her lover or that he had merely been
using her plump young body to vent his lust. She'd dress
provocatively when she met him and would let him make
love to her in that odd bestial way he liked, which hurt her
but seemed to give him such satisfaction. He'd remember
how much he loved her; after that, Aldyth of Sherborne
would seem but a whey-faced ghost.

The date for the marriage was set for the third of
December. The days passed in a blur for Aldyth, and she
slept little. Every waking moment was taken up with the
wedding. From before dawn till after dark she chivied the
castle folk in their cleaning tasks. There would be guests
occupying every spare room and every inch of space in the
hall, she reminded them, and she ordered every room newly
whitewashed, every rafter swept free of cobwebs—as if she
expected the guests to roost up there, the scullions up on
ladders grumbled. The swineherd, after hearing how many
of his charges would be slaughtered to feed the guests, fret-
ted that there wouldn't be so much as a suckling pig left after the mistress's nuptials. After talking to the shepherd, the
cowherd and the wench who minded the chickens and the
dovecote, he swore they would be living on vegetables alone
through the winter. Aldyth spent days in consultation with
Helwise the cook until the woman dreaded the sight of her

young mistress "with her fancy ideas of cookin' as if the Pope himself was comin' to bless the wedded pair." Helwise was secretly impressed that her kitchen would be serving the Earl and Countess of Kingsclere, but she had to be cajoled into promising to make any of the fancy sauced dishes that Normans prized.

As soon as she had set the household staff to their chores, Aldyth went to her solar, for the light was best in the morning for stitching her wedding gown. It was to be a wine-colored velvet, with Englishwork embroidery at the neckline, hem and wide, flared sleeves, and she was determined to do every stitch herself. Her mother had been a skilled needlewoman, Aldyth recalled, and had taught her the elaborate Saxon embroidery style. If only the long hours bent over her needle near the window did not give her so much time to think!

Turold had been the perfect swain, coming to Sherborne frequently, often with some small gift such as a pair of newly weaned kittens from Swanlea farm, one black, one white, which Aldyth promptly fell in love with and named Snow and Soot. The kittens would become valued mousers at Swanlea after the wedding, he told her, smiling in a pleased fashion at her pleasure, but for now they could amuse her with their antics.

When it was fair, they spent the afternoons walking or riding the countryside between Sherborne and Swanlea. Turold was an amusing companion, telling her funny stories about his childhood on the farm. They spoke of their future life together, laughing as they named the dozen children Turold claimed he wanted, the first six to be boys, of course, to help their father about the farm, the last six to be girls, to comfort him in his old age. Aldyth had laughingly told him that after providing him with six sons, she would be much too fatigued to bear him daughters, and he would doubtless have to comfort her, for she would be an old woman long before he was an old man!

Within a fortnight of the betrothal, he had taken her to Swanlea to meet his mother, Gundreda, who was a widow. The Englishwoman, whose thinning braids hinted at the flaxen color she had bequeathed to her son, was taciturn but civil, seemingly neither pleased nor displeased at the prospect of her son taking a wife. Aldyth hoped the woman would warm to her later; the prospect of living many years with such an uncommunicative presence was daunting. Perhaps after she had presented her with her first grandchild? Then she remembered what must precede the babe's appearance.

It was not that she found Turold's wooing distasteful; his kisses, as they walked over the countryside or sat on the settle before the fire of an evening, were gentle and loving, and he never sought to deepen the intimacy beyond what was appropriate to a betrothed couple. Of course, he let her know that the touch of her lips on his stirred the fires within him and left him sleepless on his bed, longing for their wedding night.

No, she did not shrink from his touch precisely, it was just that she was dismayed to feel—nothing. No pounding of her pulse, no trembling, no breathless desire to go further than the restrained embraces and kisses he gave her.

In Ranulf's arms she had been at the center of a fiery whirlwind. His touch had seemed to spread the burning wherever it roamed, and to places deep inside of her where his lips and hands had not strayed. Even though her brain had told her he offered her only dishonor, there had been moments in which later shame had seemed a fair exchange for the temporary bliss of being his.

Turold would not shame her. She would be his wife in all honor and the mother of his babes. If his kisses did not drug her with passion, neither would his actions clothe her in disgrace. She would be content as Turold's wife at Swanlea farm, and the devilish lure of that velvety Norman voice and Ranulf's seductive charm would soon wither and die.

"You have a new bauble, my lady?" queried Maud, breaking into her reverie. Aldyth looked up to see her servant pointing at the garnet-and-freshwater-pearl necklace that adorned her bodice.

"Yes, a betrothal gift from Turold—it is beautiful, is it not?" replied Aldyth, noting the sullen cast to her tirewoman's features. It was a familiar sight these days.

What ailed Maud? The black-haired daughter of Helwise the cook had always been of a rather sour disposition, but Aldyth had seen her brighten in midsummer. Maud's sallow complexion had blossomed and her temperament had become cheerful. There were many times when she was nowhere to be found. She frequently came back with grass stains on her kirtle after these times, and Aldyth had assumed she had a lover, probably one of the sturdy serfs whose wattle and daub hovels stood near Sherborne's walls. Aldyth had not found it in her to punish the girl, though as her mistress she had the right, for she had seemed so happy, and Aldyth was in any case so self-sufficient that she seldom needed her services. She only hoped that if the cook's daughter became with child, her lover would marry her, for if Maud bore a bastard she would be labeled a whore, fair game for any lecherous man.

Now, however, Maud's gaiety had evaporated as if it had never existed, and the girl was more sulky than before. As Aldyth marshaled the keep's women in the myriad tasks necessary to prepare for the wedding, she noticed Maud hanging back, avoiding her whenever possible. Her gaze, when she met Aldyth's eyes, was hostile.

Aldyth assumed Maud had had a falling-out with her lover and, though she was sorry for her, breathed a sigh of relief that her tirewoman's waist seemed no thicker than before. Perhaps she had thought to be wed and is envious as she sees me stitch upon my wedding dress, Aldyth thought compassionately, and resolved to be patient and understanding with her servant.

It was the eve of the wedding. They dined in great style at supper, for the guests of most prominence, the Earl and Countess of Kingsclere, had arrived and sat in the center of the high table, with the soon-to-be-wed pair on their right and Sir Nyle and Gundreda, the bridegroom's mother, on their left. Godric had come with his liege lord and was in high good spirits. He had taken her aside upon his arrival and told her how pleased he was at her choice of Turold. "A good Englishman," he had enthused. "The salt of the earth. He'll be good to you, Aldyth."

Warin, however, was not there, though he had sent a message of congratulations, and Aldyth could not help wondering if it had anything to do with his master's feelings about the wedding.

Aldyth and Turold were a handsome pair, everyone agreed, the groom a perfect example of English yeomanry, clad in a fine tunic of crimson-dyed wool, his fair hair gleaming. He sat erect and sturdy next to his bride, his demeanor proclaiming, What man would not be proud to marry such a maiden?

Aldyth wore a *bliaut* of dove gray, covered by a matching *pelisson* lined in squirrel fur, which kept out the mild draft on this early December day. Her chestnut braids were bound in gold cord, but on the morrow she would wear it loose, as befitted a maiden becoming a wife.

Turold's eyes were often upon her, his gaze warm. He was the picture of the ardent bridegroom-to-be anticipating the delights of the morrow. The castle folk seemed eager to anticipate them too, for one bold manservant shouted a demand that Turold kiss his bride-to-be.

Aldyth allowed herself to smile and shyly offered up her lips as Turold kissed her possessively, drawing a cheer from the crowd. It was but the foretaste of many such cheers tomorrow, she knew, for as the guests at the wedding feast drank the bride ale, the toasts would become bawdier, daring the groom to attempt further liberties with his bride until at last, mercifully, the bride was put to bed.

Aldyth told herself she was ready, even eager for her wedding night with Turold. She loved him, of course. Who could not love a man as well favored and kind as Turold? With such a man, the ending of her virginity held no terrors for her, she was sure.

Looking up from the kiss, she saw that Gundreda was eyeing her and her son with smugness. Well, perhaps that was a step up from mere acceptance.

Glancing to her other side, she caught sight of the Lady Nichola studying her. The countess hastily smiled and raised her cup in salute, but not before Aldyth had seen the troubled element in those cornflower blue eyes.

The countess had often told Aldyth she was like a daughter to her. Had Lady Nichola guessed that Aldyth had been in love with her son? If she had, had she favored a match between them? And if that was so, what must she think of Aldyth now, about to wed another man? Did she guess that Aldyth had tried to reach out to Ranulf, only to find him sunk beyond redemption by his own choice?

She turned back to Turold, training her gaze on his merry, round face framed in golden hair and resolutely pushing from the edge of her mind a very different visage made of lean, hard planes and hungry, dark eyes.

Aldyth had retired early, pleading a need for rest, a request her smiling groom was pleased to grant.

"Rest well, my betrothed," Turold had said, and added in an intimate whisper, "for tomorrow you will not rest alone!"

The door, well oiled at its hinges, creaked only slightly as it opened. "My lady..." came the voice from the doorway.

"Oh, there you are, Maud," Aldyth said in a welcoming voice, trying not to show her disinclination for company. "I did not see you at supper."

"I...I did not come, lady." It seemed as if the girl were determined to hug the shadows that lined the entrance of the chamber. She stood in profile to Aldyth, clutching the heavy oaken door.

"Oh?" Aldyth said encouragingly. She looked up from where she had been combing her hair by the fire. "Come in, Maud, do. It's warm over here—surely it's drafty so near the corridor. I'm glad you've come. I worried when you did not come to supper, especially since you've seemed so quiet of late."

"I did not come because Turold forbade me, lady," Maud said, coming forward from the shadows.

Aldyth gasped when the tirewoman's full face became visible. Her right eye was swollen shut, and the blue gray bruise was echoed in one lower on her chin. In addition, her lower lip was puffy and crisscrossed by a pair of small lacerations.

Aldyth jumped up and went to examine Maud's face more closely. "Turold forbade you? What do you mean? And who beat you, Maud?"

The girl shrank away as Aldyth came near, but she thought perhaps Maud was just afraid of her mistress touching her tender bruises, and was careful to lower her hands.

The girl raised her face to Aldyth, her tone as defiant as her gaze. "Turold said I wasn't to come to supper, and that I was to stay in the charcoal burner's hovel until he and ye was safely away t'Swanlea. But I thought ye should know, lady."

"Know? Know what? Who beat you, Maud?"

The girl seemed almost proud as she spat the words at Aldyth. "Who beat me? Why, Turold, o' course! Turold, the man who's been my lover for months now! The man ye're going t'wed on the morrow."

At first the words didn't make sense. Then, as she played them back in her mind, she stared at her tirewoman, feeling her mouth drop open. There seemed to be a ball of ice, steadily growing colder, in the pit of her abdomen.

"Turold was the man you went to meet? Turold was your *lover?*" she gasped at last.

"*Is* my lover," Maud corrected her archly. "We coupled only last night."

As she came closer, Aldyth could see that a tooth was missing from the front of Maud's mouth, just behind the spot where the lip was most swollen.

For a moment, she refused to think of the betrayal that her servant's words represented. She felt compelled to ask, "You made love, and then he beat you?"

"Oh, aye—but I suppose I deserved it for bein' jealous of ye. I thought the wedding meant the end fer us. But it don't, he made me see after he punished me for my sauciness."

Such a bald declaration. "It don't—doesn't?" Aldyth echoed. "And then he told you to stay out of sight, so that I would not question your battered appearance and learn of your relationship?'' Aldyth asked with a calm she was far from feeling. The cold within her was building to an icy rage. ''Yet now you appear before me, and you have told me the truth. Why, Maud?''

Any illusion she had held that Maud was telling her these things to protect her was dashed by her next words.

''I thought ye should know, lady. Ye looked so proud whenever he came t' see ye—I thought ye should know there's another what shares his love, aye, and always will!''

Aldyth hadn't known she was so close to striking the defiant Maud until she saw her tirewoman flinch. Slowly she withdrew the fist she had raised. It had never been her way to strike a servant and she would not start now. Nor did Maud deserve to be the sole recipient of her wrath, if what she was saying was the truth.

''Go to your chamber, Maud. If I find out you've lied I'll deal with you later.'' She swept from the room, not pausing to see if Maud remained or not.

Chapter Six

Lord Étienne, his countess, Sir Nyle and Gundreda had retired. Now Turold, accompanied only by Godric, sat at the high table, staring down at the castle folk who still sat laughing, singing and drinking or who lay, snoring noisily, amid the remains of the feast.

Turold wore a complacent smile. Tomorrow his dream would be realized. Aldyth would be his wife, and all this would be his to share. He planned to ingratiate himself thoroughly with Aldyth's father so that he would be like another son to him—at least until the English came into their own again, when he would denounce all those who had become collaborators with the Normans and traitors to the English cause.

Thanks to Swanlea Farm's bounty, Turold had always had enough to eat, but he had never seen such a variety of food as there had been tonight. Tomorrow, Aldyth had told him, there would be even more at the wedding feast.

He noticed his bride-to-be preferred the spiced dishes that the Normans had brought with them when they had conquered England rather than the plain boiled meats of the English. And after the initial toast, in which Turold and Aldyth had shared a gilded goblet full of spiced hippocras, he had called for ale, but his bride-to-be preferred wine, as if she were as Norman as Lord Étienne and Lady Nichola. All very well for now, he thought, crossing his hands over his full belly, but beginning tomorrow he'd cure her of her preference for Norman things! As the daughter of a castellan in service to the conquering foreigners, she'd been allowed to forget she was English, but that was over now. She just didn't know it yet, he thought, smiling to himself, feeling his groin tighten as he imagined the control he would soon exert over his beautiful bride—both in bed and at the table, and in every other aspect of her life.

"Turold, I would speak to you."

He blinked. Aldyth was standing in front of him as if he had conjured her up out of his lustful thoughts. He blinked again and rubbed his eyes, which stung from the smoke in the room and the lateness of the hour. She was still there—and she did not look happy.

What now? he wondered irritably. She had been fidgety and nervous—as was expected of a bride-to-be, when she retired. Had his dour mother disturbed her peace, making some niggling complaint about her chamber?

"Turold, I would speak to you *now*," the figure standing in front of the table repeated in an insistent tone that grated on the headache just beginning to trouble his ale-fogged brain. Soon after they married, he would lesson her about nagging a man, he vowed.

"What troubles you, sweetheart?" he said, standing up and bending over the table toward her.

"Ah, true love," Godric teased. "She can't bear to let you go for the night."

Turold gave him a cocky wink.

"Turold, I would prefer to speak to you *alone*," Aldyth said with a meaningful glance at her tipsy brother and the interested audience of die-hard drinkers at the tables below the salt.

"See, my almost-brother-by-marriage, I told you so," crowed Godric, ignoring Aldyth's glare.

"Of course, my darling almost-wife. I rejoice to oblige you," Turold said, grinning. Whatever it was, he could smooth the furrows from Aldyth's brow—maybe even in the same persuasive fashion he used with Maud, if he went about it in the right way. He hadn't met the woman yet who couldn't be soothed with the equipment God had endowed him with, he thought, the ale lending him confidence.

Taking a lantern, she led him outside, across the bailey and into the chapel in the brisk December breeze.

"What means this, Aldyth? I thought you wanted to be alone w—"

"We're alone here," she said, taking a taper and lighting the candles that flanked the altar from her lantern. The shadows fled to the far corners. "This seemed a better place for the telling of the truth, a truth that I'm long overdue to hear, it seems."

"What are you talking about, Aldyth?" he said, allowing a tinge of the crossness he felt to show in his tone as a warning. It was cold as a harlot's heart in here, and he'd be damned if he was going to indulge her prenuptial skittishness in such an uncomfortable place.

"I'm talking about my tirewoman, Maud. Just how long have you been bedding her, and when were you going to tell her it was over between you now that you were going to be a husband—or *were* you going to tell her? Were you ever going to tell *me?*"

He seemed to change in the strange, dancing shadows of the chapel. A heartbeat before, he had been the genial, indulgent bridegroom-to-be; now the candlelight from the altar reflected off the face of a demon.

Aldyth was so transfixed by the transformation of her betrothed that she missed the fist that struck the side of her head. The next thing she knew, she was lying back on the stone floor with Turold leaning over her, his features still a mask of rage.

"Don't ever presume to tell me what to do, Aldyth," he growled at her, the fumes of stale ale washing over her in a foul gust that made her stomach churn. "I'm a man, and a man has a right to do what pleases him!"

Quickly she scuttled back out from under him, all the while reminding herself she must be as understanding as she had been willing to be with Ranulf's bachelor sins. "Yes, while you were unwed, Turold, but tomorrow—"

"Tomorrow I'll be your lord and master in the eyes of man and the Church, and you'll not dare raise your voice to me!" he ranted at her crouching figure, his voice echoing in the stillness of the chapel. "You've been pampered and spoiled and allowed to forget your proper place as a woman, but no more!"

He was drunk, dangerously drunk. She knew she should meekly acquiesce while in his presence, then seek help in undoing this disastrous betrothal before it was too late. But something had snapped within her, too, something that made her ignore caution and the danger signs of his clenched fists and rage-reddened eyes.

She scrambled to her feet. "Turold, I'm sorry, but I seem to have made a horrible mistake. 'Tis clear to me I cannot marry you. I . . . I don't know what we'll have to do to annul the betrothal, but—"

"Nay, Aldyth, 'tis too late for that! You'll be marrying me, right enough, I'll see to it!"

He leaped at her, landing a stinging blow to her cheek that threatened to snap her head off her neck. The room dimmed, and for a moment unconsciousness beckoned invitingly, but she fought it.

"You can't force me to marry you, Turold!"

He struck her again. Over the ringing in her ears, she heard him snarl, "Oh, can't I? Mayhap I'll show you right now, right here, what I can force you to do!" He fell on her, grinding his body crudely against hers.

She sobbed, terrified now. "No! You can't mean to rape me in the chapel! 'Tis sacrilege! You'll be excommunicated, Turold!"

Evidently the threat was enough to penetrate his ale-soaked brain, for Turold got slowly, clumsily to his feet, then dragged her up with him. He dug his fingers cruelly into the hair at her nape, ignoring her whimpers.

Their chins were just inches apart. "You *will* marry me in the morning just as we planned." He ground the words out. "And I'll see you do no running to anyone tonight with your silly complaints, wench. To bed with you now. My bride must look radiant on the morrow."

She wanted to laugh hysterically. He must be mad! She would hardly look radiant when the blows that still stung her face had blossomed into bruises! Biding her time, though, she said nothing as he steered her from the chapel, clutching her hair with cruel strength to direct her.

Surely they would meet someone along the way back to her chamber who would intervene, she thought, forcing herself to be calm as her scalp screamed in protest at his yanking. Her father—Godric—even a scullion could be made to summon her aid!

She was not dismayed that the bailey was deserted. The hour was late. When they went into the hall, Turold would have to let go of her or arouse the suspicion of Godric. Please God, her brother had not sought his bed in the last few minutes, had he? Or if by some chance he got her up the staircase without their being seen, Lord Étienne and Lady Nichola, as guests of highest rank, were staying in the master chamber normally occupied by Sir Nyle, next to

Aldyth's. She had but to pound on the wall between them and scream . . .

But Turold did not take her into the hall, crossing instead to the range of apartments that housed the priest, her father's steward and several chambers that were reserved for guests. He did not take her to the room he had been assigned until the wedding night, but instead pushed her up the stairs, pausing to knock at Gundreda's chamber.

It took several moments of soft knocking, for obviously Turold did not want to arouse anyone else, but finally a drowsy-looking Gundreda pushed open her door, blinking as she saw her son clutching Aldyth by her hair.

"Let us in, Mother. I'll explain once we're inside."

"What—"

"Please, you must tell him to let me—" Aldyth began to plead, but then Turold clamped his other hand over her mouth. He repeated, "Let us in!"

The old woman blinked at Aldyth, struggling against her son, and obeyed Turold.

A fire still burned in the brazier, and from this Turold's mother lit a rush light. "What have ye done, Turold? Ye must've scared her with rough wooing a night too soon!" Gundreda scolded, continuing to eye them both. "I tried to warn ye! And look, ye've made yer handiwork plain," she added, raising a bony finger to trace the bruise on Aldyth's cheek.

"You must make him let me go, Gundreda," Aldyth said firmly as soon as Turold removed his hand from her mouth. "I won't marry your son! Never fear, I won't shame him before our guests . . . I'll not tell them the wedding is called off because he's a whoring brute—"

Turold raised his fist to strike her again, but at a hissed command from Gundreda, he only clapped his large hand over her mouth again.

"Silence, Aldyth!" he said, his tone soft but lethal in her ear. "Gag her, Mother."

Incredulous, Aldyth watched as his mother rummaged among her garments until she found a clean scrap of cloth and moved to obey her son.

"You'll be passing the night here, my beloved," Turold told her after the gag had been properly secured with knots at the back of her neck. "If any ask, we'll say you came here to ask Gundreda's counsel in making me happy, and then fell asleep. My mother will accompany you on the morrow until the ceremony has taken place and you are safely my wife. Then none may come between a loving husband and his wife." He smiled, a horrible, wolfish smile.

How could she have thought he was gentle and kind? He was a madman! Aldyth shook her head and tried to say, "No, I won't marry you, I'll tell the priest I won't," but only muffled gibberish came out.

"And lest you think of making some protest at the church door on the morrow, think again. My dagger will be well hidden in my sleeve, and I'll cut your throat before you ever finish your foolish words. Oh, they'll execute me for a murderer, likely enough—" He grinned. "But you'll be dead, too, so what profit is there in that?"

She stared, chilled to the bone as his words flowed on, gently chiding now. "Aldyth, Aldyth. This little... quarrel... need not stand between us forever. As soon as you learn to be my obedient wife we'll have no further néed for harsh words, will we? And once you learn the delights of sharing my bed, the same delights Maud has known—" he fondled himself crudely in illustration "—I doubt very much you'll find aught else to protest about. . . ."

"Enough, my son," Gundreda said behind him. "Get you gone this chamber. Here's another cloth. Tie her wrists and leave me your dagger. I'll sit up and guard your foolish bride.''

Once Turold had stumbled out of the door, Gundreda motioned Aldyth to the bed she had been occupying, then she pulled up a stool. ''Ye may as well sleep, for I will not,'' the old woman cackled as she settled down to watch her son's prisoner.

Aldyth had never felt less inclined to sleep in her life. She must get free, she must! She could not allow herself to be tied in wedlock to this brutish madman! Her mind raced.

She thought she could work free of her bonds, for Turold had been clumsy in his drunkenness and the knots at her wrists were loose. But the old woman was watching her like a hawk.

She whimpered under the gag to draw Gundreda's attention, then shivered elaborately.

''Oh, cold, are ye? Ye won't be cold tomorrow night, not wi' my young stallion Turold to cover ye,'' the old woman said, chuckling at her bawdy play on words. ''Well, here's a blanket,'' she said, putting it over Aldyth.

Now her hands were free to work, hidden by the blanket! Aldyth feigned a yawn and let her eyes drift shut as if she were overcome by sleepiness.

Feverishly she worked at the knots while she thought of what to do. Should she go to her father? He loved her, but he had been adamant that she choose a husband or the veil, and as there were no other men she could stand to think of marrying, he might well insist she choose the nunnery. Godric? Nay, he was so blinded by the idea of Turold as the good Englishman—much as she had been, too, she admitted bitterly—that he would likely guard her for Turold. Perhaps she should go to Lady Nichola and beg her to intercede.

But the betrothal ceremony was as binding as a marriage, she reminded herself. It might be a long, complicated and expensive process to free her from her contract with Turold. Her father had little ready coin, she knew, and what if Lord Étienne disapproved? And Turold had a vengeful nature, as she had discovered tonight. What if, during the long process of annulling the betrothal, he caught her alone somewhere? Might he not force himself on her, perhaps even causing the Church to decide they ought to wed despite her protests? Nay, it would be far better if she just disappeared.

But where could she go? A woman alone was fair game for the two-legged wolves of the world. If only there was a way by which she could maintain some connection with her family... Then she remembered Warin, who was at court with Lord Ranulf. He had written to tell her he was happy for her, but she knew that was only because she was happy; he had never met Turold and would have no conflicting loyalties. He would help her.

There! She had the knot loosened beneath the blanket. Now all depended on Gundreda falling asleep, and soon, so she would still have time to carry out her plan.

Chapter Seven

By dawn, Aldyth, clothed in the rough wool tunic and hose she had stolen from one of the sleeping scullions, had reached a cave where she had once played with Ranulf and Godric when they were children. The rocky outcrop was not far from the track leading south over the chalk hills, but its entrance was covered by a thicket, and she thought she would be safe enough here until she had accomplished her transformation.

Lighting a candle with the flint and tinder she had brought with her, Aldyth dripped some of the hot wax on a low boulder inside the cave's dark exterior so that the candle would stand up, then propped up a small square of silver-painted glass that served as her mirror and crouched before it. For a moment she stared ruefully at the bruises that shadowed one cheek. Taking the sharp knife she had brought from her sewing, she pushed back her hood and pulled her braid forward. She trembled, for her chestnut tresses had been her glory. Then she remembered Turold, and what it would mean if she was caught, and with a sigh of regret raised the knife.

Minutes later, the sun peeked over the rolling downs, illuminating the figure of a slender "lad" dressed in the rough

hood, tunic, hose and crude boots of a serf, following the
track that led south to Winchester.

"Bitch! What have you done with her? Where did you
hide her? Answer me or I swear I'll kill you!" raged Turold
at the woman he had just knocked to the stone floor of the
kitchen. He ignored the screeching of the cook, Maud's
mother, in the background.

Maud could barely breathe, let alone answer him. There
was blood in her mouth. With her tongue she felt the empty
sockets where two of her teeth had been. It felt as if he had
broken her jaw.

When she could, she raised herself up on one elbow and
stared at her erstwhile lover, though with difficulty, for his
blows had blurred her vision and one eye was rapidly swelling shut.

She spat, the broken teeth coming out in a thick red
stream. "I told her the truth—aye, I'll admit it—and I'm
glad I did! But I didn't help her escape, Turold, and I know
not where she is. I swear!" she cried, her defiance fading as
he lunged at her again.

"Lying wench! I'll make you tell me!" he shouted, ignoring her scream.

"That's enough! Touch her again and I'll run you
through!" commanded a voice, but Turold felt the prick of
cold steel against his neck before he was actually conscious
of the words.

Sir Nyle stood there, having been fetched by Helwise, who
was certain her daughter was about to be murdered by the
jilted bridegroom. His sword was bared, his expression stern
enough to make Turold let go of the neckline of Maud's
gown.

"Now, what is this unseemly uproar? My daughter has disappeared, and you're more interested in brawling with the cook's slattern of a daughter?"

"She's the one responsible for your precious daughter's disappearance," Turold retorted sullenly. "The slut told Aldyth a pack of lies about me, that's why she's run off!"

Sir Nyle eyed them both and sighed. "What did you tell her, girl?" he demanded of Maud.

Maud looked sulky. "Only the truth—that he's a lecher and a brute, an' that 'twas not likely he'd change."

"You trollop! You couldn't get enough of me!" taunted Turold, too furious to care what Sir Nyle thought anymore.

"Silence!" roared Sir Nyle. "Get you gone from this keep, Turold, you and your crone of a mother! I never want to see you darken my doorway again!"

Turold eyed the older man, who did not shrink from his gaze. "Aye, I'll be gone, right enough," he growled. "But I'll find your daughter, and she'll be sorry when I do. We're betrothed, and that makes her mine as good as if we'd wed. What's mine stays mine. Don't think you can hide her from me."

Sir Nyle kept his eyes on the angry young farmer until he left the kitchen, then had a man-at-arms follow him until he and his mother had departed for Swanlea. He was profoundly grateful that Lord Étienne and his wife had left for Kingsclere earlier. They had promised to help search for Aldyth, and to let him know if she appeared at Kingsclere, of course. But he was relieved they had not witnessed this scene, for the embarrassment would have only added to his anguish.

How could he have let his eagerness to see his daughter safely settled with a husband lead him to make such a misjudgment? The signs of Turold's true nature had been there, surely, if he had but looked.

Ah, Aldyth, daughter of my heart, I'm so sorry. I should have let you stay here, instead of forcing you to run away. Oh, Jésu, protect her, wherever she may be!

That night he wrote a long, difficult letter, telling Godric about the mistake he had made and Aldyth's flight. But days passed, and Godric's reply, when it came, merely indicated he would be looking for his sister. He said nothing about whether he believed his father's accusations about Turold.

Five days later, in the midst of a bone-chilling late afternoon downpour, Aldyth came to the castle just inside Winchester's west gate.

"Be on your way, beggar lad!" ordered a man-at-arms standing in the doorway of the guard's hut next to the wall around the outer ward. He spoke in Norman French and then repeated it in thickly accented English. "You're not near sweet enough to serve the king!"

Loud guffaws greeted his sally from within the hut, where Aldyth could see men squatting in a ring, dicing. She drew closer, hoping her disguise would hold. This was the first major test, for during the four days of her journey, she had avoided the main roads and the company of other folk, fearing pursuit by Turold.

"Please, sir," she answered him in French, remembering to keep her voice husky and low, "I'm not here to serve the king, but I must needs see my cousin Warin, who serves Lord Ranulf of Kingsclere."

The guard squinted at her more closely, then reached out a callused finger and wiped her cheek. "Well, you might do after all, once you wipe off your muddy face. It seems you brought half the downland dirt with you, lad!"

"Don't tease the stripling, Fulk! He said he wasn't here to be one of Rufus's pages," called a man over his shoulder. "Hurry up and be done with him, or you'll lose your turn, and I warn you, luck is with me!"

"All right, all right. Well, boy, I can't possibly know the names of all the lads running about here, but I do know my lord of Kingsclere. His lodging is in the west tower, there." He called to someone in the guard tower, and a moment later the gate opened to Aldyth.

Moments later she had found her way up to the chamber at the top of the stairs. Knocking at the heavy oaken door, she thought, Jésu, what if Ranulf answered it? Her disguise had fooled the guard, who had been in a hurry to get back to his dice, but what about someone who knew her?

"My lady? Is that you, Lady Vivienne?" came a voice from within . . . Warin's voice. She recognized the woman's name he called, too—'twas the name of Ranulf's mistress.

"Nay, Warin, but you know me," she called back, keeping her voice gruff and low-pitched.

She heard the sound of the bolt being shot back, and then Warin stood before her in the page's livery with the silver unicorn emblazoned on it. He stared at her, puzzled.

"Are you alone, Warin?" she asked him, resisting the urge to fling herself at her brother until she was sure it was safe.

"Aye, but who—hey, you can't just barge into my lord's quarters," he said, reaching out a hand to stop her as she walked past him and shut the door behind her.

The room she was standing in was not large and contained only a brazier, a table and a pair of chairs. There was a door at the back of it that led, she guessed, to another room, which must contain Ranulf's bed. Feeling the heat radiating from the brazier, she went to it, stretching her frozen fingers over its warmth before turning back to her brother.

"Warin, 'tis me, Aldyth," she said in her normal voice, pulling back her hood.

Her younger brother's eyes widened and he stared as if horror-struck.

"Aldyth? What *are you* doing here? I thought you had married Turold!" His mouth dropped open as he came closer and fingered a strand of the brown hair that clung damply to her temple. "Aldyth, you're as wet as a trout! *And what in the name of the saints have you done to your hair?*"

She couldn't help but smile at his expression. "I cut it so I could pass for a boy on the journey to Winchester, for my own safety. Warin, I...I found I couldn't marry Turold. On the eve of the wedding I learned he was not a kind, gentle man at all but a brute and a lecher."

"Did he...did he *hit* you?" asked Warin, reaching a tentative hand out to touch her face. She flinched from the pain. She nodded wordlessly. The bruise spoke for itself.

"But couldn't you have gone to Father, Aldyth?" Warin asked, his face worried as he took in her muddied, humble garb. "Surely this wasn't necessary—to hack off your hair and dress like a plowboy!"

"'Twas the scullion's clothes, actually," Aldyth pointed out wryly, "but they're somewhat the worse for the journey. No, I was afraid to trust that Father would get me released from the betrothal. He had insisted it was either a husband or the convent for me. Turold was so convincing...Father would never have believed what the real Turold was like under that false front. Besides, I was afraid of Turold plotting revenge for his humiliation. I do believe he'd stop at nothing, Warin!"

"I never met this Turold of Swanlea, sister, but Godric said—"

"Oh, Godric thinks Turold hung the moon merely because he isn't Norman," she snapped, then softened her tone. "He wouldn't have believed me, either, Warin. Don't you see? I had to come here!"

"Ah, you came to Lord Ranulf for aid! Aye, he'll help you, Aldyth," Warin replied enthusiastically.

She sighed. She had forgotten her younger brother's hero worship of his master. Ranulf had always been kind to Warin, so the boy saw no reason to topple him from his pedestal of knightly perfection. "Nay, Warin, Lord Ranulf is *not* to know I am here, do you understand? Trust me, I saw his true colors when we visited Kingsclere, and I know I would be no safer with a man of his repute." She had a sudden fear. "Where is Lord Ranulf?"

Warin shook his head. "Nay, he's hunting in the New Forest with the king. He won't be back this night, at the very least. But...how can I help you, sister? You know I will, for I would not have you wed to a bad man, but—"

"I need you to find me a place," she interrupted. "I need a position in a household somewhere about Winchester, as a scullion or something..."

"But, Aldyth," Warin protested, "you're a *lady*. Surely I could find you someplace fitting for a girl of gentle birth."

"Nay, don't you see? Even if I could trust Lord Ranulf and the rest of the king's nobles, I'm afraid Turold may come looking for me. He frightened me, Warin."

Her younger brother was still considering her words when Aldyth began to sneeze, and she could not stop the fit of shivering that took her afterward.

"We'll worry about where you're going to hide later, Aldyth," Warin decided, all at once in charge of the situation. "For now, we must get you out of those wet clothes or you'll perish of lung fever. Go into my lord's bedchamber, take off those wet things and wrap up in the blanket on his bed.''

Warin was better than his word. Within the hour Aldyth was luxuriating in an oaken tub full of steaming hot water within the privacy of Lord Ranulf's chamber, feeling the warmth soak into her chilled bones, while Warin went to find her a change of clothing.

She looked around her while she soaked. There was another brazier near the tub. The bed was large and hung with draperies of peacock-blue velvet. There was a clothes press inlaid with enamel. A tunic of dark wool was draped over a three-legged stool.

In all likelihood this was the very tub in which Ranulf took his own baths, Aldyth thought, then smiled at the ironic fact that the idea brought some inexplicable comfort.

She stayed in the tub until the water cooled, then wrapped herself in the blanket and sat on the stool, fluffing her hair in front of the brazier.

How odd the short locks felt after the thick tresses she was used to! Doubtless they would dry in minutes, but the thought did not cheer her. There was a silver-backed mirror on top of the chest, but she could not bring herself to look in it. All at once the loss of her beautiful, long hair symbolized all she had lost in her flight from Sherborne—home, most of her family, even the right to be herself, Lady Aldyth—and she felt utterly dispirited.

Then she heard voices in the outer room, and after the briefest of knocks, Warin came through the door, followed by a comely woman with garments draped over her arms.

Startled, Aldyth clutched the blanket around her.

''Oh, don't worry, Aldyth,'' Warin said breezily. ''This is Lady Vivienne, and she's in on our secret. She helped me obtain clothing for you, and she'll help you stay out of sight until we've found you a hiding place.''

"Lady Vivienne," Aldyth said, nodding. So this was Ranulf's mistress, the mother of his children born on the wrong side of the blanket. Of all the people to involve in her deception!

Of medium height, Lady Vivienne had the dark complexion of the Normans and black hair in two fat plaits wound with gold thread. A girdle of gold links encircled a waist that was surely too slender to be that of a woman who had borne children, and it also gave emphasis to a lushly curving bosom. Aldyth hated her.

Lady Vivienne smiled, her rosebud lips parting to reveal perfect, pearly teeth. "Hello, Aldyth, what a brave girl you are, to be sure!" she said, coming closer, and Aldyth could see the woman was staring at her bruised cheek. "When Warin told me the story of how you fled that terrible monster of a man and walked here—so many leagues from your home—I could scarce believe it. How frightening it must have been for you, my dear.'' Lady Vivienne's voice, with its slurred Norman consonants, was as pleasant to listen to as she was to behold.

"It...it was," Aldyth agreed, fighting the impulse to smile back and to like this woman, whose sympathy and admiration were like balm to her wounded soul. She would accept her help if she must, but she would never let herself forget that this woman shared Ranulf's bed.

"*Eh bien,* we will leave you to change into these clothes, which I have borrowed from one of the pages, and then you and Warin will join me in my apartments for supper.''

"Yes, Lady Vivienne. And...thank you," Aldyth called to the retreating figure. Food! The thought of it made her stomach growl, for she had not eaten anything over the last four days but the bread and cheese she had brought with her and what the monks had given her at a priory along the way. She hoped she would not embarrass herself before Ranulf's mistress with her gluttonous appetite.

Lady Vivienne's babies, a pretty two-year-old girl with hair as black as her mother's and a year-old baby boy, slumbered on pallets near the fire with their nurse, old Marie.

Aldyth, her belly full after consuming enormous quantities of good food and wine, was nearly asleep in her chair when she heard the Norman woman speak.

"I don't know if she will fool a careful observer," Lady Vivienne said across the table to Warin, over the bones of a fat capon. "The binder over her chest helps, yes, but see how slender her features and her wrists! Mayhap in a court where there are many such boys, no one will detect..."

Aldyth felt herself flushing, for the woman had been discussing her with Warin almost as if she weren't there.

"Ah, my *pauvre petite,* I'm sorry, I have embarrassed you!" Lady Vivienne apologized.

"Nay, it's all right, my lady," Aldyth said, and added politely, "and thank you for the delicious supper."

"You are very welcome, my dear. Warin is my good friend, and so I am glad to aid you, his sister. But he tells me we cannot tell Lord Ranulf you are here. Are you sure, Aldyth? I would be glad to have you as part of my household, and if he was in on the plan it would be so easy...."

The thought of having to see Ranulf coming to these rooms to spend time in dalliance with his mistress almost made Aldyth ill.

"Nay! I'm sorry, but I cannot! Ranulf must not know I am here!" she cried, jumping to her feet. "Oh, please pardon me for coming—I should have seen this would never do. I'll be on my way in the morning—"

"Nay, rest easy, my dear," Lady Vivienne said, rising also and going to put her arm around Aldyth. "You are tired, and I have upset you. I am sorry. Ranulf will not know, if that is your wish. 'Tis only that since he knows you, I fear he may penetrate your disguise rather easily, and once he comes home from the New Forest, it may be difficult to keep you from his sight. But we will make every effort. I...don't know what passed between you and my lord, but I am certain he would help you without asking aught of you. He is a good man, Aldyth."

Aldyth looked away, fatigue and distress making her perilously near tears. She couldn't tell this kind, generous woman that the last time she had been alone with Ranulf, he had tried to seduce her. "I cannot ask it of him," she managed to say at last, her hands clenched at her sides.

"*Eh bien.* Warin, take your sister back to my lord's chamber and put her to bed. It is good that Ranulf is gone a-hunting, is it not? She will feel better in the morning."

Vivienne watched them go, the young boy and his sister, the latter so defiant and so nearly dead on her feet.

She had known who Aldyth was immediately, of course. This was the girl Ranulf had told her about upon his return from Kingsclere, the girl he loved beyond reason, and as hopelessly. There could be no happiness for him with Aldyth of Sherborne while he served as his liege lord's agent at Rufus's court. His personal happiness must wait until the best of the Conqueror's sons had achieved the throne, he had insisted.

Vivienne smiled in the flickering shadows of her chamber. She knew what it was like to love secretly, for she adored Urse de Caradeuc, Ranulf's giant, one-eyed squire, fearsome-looking eye patch and all. She had no idea if her love was returned, though the Breton was teasing and amiable to her. Yet even if Urse loved her, too, how could they marry, when she was supposed to be Ranulf's mistress?

She owed Ranulf of Kingsclere so much she would never dream of asking him to end their arrangement, which had begun one night when he had found her, bruised and bleeding, at the foot of a staircase leading from a chamber in which the king's cronies had been reveling. Vivienne was a recent widow of a Norman knight who had died of a trifling wound that had become infected. With two small children to support, she had remained at court rather than go home to Normandy, because the king had promised her a rich marriage. On this night she had obeyed a summons to a supper with the king and some of his nobles, thinking that at last she might be introduced to the promised husband. Instead, she had been unable to elude the pawing hands of a pair of drunken lords and had been beaten when she resisted, then raped amidst the dirty rushes while half a dozen barons and knights cheered.

Ranulf had taken her to his chambers, summoned a laundress to help him tend her wounds and then let it be known she was his mistress. Lord Ranulf was one of the king's most trusted friends, and his protection had been sufficient to keep her from being molested again. He had obtained apartments for her at Winchester so that she and her babes could live in security.

Yet Ranulf asked nothing of her. Eventually, seeking some way to repay him for his kindness, Vivienne had offered herself to him, but he had not taken advantage of her gratitude. Instead, he had trusted her with the secret of his true allegiance and asked her to be a second set of eyes and ears around the court for him. As a woman she might hear information he would not, for as Lord Ranulf's supposed mistress she associated with other such woman around the court, the courtesans who plied their trade among Rufus's powerful circle of intimates. She was to report all gossip about the king and his nobles to him, however trivial it might seem.

She had been disappointed at first that such a darkly handsome man as Ranulf of Kingsclere did not want to bed her, but then she had come to know Urse and had grown to love the giant Breton with his merry smile. Mayhap someday Ranulf would have achieved his goal of helping, and she would be free to let Urse de Caradeuc know of her feelings.

Until then, though, perhaps she could repay Ranulf by making sure he did not sacrifice his chance at happiness for the sake of his principles. He had been so sure he should not expose Aldyth to danger, but Vivienne's first impression had been that there was a great deal more steel to this slip of a girl than Ranulf had suspected. Any *damoiselle* who was daring enough to escape a horrible marriage by disguising herself as a boy and fleeing across the country alone was brave enough to endure the dangerous intrigue Ranulf was engaged in. And she suspected that despite Aldyth's protestations of dislike and distrust of Ranulf, she still loved him.

Vivienne decided to become better acquainted with Aldyth and make certain her initial impressions of her were accurate. Then, without revealing why he had done so, Vivienne would hint that the true Ranulf might not be the Ranulf who had repulsed Aldyth by acting the lecherous lord that day in the stable.

Then it would be up to Aldyth to decide whether or not to risk all for her love of Ranulf of Kingsclere.

Chapter Eight

Aldyth awoke an hour after sunrise none the worse, it seemed, from her long trek and the drenching she had received the day before. The anxiety and depression that had dogged her steps all the way to Winchester seemed largely vanquished, and she felt hopeful, despite the radical change in her state.

She need not live disguised in Winchester forever, Aldyth reminded herself as she stretched and yawned in Ranulf's bed. Surely someday Turold would no longer be a threat. He would seek another woman to marry and find a way out of the betrothal contract, and then she would be free. The sooner he did so, of course, the better; her father would not live forever and it would be dreadful never to see him again after causing him such worry. At the very least, she must find a way to send a message telling him she was all right, without indicating where she was.

"Good morrow, sister," Warin said, strolling into the room with fresh-baked bread, a wheel of cheese and watered wine, which he put on the bedside stand. "At last I hear you stirring, slugabed! I thought we might break our fasts together today—but do not, I pray, expect such a boon every day."

Aldyth grinned. "I can't remember when I've slept so late, but Lord Ranulf's bed is certainly more comfortable than a pile of pine needles in the forest or the wayfarers' pallets at the monastery I stopped at one night. Begone for a moment, little brother, that I may dress, and then I'll gladly share breakfast with you."

When Warin came back a few minutes later, he announced, "After we've broken our fast, we are to see Lady Vivienne. She said she has already found Edward a position."

"Edward?" she said blankly, breaking off a hunk of the crusty bread.

"That's the new name I've given you, unless you've been telling castle folk a different one. You can't very well pass for a boy calling yourself Aldyth, can you?" he said with maddening logic, chewing on a wedge of cheese he'd cut with his eating dagger. "Or doesn't Edward suit you?"

"Don't talk with your mouth full," she said automatically, chagrined that she hadn't even thought of the need for a male name. "Nay, no one's asked me my name, so Edward will be fine, I suppose. I hope I remember to answer to it. But you've seen Lady Vivienne already this morn?"

"She was at mass, as always."

"'Tis well that you continue to go regularly, Warin," Aldyth said, letting her brother hear the approval in her voice. So Ranulf's mistress went daily to mass. The thought surprised her. Could such a woman be truly religious?

"Lord Ranulf told me I must, Aldyth. But I like to do it."

Aldyth snorted. "Perhaps he seeks to absorb grace by being in his page's presence."

Warin gazed at her with reproachful eyes. "'Tis not his fault if he does not get to mass most days. But the king rides out often to the hunt before dawn and demands his friends accompany him.''

She raised a hand in surrender. ''Very well, I can see you'll brook no criticism of Lord Ranulf. Hasten and finish your wine, Warin. I'm curious to discover what Lady Vivienne has found for me to do.''

Folk coming and going thronged the bailey—mailed men-at-arms drilling in ranks, noblemen in furred robes, serving women with heavy-laden arms. ''You still walk like a girl, sister,'' Warin hissed as they made their way across the sunlit bailey to Lady Vivienne's quarters in the inner wall. ''Don't let your hips sway—see, walk like this!'' He demonstrated, his stride almost a swagger.

Aldyth, still fighting the feeling of being naked in the shorter hemline of the belted tunic, tried to imitate it. '''Tis hard to do! I never realized men and women moved so differently.'' Then she colored, remembering the catlike grace with which Ranulf walked, which was nevertheless totally masculine. ''How am I doing?''

He watched her with a critical eye. ''Better.''

Lady Vivienne was playing with her young daughter when they arrived.

''I've found you a position in the chapel royal, Aldyth, um . . . that is, *Edward*. You're to go down there now. Brother Osbert, the clerk in charge of relics, knows you are coming. In fact, he nearly kissed my hand in thankfulness. He's old, and his vision is getting cloudy, so he's having trouble caring for the holy relics properly, which distresses him, poor lamb. But at least his near blindness will keep him from seeing you well enough to detect that you're a girl.''

''But I am to serve right in the castle? I had hoped for something out in the town. Isn't there more chance of

Ranulf seeing me this way?'' Aldyth asked, twisting her hands in a fold of her tunic.

Lady Vivienne chuckled. ''What better place to avoid an irreligious king's friends than in the chamber that houses the relics? You'll sleep in the adjoining scriptorium, where the clerks inscribe the many writs that go out in the king's name. In fact, I've also told him you have learning, so Osbert may put you to work with quill and parchment, as well. Go on, now. I told the good brother you'd be along soon.''

Brother Osbert squinted at them nearsightedly. ''Aye, he'll do,'' he said to Warin. ''You're not a runaway 'prentice, are ye, Edward? Ye're not a serf bound to the land? Not run off from some monastery that raised ye?'' He patted her head as if searching for a tonsure. ''I cannot in good conscience take ye in if that be true,'' he added, clucking at the thought.

''Nay, Father, I'm none of those things,'' she told him, adding to herself, *merely a runaway bride.*

He reached for her hands, his own trembling with palsy. ''Thanks be to Saint Swithin, your hands are small-boned, like the rest of you. That is good—the last great ham-handed lout of a boy that worked here broke a tooth off St. Gildas's skull when he took a notion to dust the inside of the reliquary box. Very well, come with me, for there's work to be done. You may fetch your belongings later. The holy relics must be kept immaculate, even if his grace the king never bothers to look at them.'' He turned and walked back into the scriptorium as Aldyth strove to conquer her urge to giggle. Rolling her eyes at the amused Warin, she followed the shuffling old clerk.

Osbert seemed not to require any food, or to think that those who assisted him might need to eat. He kept Aldyth busy right through the midday meal, dusting and rearranging the many ornate containers that held the relics of long-dead saints. As they handled each piece, he told her with pride the name of each saint and what the box contained. A few held scraps of cloth, others locks of hair, and there was a jeweled vial purported to contain a drop of the Virgin's milk. One elaborately gilded and velvet-lined reliquary, Osbert told her, held a splinter from the True Cross. Still others contained yellowed fragments of bone.

Preferring not to dwell on their contents, Aldyth instead took delight in the loveliness of the carved wood, silver and gold boxes decorated with pearls, garnets, amethysts and sapphires.

After she had dusted and moved everything to Brother Osbert's satisfaction, he said, "Come along to the scriptorium now, Edward. Lady Vivienne tells me you are able to read and write, and if I judge that to be true, we shall make use of you there, as well." They entered another room, where there were several clerks, all seated at desks, scratching over parchment with quill pens and ink, inscribing the king's writs. A lad clad in a rough brown tunic, who was scrubbing the floor at the clerks' feet, looked up curiously when she came in behind Osbert.

Aldyth's careful hand pleased the clerks, and she was given a writ regarding a grant of land to copy out. This took her the rest of the afternoon, but she found it interesting enough to copy the elaborate Latin legal phrases from the original copy to the one that would be sent to some baron in Dorset.

Finally, as the light coming through the chamfered windows was beginning to fail, her stomach growled loudly enough to be heard through the entire room.

The clerk in charge smiled.

"Edward, you have done well. You may go to the hall and get your dinner."

"Thank you, brother." With luck Lord Ranulf would not have returned and she would find Warin and eat with him.

The great hall was crowded with diners eating in long rows at tables set at right angles to the high table, but she was in luck, for she found Warin seated with Lady Vivienne.

"How went your first day as clerk's assistant?" inquired Lady Vivienne, inviting Aldyth to join them with a graceful gesture.

Aldyth gave a rueful smile. "Let us say it does not tempt me to take minor orders, but 'tis peaceful enough work. I thank you for helping me, Lady Vivienne."

"'Twas naught. Have some of the venison with pepper sauce, Al—that is, Edward."

For a few moments Aldyth contented herself with filling her stomach.

"The hunters have not returned?" she inquired casually of Warin, not trusting herself to use Ranulf's name in front of his mistress.

"Nay, though we had word they would arrive tonight," Warin said, gnawing with relish on a capon leg.

If her luck held, she would have eaten and returned to the scriptorium before Lord Ranulf arrived. "Brother, your manners would disgrace a serf!" Aldyth said as Warin took a particularly large bite.

"*Edward,* you sound like a peevish older sister," Warin retorted, then grinned at her discomfiture. "Don't worry, no one heard you, but you would do well to ape me, not criticize me. Boys don't eat so daintily."

Just then a trumpet flourish announced the arrival of the king. Nicknamed "Rufus" since childhood for his florid complexion, he strode in, an unkingly, thickset man with long blond hair and a potbelly. His hunting companions, still attired in short, belted tunics and cloaks, followed him.

Aldyth could not keep her eyes from immediately searching out Ranulf. He was easy to find. In his tunic and matching cloak of russet, his dark hair windblown, he was like a magnificent wild fox in the autumn woods. He was laughing at some jest of the king, his head thrown back, his white teeth gleaming in the torchlight.

Then he caught sight of Lady Vivienne and waved, and instead of following his king up to the high table, he changed course and started threading his way between the rows of trestle tables toward them.

"I have to leave!" she whispered to Lady Vivienne, panicked.

"Nay, stay, Aldyth," whispered Warin. "He'll be all the more apt to spy you if you try to dash out."

"Just keep your head down and likely he'll never notice you," added Lady Vivienne, speaking to her but smiling in Ranulf's direction.

She froze, bowed over her trencher, feeling very much like a rabbit who hoped to escape a fox's notice by her stillness.

"Good even, my lord," she heard Lady Vivienne greet him. "Was there good hunting?"

"Good even, my comely sweetheart," came his answer, just above Aldyth's head. He was standing right behind her, speaking to Lady Vivienne, who sat next to Aldyth. "Aye, the king got a magnificent stag," he said, reaching casually over his mistress's shoulder for a ripe red apple in a bowl of fruit.

"I sense there is more to this story," Lady Vivienne murmured encouragingly.

Out of the corner of her eye Aldyth could see the Norman woman lean against Ranulf's body as Ranulf laid a hand caressingly on her shoulder.

The sight of them was an arrow piercing Aldyth's heart. Beneath the table she clenched her hands into fists, wondering how long she could endure this.

"You're so perceptive, my sweet," he said. "The king made an excellent shot, but mine was better. *I* was the one who slew the wild boar that suddenly charged out of the undergrowth at the king when he dismounted to gloat over his kill."

"So his grace is pleased with you?"

"Aye. And you, my sweet? Shall you show me later how proud you are of your mighty hunter?"

The coxcomb, the braggart! Couldn't he trouble himself to lower his voice while uttering sweet words to his leman? There was a child present! She darted a look at Warin, but his brother appeared unfazed by the flirting, merely impatient to get Ranulf's attention.

"Aye, 'twould be my pleasure...."

"And who's this angry lad with Warin who looks as if he would kill me with his glare?" Ranulf said suddenly, interrupting Lady Vivienne, his dark eyes suddenly fixed on Aldyth.

"Ah, that is Edward, my lord, of—"

"He's my cousin, Lord Ranulf, from Pevensey!" cried Warin, a little too shrilly. "He's—he's come to serve at court and—"

"The pup likes me not, 'twould appear," murmured Ranulf, his gaze piercing. "I wonder why that might be?" His hand shot out suddenly and touched Aldyth's shoulder. "Why do you look so wrathful, young Edward of Pevensey? Does the color of my cloak offend you?"

She steeled herself not to tremble at his touch, to meet his eyes, then look down humbly as a page would. "Nay, my lord," she said, remembering to keep her voice pitched low.

"You mistake me. I was not wrathful. I . . . just do not see very well."

Her excuse sounded lame and she knew it, but she prayed he would be so eager to resume bantering with his mistress that he would let it go by.

For a moment, it seemed as if he would. He started to turn back to Lady Vivienne, and then he was still, his ebony stare paralyzing Aldyth.

"Aldyth! By God's toenails, what are you doing here? *And what, by all that's holy, have you done to your hair?*"

Chapter Nine

Aldyth stared up into eyes black as midnight during a new moon, eyes that seemed to gleam with anger as her heart pounded in increasing dread. She could think of nothing to say.

"My lord, she was afraid of T—" Warin began, but he was silenced by Ranulf's upraised palm.

"I have asked your sister to explain herself. Well, Aldyth?"

When she could still form no words, he spoke to Lady Vivienne. "I must sup with the king, but I would hear her reasons before I return her to her father's keep. I see you are done with your supper, my lady. I would have you take her to my chamber and wait with her there until I come."

Before I return her to her father's keep . . . It was a death sentence. She couldn't go back, not with Turold there, waiting to make her life misery!

Lady Vivienne was speaking to him now, saying something in soft, rapid Norman French. Relying on his momentary distraction, Aldyth catapulted from her seat, running between the tables toward the entrance of the hall. She would leave the castle tonight and hide in the town, then flee—flee anywhere. . . .

She made it as far as the entrance before Ranulf caught her.

"Fool! Where did you think to go? The gates are closed for the night!" There was no anger in his voice, just an irritated amusement as she struggled against the iron grip he maintained around her wrist.

"Let me go, my lord. You have no right to hold me," she raged, launching herself at him with her free hand clenched into a fist.

"Hush, Aldyth—if you would continue to pass for a lad. People are watching," he warned her in a low voice.

She looked around and saw that it was true. At nearby trestle tables, castle servants stared, and even a couple of the nobles on the dais had noticed the fracas and were smirking. She ceased her struggles.

"You *must* let me go, Lord Ranulf," she pled in a softer voice. "I—I cannot go back to Sherborne. Merely loose me and I will not trouble you further. I will go from here and you may deny ever seeing me—"

But he continued to maintain his firm grasp about her wrist, all the while studying her with that damnable amused smile.

"Interesting . . . I had heard you were about to become a bride, yet now I find you here, your lovely hair butchered, insisting you cannot go home."

"Please, my lord . . ." Was she more afraid of being returned to her home or of the mischief dancing in those devilish eyes?

By this time an anxious Lady Vivienne and Warin had caught up to them, but the king's seneschal was also approaching, an inquisitive expression on his face.

"If you would be so kind, my lady, accompany 'Edward' directly to my chamber and I will join you anon. And if he gives you any difficulty, have Warin summon Urse from the

stables to give him the hiding he deserves.'' Then he gave the
approaching steward a grin. "Nothing to worry about,
Eudo. Just a new page in sorry need of some discipline."

"Come, Edward," snapped Lady Vivienne under the
steward's watchful eye. "If you would only learn to heed my
lord, you would escape such dire consequences as you will
experience later."

A fire in the brazier had warmed Ranulf's chambers, and
the three sat down to await his coming.

Aldyth's brother was rubbing his eyes. "Warin, you look
tired," the Norman woman told him. "Go to sleep. I will
wake you if Lord Ranulf needs aught. Do not worry, all will
be well with your sister."

Warin complied, going to recline on his pallet by the door.
He began snoring in minutes.

Lady Vivienne arose and poured two goblets of wine,
handing one to Aldyth before sitting down next to her with
the other. "My dear, I think there is something you should
know about Lord Ranulf, but I tell you this in strictest confidence."

"You may trust me, Lady Vivienne," Aldyth replied, curious to know what Ranulf's leman would tell her.

"I thought I could. Aldyth, I am Lord Ranulf's mistress
in name only. He does not actually share my bed."

Aldyth felt her mouth drop open. She had expected the
Norman woman to say anything but this. "But why? Is
he...does he not...?" She couldn't bring herself to say the
words.

"Does he not like women?" Lady Vivienne finished for
her. "Oh no, that's not it at all. Lord Ranulf is very much a
man. 'Tis just that I was alone here, a widow, and defense-
less against the base scoundrels that inhabit the court. My
lord was...well, let us just say he was willing to extend his

protection, out of the kindness of his heart, without asking aught of me.''

Aldyth was more confused than ever. ''My lady, why are you telling me this?''

Lady Vivienne smiled. ''Because I think you have an image of Lord Ranulf in your mind as a wicked, dissolute man, lost to all that is good, especially between a man and the one lady who is destined to be his. But that is not the truth of it, Aldyth. 'Tis merely what he wants the world to see.''

''What are you saying, my lady?'' Aldyth asked, mystified.

Lady Vivienne reached out and grasped Aldyth's hand. ''I am not that woman, Aldyth. In fact, my heart belongs to another. But I know the right woman exists for Ranulf—somewhere.'' And she squeezed Aldyth's hand.

Her mind awhirl, Aldyth was about to probe more deeply into Lady Vivienne's words when the door opened.

She started, fearing that Ranulf had cut short his supper with the king in order to demand an explanation from her, but it was only Urse.

Lady Vivienne rose to meet him, a smile of greeting on her face, and suddenly Aldyth knew who it was that owned the Norman woman's heart—Lord Ranulf's squire. Did the giant Breton know? Could any man fail to notice the love shining from Lady Vivienne's eyes as she gazed at him?

''Lady Vivienne, well met,'' he said in his jovial, husky voice. ''And who is this young pup?'' he added, indicating Aldyth.

Lady Vivienne explained briefly while Aldyth squirmed in embarrassment. ''And as for why she is dressed like a lad, Urse, you will have to await my lord's return for the full explanation. There is no need for the poor girl to have to give it twice.''

"I wouldn't miss such a tale as this for all the coin in the treasury," said Urse, settling himself on a nearby stool with a goblet of wine. "But I must say, Lady Aldyth, you make a very fetching lad." Then he turned back to Lady Vivienne, and the two bantered on about this and that while the hour candle burned low in its socket.

It was more than two hours before the clink of Ranulf's spurs woke Aldyth from her doze.

"All right, Aldyth. I left as soon as I could escape his grace, who would have a game of tables from me first," he announced, looming over her like a vision from hell, handsome as Lucifer, and as dangerous. "Warin said you were afraid. Afraid of what? Of marriage, you spoiled, pampered wench? Of a husband's control? By the saints, I believe you need those things sorely."

"I am not afraid of marriage!" she retorted, indignant at his hectoring tone. "I fled Sherborne because I discovered the man I was to marry was a monster—worse than you!"

He had the nerve to laugh at her. "Worse than me? Hard to believe a man could be covered with more sins than I am, my innocent Aldyth. Come now, how could he be worse than me?"

"I learned Turold had a mistress, and—"

"A mistress? What of it? I have a mistress," he said, indicating Lady Vivienne. "So do most men with red blood running in their veins, despite what pious priests say."

Aldyth realized that now was not the time to admit she knew the truth about Ranulf and Lady Vivienne. "My lord, he not only had a mistress, but he had every intention of continuing to bed her after the ceremony. And he struck me when I dared to protest—aye, and would have raped me, too, right there in the chapel, on the eve of our wedding! So I fled."

He stared at her, all amusement vanished from his dark, cynical features. A long finger traced the outline of the fading bruises on her cheek, as if he'd just realized what they were. "You could not go to your father? Or to Godric?"

"No, my lord," she told him. "I felt I could not."

"And yet you did not come to me, either." Behind him, the candle flickered, lighting the angular planes of his face.

She answered softly, though Urse and Lady Vivienne were conversing together. "How could I, Ranulf, the way matters were left between us?"

He seemed suddenly thoughtful, his thumbs perched on his wide leather belt. "How indeed," he murmured. "'Twould be like fleeing from one monster to another. Well, there's only one answer for it—you must seek sanctuary in a convent."

"No, never!" she cried. "I'll not do it! You cannot make me, Ranulf! I'll only run away again!"

"Easy, easy, my passionate little one," he said, coming to run his hands down her arms, gentling her like a fractious falcon. "I meant only temporarily, while I meet with your father and the bishop and secure an annulment of your betrothal—"

"I won't go to any convent to be ordered about by an abbess and her sour old sisters in religion! How do I know I'd ever be released from the betrothal? The next thing I'd know, Turold might show up at the abbey and force me to go with him—and no nuns would be able to naysay him!"

He studied her for a long moment. "Very well, no convent for you while I get you free of this tangle, Aldyth, but what about staying with my lady mother at Kingsclere? She would—"

She shook her head. "Turold is not to be trusted, my lord. I am afraid of what he might do if he knew where I was. Please, my lord, might I not stay here, disguised as your page?'' She had not known she was going to ask such a thing until the words had tumbled from her lips.

He stared at her. ''My page? Certainly not! I already have a page—your brother, you foolish girl! And if you despised me since that day in the stables, why would you want to stay in my very household?''

Aldyth didn't know the reason herself. She only knew that something had changed since Lady Vivienne had confided in her that she was not Lord Ranulf's leman and that Lord Ranulf was not the devil he pretended to be. She only knew she had no desire to continue hiding in the chapel royal, dusting reliquaries and writing out writs in the scriptorium, if she could be near Ranulf.

''Oh, please, my lord! Let me stay, I beg of you! I appeal to your chivalry!'' she cried, flinging herself at his feet.

''You forget, Aldyth, I haven't any chivalry,'' he said, looking down at her. ''I believe you once called me a 'braying Norman ass'? You were closer to the truth then, I believe.''

His face was set in hard, sardonic lines. There was no evidence that she had reached his heart, and she began to weep in earnest. ''Oh, please, my lord, I am so afraid! Please let me stay! I'll be no trouble! I'll do anything you ask of me!''

''*Anything?*'' he inquired with an ironic lift of one brow as he cupped her chin.

''Oh, for pity's sake, my lord! Give her yea or nay, but do not torment her,'' Lady Vivienne interrupted in an exasperated tone.

Aldyth ignored her. ''Anything.'' She meant it.

''Lord Ranulf...'' Lady Vivienne began.

Ranulf suddenly let out his breath. ''Oh, very well, though I must truly be mad to even consider such a thing. But hear me—'' he raised his voice, for Aldyth was laughing and crying at once and had clasped her arms around his knees fervently "—this is only a *temporary* solution, Aldyth. It will last only until I can journey home and put the fear of God—or my sword—into this Turold you've so foolishly gotten betrothed to. I'll warrant there are enough silver marks in my coffers to cause him to abandon his dream of revenge soon enough."

"Oh, thank you, Ranulf, you won't be sorry, I swear it. I'll be an excellent page, just as good as Warin—"

"By God's toenails, one hopes you can do better than that," he drawled, the languid, fey lord suddenly taking the place of the serious, impassioned Ranulf that had been standing there a moment before. "The pup eats more than Urse here, and pays no more attention to the proper care of my garments than would a flea—just look, I pray you, at the rent in this cloak..." He bent to show her an insignificant tear in the russet fabric.

"I'll mend it, my lord, so that you need never know it was there!" she promised him.

"Hmm, perhaps this will work out very well," he drawled consideringly. "I will have Warin concentrate on the care of my horse, while your focus can be on my wardrobe. The garments a man wears are *so* important at court..."

"Yes, my lord."

He fingered a few strands of her shorn hair and clucked disapprovingly. "You will start growing this out immediately. 'Tis shorter than mine."

"Yes, my lord." How she wished she knew a magic spell so that she could comply immediately. She was ashamed at how she must look to him, like a starved sparrow.

He removed his hand. "The hour grows late, Urse, show Aldyth where she may find bedding to make up her pallet next to Warin's." He turned to Lady Vivienne. "And now, my lady, let me walk you to your chamber and collect on that loving promise you made earlier in the hall," he said, his tone velvet and seductive.

And utterly fake, Aldyth knew, even if Lady Vivienne had not managed to wink at her behind Ranulf's back as he led her to the door. Wherever Ranulf slept tonight, it would not be in Lady Vivienne's bed.

Chapter Ten

Ranulf had known as soon as he had said the words that
he was making a mistake. He should not allow his uncon-
quered love for Aldyth to cloud his judgment and allow her
to stay with him.

Prior to her coming, he had thought he had damped
down, if not extinguished entirely, the smoldering flames of
his unwise passion, but as soon as he had recognized the
green eyes staring defiantly at him from beneath that ridiculous cropped hair, he had known it was not so. He loved
her still. He always would. His task, infinitely more difficult now that she slept under the same roof as he did and ate
the bread he provided, was not to let her know.

In a week's time, her presence had become the source of
his greatest joy and his sorest torment. Just to see Aldyth
making herself busy about his quarters—setting all to rights,
fetching food from the kitchens for him when he had not
had time to eat properly, mending his garments, for all the
world like some freedman's honest wife—made him ache.
When he had come upon her yesterday, placing fresh sheets
upon his bed, it had been all he could do not to sweep her
into his arms, lay her down on the fresh linens and make her
his own. He had had to turn immediately and leave the

room. How much was a flesh-and-blood man supposed to endure?

At least in the evenings there were others about, sometimes Lady Vivienne, and always Urse and Warin. But Aldyth's little brother had a way of smiling at him and Aldyth—just as if they were one happy family! That made Ranulf cross. The silly young boy! Did he think all problems were solved because Aldyth was here? God's toenails, it was a fool's paradise!

He stared at her now as she sat making use of the morning light coming through the window to add a decorative band of embroidery to one of his hunting tunics. If anyone admired it, he would pass the work off as that of his mistress, Lady Vivienne, of course.

Hearing Aldyth swear softly as her thread broke, he smiled to himself. As he watched, knowing she was concentrating and unaware of his gaze, she pushed a strand of chestnut hair away from her face and narrowed her eyes with the effort of rethreading the bone needle.

He wished he had not made his disparaging remarks about her short hair. In truth, once Lady Vivienne had trimmed it a little, the style no longer looked like a serf's hacked-off locks. It gave her a uniquely gamine look, and the wisps of hair curling about her slender nape made him feel strangely protective. Perhaps, as long as she insisted "pon living with him in this disguise, he had better encourage her to continue to appear a slender waif. As a "boy" she could go anywhere in this licentious court with reasonable safety. Once her hair had grown back a little, though, it would be all too obvious she was no lad. When he was not there, anyone might desire to spoil her innocence . . .

The clanging of one metal goblet against another interrupted his thoughts. "My lord! Will you please attend to what I'm saying?" Lady Vivienne said in exasperation. He realized she had been speaking for several moments and had purposely banged the goblets together to gain his attention.

"I'm sorry, Lady Vivienne. I fear I was woolgathering. You were saying...?"

He saw her follow the line of his gaze, and when her eyes fell at last upon Aldyth, she began to smile. "Indeed," she murmured.

Damn the woman! Her smile said she had some idea how his loins burned and thought it was amusing!

"I'm listening now," he snapped. "Stop grinning like the court fool and tell me what you came to say."

But his testiness did nothing to dim her suppressed merriment. "I said, Lord Cross-as-a-Baited-Bear, that I chanced to pass his grace the king as he was going to the hall and he said he desired an audience with you as soon as you could attend him."

"He did? Good!" Anything to escape his supposed mistress's knowing eyes and smirking smile. "Aldyth, I'll see you later," he remembered to add before slamming the door.

"Is your new page settling in all right?" inquired the king genially, looking up from his contemplation of a map of Normandy spread out on the table before him, its curling parchment corners anchored with a pot of ink, a flagon of ale, a greasy leg of capon and a wedge of cheese.

"Yes, your grace," Ranulf replied, uneasy that the king had noted the addition of "Edward" to his household. Rufus's pages tended to be of the fair, delicate sort, like his current squire, Perrin of Petersfield, who lounged next to the king now. Ranulf hoped the king had enough young men competing for his favor that he didn't covet his vassal's new page.

"Very good, very good. Perhaps you'll choose to take him with you across the Channel when you go," Rufus said, grinning at Ranulf's evident surprise.

"Across the Channel?" Ranulf repeated.

"Yes. I've decided to have you pay a visit to the court of Normandy, to check on what my elder brother Duke Robert is about. I've heard rumors of plots. The older Norman families weren't pleased that my father gave the kingdom to me, you know. They'd be happy to see Robert with it all— the throne of England and the Duchy of Normandy—because they can control him. It may have to be a prolonged visit, but you'll enjoy a Christmas court in Rouen, won't you? Go and tell him you and I have had a falling-out—you know the sort of thing he'll fall for—and loiter about Rouen. See what information you can sniff out. Who's sleeping with whom, so to speak," Rufus concluded with a snigger.

Ranulf nodded, pretending to be intrigued with the role of traitor he was being ordered to assume.

"How soon do you wish me to leave, your grace?" he asked, his mind racing ahead. It was a godsend. He would inform Aldyth she was not going, of course. Though it might take some doing, he could arrange for her to stay somewhere safe, even if it meant placing her back with the clerks in the chapel royal. Before he left he could begin the process, through his church contacts, of canceling Aldyth's betrothal contract. But the advantage of being sent away right now was that with the Channel between himself and Aldyth, at least for a time, he could somehow find the strength to give her up. He could not ask her to wait for him for God knew how long.

"You're...you're going to Normandy? Without me?" she said an hour later as they took the midday meal in Ranulf's outer chamber. Her lower lip quivered and she looked away, but not before he had seen tears well up in the jade eyes.

"Of course without you. It's too dangerous to even consider. There are even more scoundrels and scapegraces about Duke Robert's court, and the road from the coast is rife with brigands."

"But that doesn't stop you from taking my brother," she pointed out, her jaw jutting out pugnaciously as she indicated the excited boy beside her. "I don't like you exposing him to danger—"

"Aldyth!" her brother cried in anguished embarrassment.

"He's my page. He's a *boy*," Ranulf pointed out, guessing from the sparks flashing in her green eyes that his deliberate tone was maddening to her.

The real danger was of Aldyth ever guessing the fantasies his mind had been spinning about her accompanying him on the journey. He could picture them together, compelled to share a tiny room with a single bed at some harbor inn at Honfleur. The idea was enough to make him throb with need. Perhaps it would be better if he made her angry enough that she would be glad to see him go.

"S-so am I, as far as anyone else would know," she sputtered, putting her arm protectively about Warin.

"Aldyth!" Warin squirmed out of her sisterly embrace. "I'm not an infant in swaddling bands!"

"I'm sorry, Warin," she said, her voice contrite. "Of course you're not. But I want to go, too! I can't bear the idea of being left to dust relics and scratch out Latin writs under Brother Osbert."

"I have given you another option, that of staying with Lady Vivienne's babes," Ranulf reminded her. "They'll have their nurse, of course, but I'm sure old Marie would appreciate help with those lively children."

"Oh, they love you, Aldyth," Lady Vivienne said encouragingly, "and I'd feel better knowing you were with them." Lady Vivienne, of course, was going; it was expected that Lord Ranulf would want to take his "mistress" along.

"Please, sister, don't take it so hard," Warin pleaded, laying a hand beseechingly on her arm.

Aldyth clutched her head and seemed about to make an angry outburst when there came a pounding on the heavy oak door.

"Lord Ranulf! Are you within? Lord Ranulf!"

Ranulf looked at Aldyth, who had gone white as a winding sheet. She stared at the door, then at him, her lips shaping the word *Godric*.

She obeyed instantly as Ranulf motioned her into the inner bedchamber and directed her to conceal herself under the bed. The pounding began again.

Lady Vivienne went to the door, and a moment later Aldyth heard the sounds of booted feet entering the room— two pairs of booted feet.

"Godric!" she heard Warin shout in welcome. Oh, Jésu, had Warin believed her when she'd said that Godric would not have helped her escape Turold? Would he be able to keep the secret of her presence from his older brother?

"Greetings, Godric. This is a surprise," she heard Ranulf say in his lazy, drawling manner. "I hope you bring no ill news of my lord father or my lady mother?"

"Nay, my lord. They are well, and I am here with the earl's leave. Lord Ranulf, I would present Turold of Swanlea to you, the betrothed of my sister."

Turold was here, in the next room! Her blood froze in terror. She inched forward beneath the bed until she had a narrow view of the outer room, and she could see the two pairs of dusty, booted feet and a few inches of their braies.

"My lord," she heard the hated voice murmur respectfully. She could not hear Ranulf make a reply.

"My lord, are you aware that my sister disappeared from Sherborne keep on the night of her wedding? We come seeking her," Aldyth heard Godric say.

"We had word, of course, from my father, who felt Warin should be aware. But why come you here? Surely your runaway bride would be found closer to home, Turold."

"My Aldyth did not run away, my lord," Turold corrected him defensively. "We were in love. I fear the worst."

"The worst?" she heard Ranulf murmur in languid tones. "Surely the worst is being shackled to one woman forever. You have had a lucky escape, my good Turold!"

"You are pleased to make jests, but I mean I fear foul play," she heard Turold respond stiffly. The scoundrel, to try to paint himself as the grieving lover!

"If she's been abducted, then surely they would not bring her here," Ranulf drawled. "Unless, of course, you are accusing *me* of stealing your bride? God's toenails, the idea is ludicrous!"

Did he have to make it sound as if she were the last woman on earth he'd want? Aldyth thought wrathfully from her hiding place under the bed.

"My lord, I accuse you of nothing," Turold said hastily. "I merely thought she might come here seeking her younger brother."

Ranulf pounced on the remark. "Ah, so you don't feel she's been abducted after all. You really do feel she's bolted from your marriage bed."

"My lord, we're just trying to find her, to make sure she's all right," Godric put in. "Turold and I have combed the area around Sherborne and Kingsclere, so 'twas natural to come to Winchester next. Not only is our brother here, but

I'm aware that once my sister had ... feelings for you ...''
Godric's voice trailed off. Aldyth wondered if Ranulf heard
the undertones of hostility and defiance.

"Feelings? For me? That pure maiden? What an
astounding idea!" Ranulf said, laughing. "I can assure you
gentlemen that I had not guessed."

"Would that I could share my lord's merriment," Turold
said in a pompous voice, "but as I have told you, I am a
worried bridegroom bereft of his bride. Am I correct that
you would have me believe you have not seen her?"

"I don't care what you believe, fellow," came Ranulf's
voice with silky insolence. "But nay, the maid has not
sought sanctuary with me."

"Warin?" she heard Godric ask, and she could picture
the piercing gaze her elder brother would be leveling at this
moment at their younger sibling. *Jésu, please forgive him
for the lie, but make him able to tell it* ... She held her breath
and squeezed her eyes shut. Godric had always been able to
pry the truth out of Warin, whose guileless eyes held no secrets.

"Of course I haven't seen her!" she heard him respond
stoutly. "Why wouldn't I tell you if I had?"

She dared to breathe again.

"But I'd like to know why my sister ran away from you,
Turold of Swanlea," she heard Warin declare with defiant
boldness. "You must be an evil man if Aldyth won't have
you as husband."

"Why, you impertinent little puppy. I'll break you like a
twig," Turold growled, and Aldyth heard scuffling sounds
as the feet belonging to Godric and Turold mingled. Godric
was holding Turold back.

"Warin, you will apologize to Turold," snapped Godric.
"Apologize, or I'll give you a hiding—"

"I believe my page is mine to beat," drawled Ranulf, and she saw him interpose his silly shoes with the curling toes between Godric and Warin. "I have told you I am not concealing Aldyth here, so you may both be gone."

"Oh, I believe we will linger about Winchester for a time, my lord. We have journeyed far in our quest, and we are weary," Godric said. "Since I have his lordship's permission to help Turold find my sister, I need be in no haste to leave." His voice diminished as he and Turold moved toward the door. "Perhaps it is merely that she has not arrived yet."

"Aye, she will show herself eventually," Turold said. Then, his voice heavy with menace, he added, "And when she does, I'll be waiting."

The door was shut, and she heard them stomping down the stairs. She went to the window, peering cautiously over the edge, and a minute later saw them stalking across the bailey, deep in conversation. Then Turold looked back and up, in the direction of her window, and she ducked down just in time.

She straightened and went into the other room, where Warin and Lady Vivienne and Ranulf were all staring at one another ruefully.

"See, my lord," she said triumphantly. "You have no choice—now you *must* take me with you."

Chapter Eleven

It was the only solution. He was caught, and he knew it, but Ranulf misliked having this slip of a girl tell him he must do what he knew he must do—unless he was to deny her the help he had promised. But he struggled against the tightening noose anyway.

"The devil you say!" he retorted, slouching in his chair. "What makes you think the presence of those two will make me do what I do not wish? I'll merely think of a better place about the castle to hide you."

He saw her eyes glitter with unshed tears, but she raised her chin defiantly. "Very well, if you do not care what happens to me—if you want that brute to find me—he'll kill me, you know, and then I'll haunt you, I swear it!"

"Oh, be reasonable, my lord," snapped Lady Vivienne in exasperation. "This is but a small castle, and they would see her eventually or hear someone gossip about Lord Ranulf's newly arrived page."

"Such a pother about nothing," he drawled. "There's always my keep at Beauworth. I don't know why I didn't think of it before."

"And if you've thought of it, Godric will, too," Lady Vivienne pointed out. "You'd take a chance of that Turold finding her? She does not exaggerate—I've seen his type before,'' Lady Vivienne said. "He will kill her, the moment she crosses him. He had the cold eyes of a stoat."

"Very well, I'll take her to Kingsclere before I go," he said irritably. "She'll be safe enough behind my father's moated walls, I dare swear."

"I've told you why that will not answer, my lord!" Aldyth said. "And anyway, did not the king say you were to leave by day after the morrow? You have no time to be shepherding me back to the earl and the countess if you are to leave for Normandy in two days' time."

She was right, and he knew she knew it.

"Surely there's no harm in takin' the girl," boomed Urse. "I'll watch out for her, my lord."

Both Aldyth and Lady Vivienne shot him a grateful look. He had but one arrow left in his quiver.

"What say *you*, Warin? But before you answer, know that I cannot take you both. If your sister comes as Edward, my page, I will not be able to take you. We must travel far and fast, you know. I'll have to find something to keep you occupied about the court."

There was a long silence during which Warin looked crestfallen as he stared at Ranulf, then at his sister, and back to Ranulf again. A sudden thought seemed to strike him, and he grinned in a cheeky fashion.

"I won't mind if you take Aldyth, my lord, if you will give me leave to visit my father at Sherborne for Christmas while you are gone."

Aldyth's face wore an expression of total incredulity.

"Oh, it is the perfect solution, my lord!" she said, clapping her hands together. "Thank you, Warin, thank you! I am so proud of you!"

Ranulf held his hands out in defeat, conscious of a current of joy running perversely through him even as he conceded defeat. Aldyth would be accompanying him to

Normandy. "You are too well championed for me to refuse you, Aldyth, it seems. But hear me well—you will dress during the entire journey as Edward and you will obey me instantly in all things. Is that perfectly understood? It may well mean your life. Nay, don't weep now—you will unman me."

"Aye, my lord," she said, smiling through tears that threatened to spill over onto her cheeks. "I will carry out your every command. Turold will be on this side of the Channel and I will be on the other, not having to fear him. I am so relieved! I'll make certain you are not sorry, my lord, that you rescued me."

So that was it. While he was imagining the intimacy of traveling with her, she was merely grateful to be escaping a brutish husband. She had gotten over her love for him. Ranulf called himself every kind of a conceited fool. She not only was no longer in love with him but probably feared and detested all men, after what Turold had shown her of his sex, God rot him!

He must show her she need fear no lustful attentions from him.

"*Eh bien*, part of your obedience will entail giving my leman and me occasions of privacy, eh, Lady Vivienne?" he said, leering at Vivienne.

Vivienne was paying him no attention, so lost was she in gazing adoringly at his squire, who was grinning back at her. He turned back to Aldyth.

Her face was a mask. "I understand fully, my lord."

"Good. Then we need to discuss how we're going to spirit you out of the castle under that pair of louts' watchful eyes and get you onto a cog without being seen. You may have to be hidden until we set sail, you know. I wouldn't put it above those two not to shadow us all the way to the coast. Now here's how I think it should be done..."

* * * *

"Such a heavy-laden wain, my lord," she heard Turold say to Ranulf two days later. The voice was muffled, for Aldyth, curled into a tight ball, lay concealed in one of the two large iron-bound chests stowed on the ox cart behind four tuns of mead.

"Yes, the king is sending the mead as a Christmas gift to Duke Robert, and of course I could not *think* of skimping on my wardrobe for a visit to the Duke of Normandy's court, even though my squire twits me about my notorious love of fine garments in peacock hues..."

Within the confines of the chest, Aldyth rolled her eyes. Ranulf was really playing it to the hilt. She could almost see the elaborate gestures, the eyes raised heavenward...

"In troth my feelings are a bit stronger than that, I don't mind telling you," Urse said in long-suffering tones. "For who gets to carry these chests full of robes and tunics for my lord the peacock? I do! And if *his* clothing weren't enough, there's my lady's clothes..."

"Well, naturally! My leman need not play peahen to her peacock. Lady Vivienne must appear before his grace as gloriously arrayed as I. 'Twould not be chivalrous else. And then there are our jewels and gold chains."

"Naturally," Turold echoed, his voice heavy with irony.

"You're a good man to understand so well," Ranulf said with hearty gratitude. "Perhaps you'd like to consider service in my household—since it doesn't appear that you'll be getting married, that is."

There was silence for a moment. Aldyth could imagine Turold's astonishment. After all, he'd as good as accused Lord Ranulf of harboring his betrothed, and now the man was offering him a position. What a fool Ranulf must seem to him.

"I thank you, my lord, but I must continue to seek Aldyth. In any case, I do not think I'm suited for such a role. I'm used to being my own master—as much as any Englishman is allowed to be these days, even as a freeholder."

Ranulf seemed not the least put out by the barely veiled hostility. "Ah well, I just thought I should make the offer. 'Tis the least I could do, since your lady ran away."

Aldyth grinned from her place of concealment. She could visualize Turold stiffening at the needling hidden within the apparent sympathy. He did not dare react with anger, however.

"You do not take your page, my lord?" she heard Godric ask.

"Nay, I thought to give him a holiday," Ranulf replied casually.

She was less amused when she heard Godric and Turold tell Lord Ranulf they would be accompanying them to the coast. Godric insisted Lord Ranulf's father would want him to do so, for it was well-known there were outlaws preying on travelers on the road south. In vain did Ranulf point to his six mounted men-at-arms as evidence they were not needed, but she knew he dared not protest much. He could not refuse to let them ride with them without it looking suspicious.

Their presence meant she would have to stay hidden in the chest all day. The wain lurched and jolted over the road south while she remained in her cramped position with her nose pressed to the holes Urse had cut in the ornamental carving on the sides of the chest. It was very little comfort to know that she was more sheltered than the others from the bone-chilling rain and wind.

By the time the chest was loaded on the bobbing cog, Aldyth was sure every bone in her body had been shaken apart, and her head throbbed. But she was thankful for the change of travel, as well as for the soldier's presence. She guessed Turold and Godric might have tried to overwhelm Ranulf and his squire and force an inspection of the chests. Instead, with terse farewells, they departed.

The crossing had been a horror. One of the storms that could blow up so quickly, especially in winter, had seized the ship and tossed it about mercilessly. By the next afternoon, when they were about to dock at Honfleur, Ranulf looked every bit the effete noble he pretended to be.

Urse, however, suffered from no *mal de mer* and teased him. "Lord Ranulf, I expect you'll grow scales next. Your visage has the same hue as the belly of a cod." He chuckled at the sight while Ranulf glared and attempted to hide the fact that his gorge had risen at the very thought of fish.

"I thought we were going to be food for the fish at one point, when the cog heeled over so far that the next wave poured right onto her deck," Ranulf said with a shudder. Like most knights, he was no sailor, enduring the Channel only when he must and avoiding any further travel by sea. Everyone knew the waters beyond Europe to be the province of monsters.

"For shame, Lord Ranulf, I don't see Aldyth whining and moping, and she's but a slender maid," Lady Vivienne said, taking up the game and pointing to the girl, who was obviously so glad to stretch her cramped limbs that she seemed actually to enjoy adjusting to the rolling of the vessel.

"Bedevil me not, you two," he moaned, swallowing with difficulty.

"Cheer up, my lord. Fresh air and a good meal at that tavern in Honfleur will soon set you right. Nay, you must put something in that empty stomach or you'll fall off your horse long before Rouen," insisted the huge Breton squire.

The tavern was not far from the docks in the Norman port city. It was comfortably furnished, though not ornate, but Ranulf could not feel at ease when he spotted the six men staring at them from the far corner of the dimly lit common room. There were no other customers.

Too late, Ranulf remembered that he had been so preoccupied with his seasickness that he had neglected to change his clothes to plain, sturdy traveling garb. Under the sea-dampened cloak, he was still wearing a costly tunic with long, trailing sleeves and the shoes with the curling points affected by all Rufus's favorites. The loitering rascals in the corner were taking note of the richness of the velvet, pointing and sniggering.

"Urse," he said quietly, "look behind you at yon collection of blackguards. I think we're in for trouble."

The Breton squire had to swivel completely around because of his patched eye, but even a quelling look from the giant was not enough to stifle the rough group's amusement.

The tavernkeeper promised Ranulf roast capon for him and his party and provided each with a cup of his finest wine, then went out to the kitchen behind the common room. The baiting began.

"'Twould appear that we have visitors from the English court," remarked one in a voice that was meant to carry to Ranulf's ears. "One of William Rufus's fancy, scented lordlings, I doubt not. One can tell by one's nose, *hein?*" He pantomimed sniffing the air.

With a growl, Urse made as if to rise, but Ranulf's hand on his wrist stayed him.

"Let it go since the ladies are with us, and we may yet avoid a fight," he whispered to his squire, conscious that Aldyth's eyes were rounded jade orbs in her pale face. "In any case, I find I *am* hungry after all."

But the rascals were not about to let them relax and enjoy their wine. They were strolling past as if about to leave, when one of their group ran a finger inquiringly down the velvet of Ranulf's tunic.

"Lovely," he murmured with sarcastic emphasis.

"Be careful, Guillaume," one of his friends said. "Likely the popinjay will scratch your eyes out." At this sally they all snorted with derision.

Feeling himself flush with rage, Ranulf fought for control, knowing it was better not to give in and give them the brawl they wanted, lest Aldyth and Lady Vivienne be hurt in the midst of it. He had almost reined in his temper when another of the troublemakers reached down and felt a lock of Ranulf's long, curling hair.

"Do all the English *damoiselles* have hair so soft?" he cooed directly into Ranulf's ear.

Rage won over self-control. Ranulf jumped up, knocking his bench back on the rough-planked floor. The clatter and his roar of fury drowned out Lady Vivienne's scream and the low cry Aldyth smothered behind her hand as both backed out of the way.

Snatching up Urse's wine cup—for he had already spilled his own when he arose so precipitately—Ranulf threw it full in the face of the man who had touched his hair. This action enabled him to follow quickly with a stunning blow to the head, which momentarily staggered the ruffian.

The remainder of the group would have jumped Ranulf *en masse* at this point but for Urse, who had decided to wait no longer to join the fray. The giant had grabbed the nearest two scoundrels and crashed their skulls together. With twin grunts both sank to the floor, senseless. He bellowed a challenge to one of the others. "Come on, ye whoreson, and by God's fist, I'll pound ye into the floor!" The lout foolishly, if obediently, charged the waiting giant.

Ranulf was far too busy to admire the neat way his squire had put a pair of their attackers out of commission at once. Two of the pack circled him, wary now, but waiting for an opening.

He watched them, wishing for the dozenth time that he had not worn the attention-getting tunic with its scalloped, hampering sleeves. The feel of the cold metal links in his hauberk certainly would be comforting now, but his stomach had been roiling as they disembarked and his mail was packed away at the bottom of one of the trunks he would have to reclaim back at the dock. Both his tormentors had daggers in their belts, but if he took time to draw his sword from its scabbard across his back, one or both of them would be upon him before he could accomplish it.

Out of the corner of his eyes he saw Aldyth and Lady Vivienne hugging the wall, stealing toward the ladder that led to the tavern's few bedchambers for hire. All the better. If they could get out of sight, he would not have to worry about them. The tavernkeeper, drawn by the commotion, was peering into the room from the door to the kitchen, but he was useless, merely making moaning protests about the damage.

Turning slightly to place the wall at his back, Ranulf lured the two closer. Then, in a lightning-fast motion, he threw his left shoulder forcefully against the attacker on the left, pushing him backward so that he fell head over heels over another bench.

There was still the other to deal with, and he had drawn his dagger and was dancing on the balls of his feet, shifting the knife from hand to hand and grinning evilly at Ranulf.

Urse, meanwhile, had dispatched the lout who had charged him. Four bodies now littered the hard-packed earthen floor in addition to the overturned bench and discarded bones of previous meals. Urse readied himself to take care of the knife-wielding knave who faced Ranulf.

He had forgotten, however, about the brigand he had first knocked down. That one had been dazed but not unconscious, and he now stole up behind the Breton squire, clutching a wooden bench, and brained Urse with it. The giant sank with a groan.

There were now two to his one, surmised Ranulf. If only he could have the time to draw his sword ...

Movement blurred past his eyes from the direction of the ladder. With a cry worthy of a demon from hell, Aldyth launched herself at the scoundrel who held Ranulf at bay and clonked him on the head with a warming pan. The miscreant fell like a poleaxed ox.

Now there was only one left on his feet, and he seemed more interested in escaping alive than continuing the fight. Ranulf stood, however, between him and the tavern's one door. While the brigand turned to gape at the "boy" behind him, who scowled and swung his impromptu weapon threateningly, Ranulf had the leisure to draw his blade. "Come at me, fool, and I promise to bury my blade in you to the hilt. Leave me alone, and you may live to tell of how an English *damoiselle* refused your attentions."

The lone survivor of the ill-advised mêlée didn't seem able to laugh.

With both Aldyth and now Lady Vivienne in the room brandishing warm pans at the man, Ranulf crossed to the fallen Urse. Keeping an eye and his sword trained on the last bandit, Ranulf shook his squire awake and helped him to his feet with his free hand. Urse shook his head as if to clear it, then glared at the man, who shrank before him.

"Let him live, Urse," Ranulf commanded the Breton, who contented himself with merely knocking the man out. Ranulf then motioned to Aldyth and Lady Vivienne to go past him out the door. They obeyed, after dropping their pans with loud clunks perilously close to two of the fallen knaves' heads. Last of all, Ranulf and Urse backed out the door, but not before Ranulf paused to toss a silver mark in the tavernkeeper's direction. "For your troubles, mine host."

When they reached the outside, all took deep breaths and looked at one another.

"Damn the lot of them," Urse grumbled. "Couldn't they have waited till we'd eaten? The next town is a goodly way up this road."

"Can this be Urse de Caradeuc I'm hearing? Admit it, you love a good fight!" retorted Ranulf with a grin. "I must confess, I haven't felt so alive since we rode on campaign with the Conqueror."

Aldyth watched him, marveling at the change. Gone was the languid courtier he pretended to be, and in his place was a panting, tousled and very handsome Ranulf of Kingsclere—the very image of the hero of chivalry she had imagined before seeing him again at Kingsclere.

As if aware of his eyes on her, he turned to her then. After a quick glance assured him no one but Urse and Lady Vivienne were around, he took both her hands in his. "I owe you a vote of thanks, as well, Aldyth. You were magnificent, swinging that pan. You saved my life, of that I am certain."

His praise and his dark eyes joyously shining down at her were too much to resist. Impulsively she threw her arms about him, crying, "You were splendid as well, my lord! What a cool, calculating fighter! You never panicked, even though you were outnumbered and might well have despaired." And then she kissed him.

His lips were salty, for he was sweaty from the battle, but more than salt she tasted desire—and danger. For the space of a few moments she savored both, allowing him to deepen the kiss, opening her mouth in response to the increasing pressure of his, shivering with delight at the delicious tickle of his mustache and short beard against her skin. This was what she had been born for. It was destiny to be here in the circle of his arms, to be kissed like this. She felt his arm at her back, pulling her closer, and his heart thudding against hers.

His other hand reached between them and cupped her breast, stroking it even through the binding cloth, and suddenly the danger of her position overpowered her desire.

What had made her do such an impulsive thing? She struggled in his embrace, against the arm that held her imprisoned against the hard planes of his chest.

She lifted her mouth from his. "My lord—"

"Nay, don't stop now," he said, his dark eyes gleaming with surprised hunger. "Let us continue with our victory celebration, Aldyth," he murmured, bending his head as if he would resume kissing her.

She no longer wanted to kiss him. After a battle, small or large, a warrior often sought the nearest available, willing woman. It was merely the metamorphosis of blood lust into lust of the more ordinary variety. She meant nothing to him as Aldyth, but Lady Vivienne was the only other woman there and she was absorbed with Urse. If he wanted her, she wanted to be certain it was for herself.

"Loose me, my lord—immediately," she commanded, and with a ragged breath, he complied.

"Coward," he breathed.

"You mistake me, my lord," she protested. "I kissed you because I was happy that we all escaped unscathed, 'tis all..."

The dark, fathomless depths of his eyes became shuttered, and he looked away from her, a muscle twitching in

his temple. She whirled around, hot with embarrassment.
What an idiot! One should not poke a sleeping leopard if
one fears seeing it leap.

He chuckled suddenly, and she turned back, indignant
that he would be laughing at her for reacting like a frightened abbess, but then she saw that she was not the source of
his amusement but rather Urse and Lady Vivienne, who
stood a little way off, wrapped in a passionate embrace. As
Aldyth watched, they raised their heads and stood gazing at
each other in adoration.

"I should have guessed," he called. "My felicitations, my
lady! It seems you have captured my squire's heart!"

Urse looked stunned. "How could you guess when I had
not, my lord? How could I imagine such a winsome lady
could care for a one-eyed monster such as I?"

"You're no monster, merely a giant," Lady Vivienne informed him, "and I don't just care for you, I *love* you, you
big oaf!" Then she seemed to remember Ranulf. "But what
of our arrangement, my lord? I would not—"

"I make no doubt we can find a Norman priest somewhere," Ranulf said easily. "Perhaps we will need to continue the pretense of your being my leman while we are at
the ducal court, but when others are not present..." His
voice trailed off and he winked at them. "I do not see why
you two should continue to deny to each other what is now
common knowledge among us."

"Oh, thank you, Ranulf," Lady Vivienne cried, and left
her giant's arms long enough to give Ranulf a kiss on the
cheek. "You are the noblest of men."

The Norman woman, who had gone back to Urse, didn't
see the rueful look Ranulf leveled at Aldyth after both heard
Lady Vivienne's high opinion of him. Aldyth saw it, though,
and had to fight the urge to giggle. In the space of a few

moments, two women had kissed Ranulf, neither of whom would do more.

It wasn't amusing, though. She was sure now that Lady Vivienne didn't long for Ranulf's love or he for Lady Vivienne's. But Aldyth nevertheless realized that didn't mean he could feel love for *her*—not a true love, which endured longer than it would take a skilled lover such as Ranulf to lure a vulnerable maiden into his bed. Lady Vivienne saw Ranulf through idealistic eyes, Aldyth thought.

In her own week at court, though, she had learned Lord Ranulf was known for his appreciation of women—many women. He would never confine his attentions to one daughter of a poor English castellan, and he would give his heart to no one.

Ranulf cleared his throat. "Perhaps we had better get on the road, you lovebirds. I won't feel secure until I've put on my hauberk."

"Yes, but wait—I heard something," Urse murmured, though he didn't seem apprehensive. With a gesture he indicated they were to follow him to the rear of the public house.

They were in luck. There were six horses tied up at posts there, still saddled and bridled. They could only belong to the ruffians.

"I thought I smelled horses. Here's our mounts, my lord, ladies," Urse said with a grin. "They're not much to look at, but now we won't have to hire horses of our own. There's even two left over to be packhorses. I'd say the ruffians owe us that much, wouldn't you?"

The rest agreed. The horses were a rawboned, unhandsome lot, but they were already saddled and immediately available. It was a godsend.

Mounting quickly, they trotted down to the dock, Ranulf and Urse whooping gleefully. Ranulf seemed to take disappointments in seduction in his stride, Aldyth thought sourly.

After a quick stop to load their belongings from the trunk onto the designated packhorses and for Ranulf to don his hauberk, they galloped down the road that led east out of Honfleur toward Rouen.

They stopped that night at Tancarville, on the other side of the curving river Seine. Here they found an inn, thankfully one free of ruffians this time, and bespoke supper. Then Ranulf gave the host silver coins for three rooms.

With Urse and Lady Vivienne intent on each other, Aldyth gave Ranulf a questioning glance.

"One chamber is for my lovesick squire and his lady-love, who obviously cannot wait to be alone with each other," he explained to her. "One is for my page, Edward, who I have told mine host has a cold and would keep me awake all night with his sniffling and coughing, and the other is for myself. Does that satisfy you, my innocent 'Edward'?"

"Perfectly, my lord," she said with unwonted primness. "Indeed, you are too good."

Chapter Twelve

In the morning, the four left the inn to follow the serpentine Seine deeply into the heart of Normandy. The rain that had led the way south from Portchester in England had been replaced by a chill December sun.

Of the four of them, only Urse and Lady Vivienne seemed oblivious to the discomforts of the road. Even when their eyes were not upon each other—which was very seldom— Lady Vivienne radiated a serene contentment, while Urse bore a silly smile utterly at odds with his fierce appearance.

Aldyth rejoiced for them, for Lady Vivienne had been very good to her and surely deserved some happiness and a man to help protect her babes. Aldyth had come to appreciate Urse's merry wit and rock-solid dependability, too. If fate was kind, they would not have to wait long before they could openly live as man and wife.

Their happiness made Aldyth glad, true enough, but she was also conscious of an aching yearning as she gazed at the lovers, so intent on each other as they rode along. If only Ranulf would look at her that way. If only true love made Ranulf so solicitous of her comfort that he held his hands cupped for her to mount, and so inflamed with desire for her that the looks exchanged between them could set tinder afire.

Aldyth resigned herself to the knowledge that she would never enter such a state of paradise. She must have dreamed that moment of fiery sweetness when she had first touched her lips to his outside the tavern. Ever since she had halted that kiss, Ranulf had been remote—kind, considerate, but treating her just as he would if she actually were his page.

Ranulf would not suffer, though, because she was not willing to be just another partner in bed sport with him. She had seen how women looked at him at court. Handsome devil that he was, Ranulf would never lack for a woman whenever the opportunity for dalliance presented itself. And eventually he would marry some great Norman lady who would bring him lands and increased power.

The journey to Rouen on the ruffians' sorry nags took a day and a half. By the time they neared the capital city of Normandy, Aldyth was sure she would rather walk than ride for the remainder of her life. Her thighs were rubbed raw by the poor quality saddle, and her head ached from the cob's ragged trot. She thought longingly of her smooth-gaited palfrey, Robin, back at Sherborne.

She was not the only one discontent. Ranulf knew he was being morose and curt with her, though he let her believe his ill temper was due to his stubborn bay's penchant for sudden starts and bucking.

"Don't worry, we shall be trading these skinny plodding beasts for more suitable ones before we arrive at the ducal palace in Rouen," he assured Aldyth.

"Oh, I *hope* so," she sighed, rubbing her hose-clad knees during a stop.

His mouth went dry as he watched her and he had to look away lest he reveal his feelings. Saints, the innocent girl truly seemed to have no idea how she tempted him, how her presence had become a source of aching torment for him! It was becoming harder and harder to remember to maintain his languid, drawling manner with her, particularly since he wanted to take her into his arms and kiss her until both of them were breathless!

But because of her experience with the Englishman, such an action would only frighten her, he reminded himself. He must maintain his disguise, must not let her know how he truly felt.

He made one of his elegant gestures and said, "After all, if we were seen upon such creatures masquerading as horseflesh, 'twould certainly be damaging to my consequence."

Lord Ranulf's consequence was soon put right by a visit to the horsemonger's yard within sight of the red-tiled roof of the palace. Here they purchased four mounts, a spirited black with barb blood for Ranulf, a large gray capable of carrying Urse's weight without tiring, a beautiful bay mare for Lady Vivienne and a short, stocky, piebald cob for Aldyth.

The horse's markings gave him a gaudy, almost comical appearance, but Aldyth realized it would not have been appropriate for a page to be riding an expensive lady's palfrey. She named him Motley.

Thus remounted, they rode the short distance to the palace, where the sergeant at arms took Ranulf's name. Moments later they were shown up to the duke's apartments, where Duke Robert roused himself from dicing with several knights to greet Lord Ranulf and his party.

"You are welcome to my duchy, my lord. Always pleased to welcome envoys of my *dear* brother the king, especially at this festive time of the year. You will keep Christmas with us, I trust?" Robert inquired hopefully.

Though older than Rufus by two years, he was several inches shorter, which had earned him the hated nickname "Curthose." He had the same slightly bulging hazel eyes as his royal brother, but his manner was more genial and easygoing.

"Yes, I thank your grace, we would be honored to celebrate Our Lord's Nativity with you and your court. But I would not mislead you, by my troth. I fear I am not precisely an envoy of your royal brother," Ranulf said vaguely, gesturing with his hands but making the movements a trifle less flamboyant than he would have at Rufus's court. "I fear the king is—how shall I say this?—*displeased* with me." He added an expressive sigh and rotated his eyeballs toward the ceiling. "But I'm sure I need not explain further to your grace, wise as you are. You know how he can be."

"Indeed," Robert said wryly. "You are very welcome to Normandy, then! You shall find loyal men are always appreciated in my duchy."

His sentiments were echoed by the duke's dicing partners, who greeted Ranulf and his squire and bowed to Ranulf's lady as if they were long-lost allies.

Aldyth, of little importance as a mere page, was free to study the scene and marvel. The duke tested Ranulf's allegiance no further and was already making vague promises of lands in Normandy to be given Lord Ranulf in reward for his shifting of allegiance.

She caught Urse's eyes. *That's all? Lord Ranulf's his man, just like that?*

Urse read her gaze correctly, for he nodded, his mouth twitching with amusement. It was apparent that Robert of Normandy's reputation for carelessness and uncritical acceptance of any who made friendly gestures was well earned.

The duke was speaking again, inviting Ranulf and his lady to sup with them that evening in his apartments as his guests of honor.

That evening, Aldyth, bathed and dressed in Lord Ranulf's livery, helped the duke's pages serve the meal and listened to the duke's amiable, artless chatter. Lord Ranulf and his winsome mistress must join the party as they hunted the red deer on the morrow, Robert insisted, after kissing Lady Vivienne's hand and complimenting Lord Ranulf on his taste in ladies.

Proffering a dish to her lord on bended knee as if she had been Lord Ranulf's page forever, Aldyth was able to catch the flicker of distaste in Lady Vivienne's eyes as she retrieved her hand. How she must hate acting the lord's leman now that she had given her heart to Urse, Aldyth thought. How she must long for the supper to be over so she could escape to Urse's arms.

One of the duke's pages, a lanky bean pole of a lad named Bertrand, invited her to join them as the pages trooped down to the hall to seek their own supper.

"Do you like serving Lord Ranulf, Edward?" he asked as he heaped a trencher between them with grilled fish, roast pheasant and crusty bread.

She found his Norman French, so much thicker than Ranulf's, hard to follow, but eventually she comprehended and nodded. "He's very kind."

Unfortunately, her slow response gave another of the pages, called Fat Louis by the others, the idea that she was slow-witted.

"He's very kind!" he mimicked in a carrying falsetto. "Bah, he'll never make a squire, let alone a knight, this *gringalet* from England who speaks such terrible French."

Aldyth glared at the stocky, pimply Louis and clenched her fists, trying her best to make it look as if "Edward" would be a formidable opponent in spite of his slender frame.

Fat Louis continued his goading. "And your lord, the so elegant one with his flowing black locks and exquisite gestures—are all of the lords on the other side of the Channel

Lord Liar

such popinjays? It seems he cares more for the fineness of his garments than knightly skills, *hein?*" he jeered from across the table.

Aldyth jumped up. "Come here and I'll show you what a fine squire I'll make, under my lord's training—"

She felt a hand gently pushing her back onto the bench. "Let him be, Fat Louis," Bertrand said imperturbably. "You're being insufferable, as usual. I'll bloody your nose if your antics get us kicked out of the hall by the seneschal again. I haven't even finished my supper."

Fat Louis subsided, but the look he gave Aldyth promised trouble.

It had been an endless evening, and Ranulf was glad to seek his bed. He had played the genial coxcomb all evening, languidly fondling his leman while boasting of his influence among the young lords in England. Robert had lapped it up, as had the half dozen barons and *comtes* invited to share the meal. There had been much backslapping and *bonhomie* exchanged between Robert's cronies and their new Anglo-Norman ally.

He found himself wondering, as he followed the flickering path the torches lit up the stairs, what Aldyth had thought of it all. She knew now, of course, that the caresses he gave Lady Vivienne were but an act, but what did she think of the plotting he seemed to be entering into with the deep-drinking nobles of Duke Robert's court? Did she think that he really did intend to intrigue with the eldest of the Conqueror's sons against Rufus, the anointed King of England? If that was what she thought, did she approve, thinking Robert Curthose, with all his weak amiability, would be a better king for the English? Or did she know that Rufus had sent him to spy on his elder brother? If she knew that, did she think he was doing the right thing?

What would she think of Ranulf of Kingsclere if she knew where his true allegiance lay? Ah, it was too many dizzying circles of thought, given the lateness of the hour and the amount of good Gascon wine he'd consumed.

He entered his chamber quietly so as not to disturb Urse and Vivienne in their bed behind the curtained alcove. He'd sent his "mistress" from the table an hour ago to "warm the bed for me, my sweet friend."

His own bed would be cold, but he was glad his squire and the Norman woman had finally given in to the passion he'd guessed each felt for the other for months. Urse would make Vivienne de Lisieux a good husband.

Someone had left a fat tallow candle burning on the low table beside his velvet-hung bed. By its flickering light he could see Aldyth asleep on a pallet between the table and the bed curtain.

He stood over her for several long minutes, watching the candlelight illumine her high cheekbones, her vulnerable chin, her sensitive mouth, relaxed now in sleep. The loose neck of her tunic had fallen low, exposing one alabaster shoulder and the upper edge of her breast. He felt his groin tighten in response to the sight.

You could take her. The thought came to him unbidden, but he knew it was true. He could stretch out beside her and begin kissing her and stroking the womanly curves she'd kept so well hidden under her page's livery. Very likely he could have her on fire for him before she—and that stern conscience of hers—was fully awake. He imagined touching her until she was wet and whimpering and slipping inside her, breaking the barrier of her virginity effortlessly because she was so relaxed, then bathing her in the pleasure of passion.

He almost groaned out loud, biting his knuckle with the effort it took him to turn away. *You lecherous fool, she trusted you enough to flee to you, in spite of how you treated her in that stable. She's terrified of what men do to women, especially after what that bastard Turold of Swanlea put her through. What would she think if she woke to find you leaning over her, leering?*

Putting the bed firmly between himself and the sleeping Aldyth, he undressed in the shadows, then entered the bed from that side. It was not as chill as he'd feared, he discovered as he got beneath the blankets. Aldyth had put a large, heated stone at the foot underneath the covers.

He could not stop himself from pulling back the bed hangings and gazing down at her. *Just for a moment,* he promised himself, *before I blow out the candle.*

Ranulf smiled as he saw her clutch a fold of the blanket and yank it determinedly over the bare shoulder. *Thank you, little one, that makes it easier for me to conquer the devil.* It made it no easier to look away, however. He stared at the slumbering, innocent girl until his eyelids grew heavy and drifted shut. The candle eventually guttered out in its holder sometime near dawn.

It was the eve of Christmas. Aldyth, helping the other pages decorate the hall after supper with holly and evergreen boughs, was relieved to see that the Normans had some of the same ways of preparing for the Nativity as they had in England. The two peoples, English and Norman, owed much of their heritage to mutual Viking ancestors, after all. There would be a boar's head—she'd spied it being prepared in the palace kitchen—roasted and decorated much as the one that always adorned the high table at Sherborne. There was a Yule log, only the French called it a *souche de Noël*. Tomorrow there would be feasting, Bertrand told her, and games.

She wondered how Christmas would pass at Sherborne. It was the first time she had ever been away from her father and brothers on that holy day. Had her father received the letter she'd sent by secret messenger, telling him she was safe? Did he nevertheless fret about her? Was Warin enjoying his holiday at home, yet managing to keep her secret? Had Turold resigned himself to the fact that she had evaded him, or was he harassing her father about her? And what of Godric—had he yet realized the folly of dreaming of an English return to power? She would give so much to be home and celebrating Christmas with her family instead of at a foreign court—and dressed as a boy!

A wave of homesickness swept over Aldyth, and her eyes misted over so that she could not see the wooden peg she was endeavoring to drive into the wooden rafter and dropped the hammer.

''Hey! You there up on that ladder! Have a care—you barely missed my head!'' shouted the aggrieved voice of Fat Louis below. ''Oh, I should have known it was Edward, the clumsy English—I've a good mind to topple that ladder and thrash what's left of you,'' he growled, giving the wooden structure a shake as if in promise of what was to come.

Aldyth clutched the swaying wooden sides, trying not to cry out in fear, but the rafters were two stories high, and if he made good his threat, she would end up with broken bones.

She smothered the urge to tell him to go to the devil. ''Sorry, Louis, I was butterfingered, it's true,'' she called apologetically. ''How about if I creep into the buttery after the steward is asleep and get you some of that good Gascon wine by way of apology?''

That placated the pudgy page. It would be an easy theft, she knew. The steward fell asleep in the buttery, the victim of the very wine he was supposed to guard. If she had help she could filch a tun of wine with him none the wiser. The other pages chimed in enthusiastically. Before long an informal party had been arranged in the stable to commence after the fires were covered. She would bring the wine, Aldyth figured, then leave as soon as her fellow pages were well into their cups. Ranulf would never miss her. He was no doubt reveling with the rest of the wine-soaked nobles of this court, aye, and had probably managed to arrange an assignation with some available lady, too, in spite of his supposed mistress, Lady Vivienne.

She should have known Fat Louis wouldn't let her escape so easily.

Two hours later, half a dozen of the pages sat in an empty stall lit only by a lantern. Drinking sparingly while appearing to consume great quantities of the Gascony was easy enough for Aldyth—just a flick of the wrist when no one was looking and the wine trickled harmlessly into the straw. But then Louis, whom she had seen guzzle prodigious amounts as easily as he drank water, added a new challenge, leaving the barn for a few minutes and coming back with Margot, the blowsiest of the palace kitchen wenches. Margot, whose brassy gold locks owed much to saffron dye, waved and smiled blearily at the boys lounging in the straw. It was evident she had been filching wine, as well.

"Margot is desirous of earning some extra coin for her New Year's gift for her poor old mother," he said with a snigger. "I brought her out so you boys could fill her, uh, pockets."

At first Aldyth, listening to the excited catcalls from the wine-flushed youths around her, did not understand. Then the wench pulled the neckline of her dirty bodice down, exposing one enormous breast, which she stroked suggestively to the accompaniment of the pages' cheers. Finally, with a meaningful wink over her bare shoulders, she strolled into an adjacent empty stall.

"I'm ready, boys," she cooed. "Which of you wants to be first?"

"I think Edward should be," Fat Louis announced. "It should be interesting—I doubt he's ever had a woman before!"

The pages guffawed and looked at Aldyth expectantly.

"Well, go on, Edward," Bertrand urged her. "Margot usually isn't so generous with her favors with mere pages. You might as well take advantage."

Jésu, what do I do now? This was a problem she hadn't anticipated.

"I, uh, I'm afraid I'll have to pass her up, Louis, though 'twas a good idea," she said, hoping she didn't look as dismayed as she felt. "I...my lord didn't leave me with so much as a sou in my pockets."

"Oh, we can't let that stop you, my good man," Louis said with an evil chuckle. "There would have been no party without you. See here, just to show we're friends now, I'll pay for your turn."

There was much hooting and applause as Louis turned back to her.

She swallowed hard and prayed for inspiration. "I, uh, I'm not ready. As you say, 'twill be the first time..."

"Don't let that stop you, lad! Margot will show you what's what," someone suggested.

"Why don't you go first, Louis? I'll just have a few more swigs...get up my courage, you know," Aldyth said weakly, raising her cup for a refill.

"Your courage isn't the only thing that must rise!" tittered another of the pages.

"Well, all right, if you insist." Fat Louis seemed pleased by the idea. "Why not watch through the cracks, little

Edward? Margot won't mind, and you can pick up some pointers."

She looked over her shoulder through the cracks in the stall divider. Indeed, she could see the wench lying on her back in the stall, her legs bent and her skirt pulled up to her waist as Fat Louis entered and began unfastening the points of his hose.

Aldyth looked away, but it didn't help. She could still hear them—Fat Louis grunting and panting like a boar hog, Margot squealing like a sow as the fleshy page rode her.

"Edward's turning green," one of the pages tattled as Louis came back. "I'll go next, and you see that he keeps drinking, eh? We'll either make him sick or make a man of him!"

Aldyth squeezed her eyes shut in an agony of embarrassment. How could they do this? How could a woman like Margot allow these awful boys to shame her—and through her, all women—especially on the very eve of the Savior's birth?

"Please, I *am* going to be sick," she murmured when they insisted it was now her turn. It was not a lie, for she was frightened to the point of nausea. If she refused, they might either beat her up or strip her with the intention of throwing a naked Edward at Margot. Either way, they would find out she was no boy.

"Hurry up, English. Margot doesn't like to be kept waiting," Fat Louis jeered, waving his eating dagger threateningly in the direction of her belly.

Aldyth stood up on trembling legs, then backed out of the stall. She hoped she could run fleetly enough to outdistance them and reach the safety of Lord Ranulf's chamber....

All at once she felt herself being snatched backward by the neck of her garment.

"So this is where you've been hiding! You English puppy, you're about to rue the day you were born!"

Lord Ailric   143

All at once she felt herself being snatched backward by
the back of her garment.

"So this is where you've been biding! You English puppy,
you're about to rue the day you were born!"

Chapter Thirteen

"**M**y lord, thank God. I—" Aldyth began, twisting in his
grasp to look at him.

"Silence!" he snapped, and gave her a shake. "And what
were the lot of you about, anyway?" he asked the group,
raising the lantern he carried. His manner had gone back to
his usual one of the elegant, languid lord, now vexed by a
disagreeable sight.

"Just drinking wine, *if* it's any of your concern," Fat
Louis retorted with wine-induced boldness.

Ranulf pointedly ignored him.

Margot, already wearying of putting up with sweating,
grunting striplings for a few paltry sous, apparently hoped
to net a bigger fish, for she chose this moment to poke her
head over the stall divider.

"Just having a little fun, my fine lord. But now Margot
is ready for a lover with some . . . finesse, eh? I could come
up to your chamber and show you how we celebrate a holiday in Normandy, yes?"

Aldyth watched as Ranulf raked Margot with a single,
scathing glance. "*No.* Begone, wench, or I'll show you how
we treat trollops desecrating a holy day in England! And as
for you pimply young lechers, you're disgusting the horses.

Get you back to the hall and I might forget to tell the duke how you've disgraced his livery—''

One of the pages who hadn't yet enjoyed Margot's charms was too drunk to know caution. ''Hey, you can't tell us what to do!'' He charged the Norman lord like a young bull.

In spite of his grip on Aldyth, Ranulf easily sidestepped the head-down charge. Almost negligently, he raised a fist and knocked the youth out flat as he ran by. Still holding on to Aldyth, he faced the rest. ''Anyone else?''

No one seemed inclined to face the challenge and, following Margot's example, gathered up cloaks and cups and began to disperse.

Ranulf kept his grip on Aldyth's neckline and pushed her out into the bailey.

''My lord, let me explain! I was trying to get away. I had taken them a bottle because Fat Louis was angry at me and I thought he was going to beat me up, but I didn't bargain for them inviting Margot and insisting I have a go at her. Lord Ranulf, where are you taking me?'' she asked, for they were headed for the gatehouse, not the tower in which Ranulf's chamber was located.

''Keep your mouth shut, Edward,'' came the grim voice attached to the hand that held an iron grip about the neck of her tunic.

Whatever did he plan to do with her? Was he so sickened by her knack for getting into trouble that he would put her outside the castle gates tonight?

As the captain of the guards listened to Ranulf's request to be let out into the city, she saw Urse loom up out of the darkness, carrying her hooded cloak. ''I see you found him, my lord.''

Perhaps she could enlist the giant squire's sympathy.

''Urse! He means to put me out! Please don't let him, not on Christmas Eve!''

"Stop your babbling, Edward. I'm not putting you out," Ranulf said, loosing her at last. "Yes, it's Christmas Eve, and, not finding you abed, I came looking for you, thinking you might like to celebrate properly—certainly in a more fitting fashion than what I found you doing." The rising portcullis made a loud creaking in the cold, frosty air. "Urse, do you know what I found my page doing?" Ranulf asked conversationally as they strolled across the drawbridge and into the dark streets of Rouen.

The Breton shook his shaggy head.

"He was guzzling wine in the barn with the other pages, while each of them took turns between the legs of one of the palace whores."

"Urse, it's not like he says!" Aldyth protested, hearing the squire's gasp of disbelief. "I agreed to drink with them, no more, and I didn't even drink that much! It was horrible, each of them going at her right in the next stall, with any who wanted to watch peeping through the cracks—" She broke off, giving an elaborate shudder. "They were saying I had to try her, since I'd never had a woman. Believe me, Urse, my lord Ranulf, I only wanted to get out of there without them discovering—"

"That you're a girl!" There was something odd about Urse's voice, and she looked up to see his huge shoulders shaking, not from horror but an effort to suppress laughter. "And they didn't know you lack the proper equipment!" He gave up the struggle and let loose a hearty belly laugh. "I can just picture it, my lord, can't you? Our Aldyth trying to pretend she's but a shy colt when really she's a filly. Oh, wait until I tell Vivienne. She went to bed early, but she'll wake when I return."

She glared at Urse. It had been horrible, not funny. And the thought of him telling Lady Vivienne of her humiliating experience added to her shame. Aldyth then looked at Ranulf, only to find him fighting a grin, too.

"I don't see a single thing humorous about it," she grumbled. "You men are all alike—coarse, disgusting creatures. And you, my lord," she said, rounding on Ranulf as he ran a hand down his bearded chin. She could see the amusement dancing in his dark eyes, as much as he strove to conceal it. "What right had you to call that misguided girl a name? You, who've bedded the finest trollops of the English court—yes, and of Normandy, too, in the last few days—though I do not suppose they call them such a common name when they service the nobility. I've heard you come to bed in the wee hours of the night, reeking of wine and expensive scent."

He saw the hurt glistening, along with tears, in Aldyth's eyes and longed to pull her into his arms and comfort her. *Oh, if only you knew the truth, little one. If only you knew how I sat up drinking with Robert and his hangers-on simply to keep myself out of your bed. And yes, I admit it—I went to one of the court harlots the other evening, because if I hadn't I don't think I could have kept myself from lifting you into my bed and kissing you awake before I made you mine. But once there I found I wasn't interested in the painted, perfumed courtesan, lovely and available as she was. I left her a silver mark or two and went back to my chamber. There I listened to you sighing in your sleep and wished I could let you know how much I wanted you—but I knew 'twould only frighten you, my sweet Aldyth...*

"Well, where *are* we going, if I might be allowed to ask?" he heard Aldyth say as they continued to walk along in silence. "Are you taking me to the dock to put me on a boat, or did you just think it was a fine, clear night for a walk?"

"We're going to midnight mass at one of the smaller cathedrals in Rouen, my grumpy Aldyth," he told her. "Oh, there'll be high mass at court in the morning, with the Bishop of Rouen in gorgeous state, but I thought it might mean more to celebrate our Lord's birth with the ordinary folk,'' he said with a gesture pointing out his own garments, which were sober and plain compared to his usual peacock style. "'Tis Christmas Eve, Aldyth. Can you forget your grievance against me for a few hours? Shall we cry peace?''

Eyes wary and still suspiciously bright, she nodded.

As they neared their destination, they came upon several groups of men dressed like shepherds who were singing. These men were led by others playing on pipes and viols.

"God sirs, now hark ye!
From far lands come we,
For it is Noël!''

Moments later, they reached the church. "This is the oldest cathedral in Rouen. 'Twas built by Saint Vitricius in the fourth century,'' he told Aldyth as they entered.

Inside, the darkness of midnight was dispelled by blazing torches along the walls and countless candelabra on the high altar, and the scent of incense mixed with more earthy smells. All around them the humbler folk of Rouen hastened in to worship as the bells began to toll above them.

As their eyes became accustomed to the light, they saw a manger upon the altar and in it a sleeping baby whose mother was no doubt the white-veiled, blue-robed woman who knelt beside it, acting the role of Mary. But Ranulf noticed that Aldyth's eyes shone at the sight of the animals sharing the altar and the space in front of it, several heifers, a pair of oxen and a donkey, as well as lambs held by more "shepherds.''

"The people believe the animals warm the baby Jesus with their breath," Ranulf whispered to Aldyth, and was rewarded by her smile. "They also believe that in olden times, the animals spoke Latin and do so again at midnight on Christmas Eve if no people are around."

Afterward, bells tolled all over the city, and they walked back to the palace. Instead of returning to Ranulf's apartments, though, he asked permission of the captain for them to climb the stairs and go out onto the parapet.

He felt Aldyth eye him curiously as they went out in the moonlit, windswept wall walk, followed by Urse.

"I know you're more than ready for your pallet, Aldyth, but there's a sight I thought you might enjoy first." Laying a hand gently on her shoulder to redirect her attention, he pointed across the darkened capital and out onto the distant hills.

He saw her gasp of surprise as she caught sight of the distant bonfires.

"The country folk build them to welcome the Christ Child," he said simply.

She turned a moon-kissed, glowing face to him. "'Tis a wondrous sight, my lord. Thank you."

She looked so winsome. Only the presence of Urse behind him kept Ranulf from kissing Aldyth there and then.

"Now is as good a time as any to tell you both that Christmas Day will be our last day in Rouen," Ranulf told Aldyth and his squire. "His grace the duke has asked me to pay his brother Henry in the Cotentin a little visit."

"Ah, but that's excellent—" began Urse.

"He couldn't have played better into my own hands, true," Ranulf agreed. "I had wanted to pay the prince a visit in any case and was wondering how I could do it without offending Robert before Rufus orders me home. And now the duke himself has asked me to do what I wanted to anyway."

"Well then, perhaps this is the best time to request a Christmas boon of you," murmured Urse. "But before I do, my lord, know that it's all right if you don't want to say yes."

Ranulf looked up. It wasn't like the big man to ask for favors or to be hesitant about anything, for that matter.

"Yes, what is it? You never ask me for aught—don't go about it like a stammering boy."

"'Tis not me, my lord, 'tis for Vivienne I ask. She ... she misses her babes, my lord. Being away from them at Christmas is—well, it's harder on her than she'd thought 'twould be...."

"And she wants to go home to them? Of course she does—I was amazed she consented to come in the first place. Very well, I'll give her passage money—but only if you'll escort her and find somewhere to marry her between here and Winchester."

"Oh no, that's not necessary, my lord, though 'tis good of you to offer. I couldn't desert you in the middle of all this. If I could just see her safely aboard ship, I'll catch up—"

"What, don't you want to marry her?" Ranulf asked with a tone of mild menace. "I'd hate to think you were trifling with that good woman, my Breton friend."

"Nay, of course I'm not! Of course I want to wed her, just as soon as possible. 'Tis just that—"

"Nonsense, Urse. I can handle it from here. Very likely we'll sail home from the peninsula, and there's naught I can't handle with the help of my good page Edward." He grinned over his shoulder at Aldyth, who grinned back, though she appeared dazed by this new development.

Urse still looked skeptical, but he recognized when his lord's mind was made up. "Very well then, Lord Ranulf. I—we—thank you. We'll pray for you every day of our lives."

"And name your first son after me."

Urse's eyes darted to Aldyth, then back to Ranulf, and a huge grin split the big man's face.

"Oh, I think you'll have your own son before long, my lord. Two little Ranulfs playing together would be too confusing, don't you think?"

Ranulf snorted. "You're talking nonsense, Urse."

They left the day after Christmas, as planned. In the five days in which they had lounged at the ducal court, Ranulf had been at pains to show Robert and his nobles exactly what they expected to see—a genial popinjay who asked nothing more of life than an overlord who would make it worth his while to sit decoratively in his hall, showing off his gorgeous raiment and singing the duke's praises. Thinking him harmless, Robert's men talked freely in front of Ranulf, so he had seen and heard much that would be of interest to Rufus—and Ranulf's true lord. He learned who truly favored the duke, and who merely hung around court for the easy life Robert offered, and who would desert the duke if offered a better deal.

He saw that Bishop Odo, the Conqueror's half brother and uncle to Rufus, Robert and Henry, was firmly in Duke Robert's camp, for he had realized that he was considered of no value to England's new king. He saw that Robert counted as best friends such men as Robert of Belesme, a man already famous for his bloodthirsty unscrupulousness, and Edgar the Aetheling, who had once been heir presumptive of England long before the Conquest. It was easy to see that Edgar and Robert had a common interest—

the throne of England—but less easy to see how they could both be satisfied if one of them got it.

What would be more disturbing to Rufus, however, was the number of members from the most prominent Norman families in England—men who had supported the Conqueror, or whose fathers had—who now sought to throw their support to Robert rather than the Conqueror's chosen heir, because they felt Robert more amenable to their control than Rufus ever would be.

Rufus was right to suspect a plot. Ranulf could practically see it beginning to hatch in front of his eyes. He could not decide, however, how much to communicate to Rufus. Obviously Ranulf would have to feed his king some information to keep him content. But it would have to be facts that would not harm Ranulf's liege lord, and where that lord stood had not yet become apparent. Ranulf wanted to be able to help him, though, whenever his liege made his plans clear.

In any case, no immediate action had been demanded of Ranulf by Robert Curthose. After the few initial questions, he had been made welcome to enjoy the lazy, generous lifestyle of the duke, whose most strenuous pastimes were hunting and hawking. The wine flowed liberally, the food was excellent, and women had been available for the taking, had Ranulf been interested.

He realized he had been preoccupied by his thoughts all morning. Scarcely a word had passed between him and Aldyth ever since they left the abbey where they had passed the night.

"You haven't said what you thought of Christmas at the ducal court," he said. "Or are you still sick from stuffing yourself with *dedells en burneaux?*"

She gave a rueful smile. "I'm not sure if it was that or the roast porpoise—I'd never had either before. And what of you, my lord? You visited the wassail bowl rather often, I noticed.''

"And paid for it the next morning, by God's toenails! The pantomimes were funny, were they not?"

"I enjoyed the horse racing and the jousting more," she replied, "for you won both of them over those braggarts of Duke Robert's court."

He rolled his eyes and made a deprecating gesture. "I'm not sure the race was worth it, for the mud *ruined* my best cloak," he groaned, trying to put on the persona of the languid Lord Ranulf again. But somehow, out here alone with Aldyth, it was difficult to be false with her. There was something about the solitude of this sandy coastal road, with the seabirds screeching overhead in the cold winter air and the waves rolling in to shore off to their right, that demanded honesty.

As if she sensed his mood, she said, "I'm not sure I understand why we're going to see Prince Henry."

He shrugged. He wasn't sure he was ready to be completely honest with Aldyth yet, for he didn't know how she would react. "I told you—Duke Robert asked me to go. He wants to see where Henry's loyalty lies—currently, that is."

"So cynical! Yet there is more to this journey than a ducal request, and you know it. You're playing some deep game, my lord. What is it?"

Inwardly he marveled at Aldyth's perception. "My games are my own, little one, and I think it best to keep it that way," he said, avoiding those honest green eyes that saw too much.

He could feel her studying him.

"All right, we'll discuss something else. I still don't understand why I have to continue this masquerade as a page," Aldyth said then.

"You might as well continue acting the boy—your hair's still too short to convince anyone you're a girl," he retorted, but was sorry when he glanced at her and saw his flippancy had only made her grit her teeth with frustrated fury.

"I can hardly make it grow any faster! And anyway, I'd be wearing a veil most of the time so my hair wouldn't show anyway," Aldyth shot back. Then, as if striving to match his flippant tone, she added, "or if any saw it, you could tell them it was the latest style in England!" Then she grew serious again. "Now that Lady Vivienne's gone home, I don't see why *I* cannot pose as your mistress. I'm so tired of wearing boy's clothes and remembering to speak in a low voice and walk just so...."

He smiled inwardly, for he knew the masquerade was becoming trying to her feminine spirit, yet he secretly enjoyed being the only one to know that his gruff-speaking, rough-and-tumble page "Edward" was really very much a woman. *I could not have you acting as my mistress, dressing in seductive clothes and letting me caress you before others as a leman would, my foolish blind darling, for then I'd want you to be mine in truth,* Ranulf thought, but he did not say so. If only Turold had not made you fear my sex....

Aloud, he said, "I've told you why. I've been saying it ever since we left Rouen, Aldyth—I don't trust Prince Henry—not around an innocent like you. He's a womanizer *par excellence.* If he thought you were my mistress, it would be only too like him to want you, too—and as he outranks a mere baron like me, I'm afraid I would be pressured to let him, uh, sample you. I don't want to be put in that position, Aldyth, and you don't want to be in it, either, do you?"

Aldyth shook her head, aghast at the thought. "He sounds like a monster."

"He's not," Ranulf said, but an incident long ago had taught him to be wary. He doubted Henry would still use his rank to take a vassal's woman, but he would take no chances, not with Aldyth. "He has many excellent qualities—a keen mind and a talent for strategy not the least of them—but he's been denied the thing he wants most, real power. He had to buy his county, you know, with the silver that was his only legacy from his father, for the Conqueror had given all the land to Rufus and Robert. As a consequence, Henry thinks he should have whatever else he wants, such as any woman who attracts his passing fancy."

"Yet you were going to bring Lady Vivienne here," Aldyth pointed out.

"Yes..." Aldyth's mind was ever sharp for holes in his carefully constructed reasons. "But Vivienne is not an innocent babe such as you are. She could have taken care of herself."

"And I cannot?" Aldyth cried, stung. "*Grande merci,* my lord, for your faith in my abilities!"

She dug her heels into the cob and shot ahead of him down the coastal road to Henry's castle.

Chapter Fourteen

"Ranulf of Kingsclere, it's good to see you!" the prince cried, rushing into the bailey as Ranulf and Aldyth dismounted. "I was hoping when you sent word you were going to Rouen you'd find a way to visit me here."

Ranulf bowed. "My prince, I am happy to be here."

Henry caught him into an embrace as he straightened. "But you travel in little state, Ranulf—with just a page?" Henry exclaimed, indicating Aldyth. "Where is your giant Breton?"

"Edward, stop staring and do as I taught you," Ranulf commanded.

A blushing Aldyth, who *had* been staring at the best looking of the Conqueror's three living sons, hastily went down on one knee and inclined her head.

"Prince Henry, I have the honor of presenting Edward of Pevensey, my page, whom I'm still training in courtesy, as you can see," Ranulf said dryly. "Urse, my squire, had the temerity to fall in love with my leman and ask her to wed him. He has taken her home to celebrate the New Year with her babes, so I had only this young pup to bear me company up the road from Rouen." He ruffled Aldyth's hair playfully. "A sore trial, that," he added, chuckling.

Under the cover of her tousled hair, Aldyth glared at him. She'd teach him to patronize her!

"And you did not mind your squire filching your *chère amie?* You do not seem brokenhearted. No, I see you are not. No matter, there are other delights here to tempt your— ahem!— palate. You have come to bring in the New Year with us. Excellent!''

"Your court is always most comfortable," responded Ranulf. "And I would somewhat belatedly congratulate you on your new lands, my prince. May I ask how you like being Count of the Cotentin and Avranches?"

Obviously forgotten, Aldyth was free to study Henry once more. He was taller than his older brothers and his sire, Aldyth noted, but shorter and more stockily built than the Norman knight who stood before him. He was tawny-haired and lacked the floridity and uncouthness of Rufus's face and the dissipation that marked Robert's.

"Ah, I'm quite fond of having any land, since before I had nothing to call my own, thanks to the inequities of Father's will—even if I had to buy my county myself. But I think you know this Norman peninsula is not the end of my ambitions, Ranulf." He grinned wolfishly and his gray eyes gleamed.

Ranulf darted an uneasy glance back at Aldyth. "You come right to the point, as ever, my prince. Let me just send my page up to my chamber with my things to unpack—''

"Nonsense, my lackeys can take them. The boy wants to be a knight one day, don't you, Edward? And perhaps more?" the count said, patting Aldyth on the shoulder in a friendly fashion.

"Y-yes, my lord," Aldyth said, lowering her head in hopes that the keen gray eyes would not see too much.

"Of course you do, that's a good lad. And where better to learn statecraft than at our knees, eh, Ranulf? Let us just go into the hall, where we may be more comfortable, for it's a chill wind blowing in off the Channel, eh?''

He ushered them into the hall, where a great stone fireplace did an excellent job of keeping the December cold away. A trio of women sat stitching by its light and looked up curiously as the count approached with Ranulf and his page. Henry shooed them away, saying, ''Ladies, please excuse us for now, for we must talk of tedious manly things, but later, I promise you, you shall meet my most trusted vassal.''

The three women gathered up their stitchery, giggling and eyeing Ranulf appraisingly. Aldyth darted a surprised glance at him herself and met dark eyes that told her nothing. Henry's ''most trusted vassal''? Wasn't he supposed to be Rufus's man? *Whom did he serve?*

''Tell me,'' Henry said, sitting down on one of the chairs the women had vacated and indicating that they were to take the other two, ''how fares my brother?''

Ranulf took a deep breath. ''If I may be frank, my prince—''

''I have always trusted you to be so, Ranulf,'' Henry put in dryly.

''But perhaps I must carry frankness to extremes if I am to be honest at this time, Prince Henry. I found the duke as devoted as ever to the pleasures of the flesh, practically to the exclusion of all else. It's wine, women and song all day in Rouen. But just before I left, all the barons of the duchy began pouring in for the Christmas court—including several who should have been in attendance upon your royal brother in England.''

''Nay, Ranulf, you have mistaken me,'' said Henry with a wave of a regal hand. ''I see you thought I meant Robert. Believe me, I know all about my brother the wine sot, for he tells me everything, the gullible fool. I know all about the rebellion he's brewing, for he's invited me to be a part of it. Does that surprise you? He also sent you to spy on me, did he not?''

Ranulf nodded, looking a little startled at Henry's words.

"Well, you'll tell him exactly what he wants to hear, that I'm in it heart and soul, boots and purse—if I *had* a purse, that is. No, I meant to inquire about the state of my *royal* brother, William Rufus. How is the dear boy?''

Aldyth was chilled by Henry's cold-blooded tone as he discussed his brothers. How sad that one could be so coolly cynical about one's siblings. She certainly did not agree with Godric's loyalties, but she could never stop loving him. Apparently princes could not afford to be sentimental.

"He is well, my prince, though he suspects Robert to be plotting. He sent me to spy on the duke, you know. He didn't mention you in his suspicions, however.''

"Which doesn't mean he doesn't know that I'd jump whichever way my advantage lies,'' Henry said thoughtfully, making a tent of his fingers and staring at the tapestried wall without seeing it. "Ah, Ranulf! What a family we are, we sons of William the Bastard and Matilda. I'm sure you cannot imagine plotting against your brother, or him scheming to steal your inheritance?''

Aldyth thought of Ranulf's younger brother Richard, who was a squire in the Earl of Chester's household.

"No, my lord, but then, we are not royal, and a kingdom and a duchy are at stake here, not a mere earldom,'' Ranulf said diplomatically.

"How tactful of you, Ranulf. Yes, I know we're an awful lot, but what else can you expect when a king has too many sons? I suppose one of us should have gone into the Church, but I'm sure you knew early on I wouldn't suit. I like mischief too well! Do you remember the time we all dropped the contents of that chamber pot on Robert's head?''

Ranulf threw back his head and laughed, a deep, rich sound that wrapped itself around Aldyth's heart before she could think to guard herself.

"Nay, I had forgotten!'' he said, slapping his knee.

"Your page is looking at us as if we both have two heads,'' Henry observed. "I will explain, boy. Once upon a time when we were all young, your master assisted Rufus and me in dousing Robert's pretensions of elegance when he was being most insufferable. He was dressed in an elegant new cloak of purple silk.'' He seemed to wait for some reaction on Aldyth's part.

"I—I see, my lord,'' she said hesitantly, not knowing whether it was all right for her to laugh or not. It *was* funny when one thought about how it must have looked. It was easy to picture Ranulf participating, for even now, as he remembered the prank, Aldyth could see that his eyes danced with devilry.

"That was the beginning of the rift, you know,'' Henry said wistfully. "Our father wouldn't discipline us enough to salvage Robert's youthful pride, which had been damaged in front of his friends.''

"His grace the duke made no mention of it while we were in Rouen,'' Ranulf murmured.

"That alone ought to convince you that Curthose is either forgetful of your role in it or a forgiving fool. But enough of my family woes. Are you enjoying being known as an elegant popinjay, Ranulf?''

Ranulf studiously avoided Aldyth's gaze as he forced a tragic look into his eyes and effortlessly took on a languid manner. "You've no idea how *fatiguing* it is to set the standards of raiment around his grace's court. 'Tis so expensive to always be wearing the latest mode, the thickest velvet, the softest silk...."

Henry gave a hoot of laughter and applauded. "You're utterly convincing, Ranulf! I salute you!"

"Well, I'm heartily sick of playing the role, I can assure you, my prince. I'll be happy to drop the pretense during my visit here—that is, if you're certain of the allegiance of all your men."

"Absolutely. Most of them either came with the land or are ones you'll recognize as having been around me since our boyhood days. Feel free to dress as you wish and be yourself. And now I must bid you to excuse me, but I will see you at supper. You will find a hot bath awaiting you in your chamber. You might want to continue being the peacock and come down betimes, my friend, for I will have a surprise awaiting you." He smiled mysteriously as he left them.

"You're very quiet, Aldyth," Ranulf said as he stood at the arrow slit window, watching the waves crashing in upon the rocks below in the waning light. "Are you sorry you came on to the Cotentin with me? I could have sent you home with Urse and Vivienne, I suppose, though you would have felt prodigiously in the way. Three's a crowd when two are in love, you know."

Aldyth looked up from the tunic she was shaking out from its folds. "Nay, I did not want to return to England, my lord...." She looked away. Below he had avoided her eyes; now it seemed as if he probed too deeply and would reach her soul.

"I sense a 'but' coming."

"I... 'Tis just that ever since we reached Rouen, I've felt less and less as if I know you, my lord."

He stared at her for a moment, stroking his mustache and bearded chin. "Surely when we are alone you can drop the formality, Aldyth. I am Ranulf, the same Ranulf who used to try to rescue your hair ribbons, not 'my lord.'" He waited.

She spread the garment out upon the bed, then turned back to him. She felt as if she were about to step out onto a precipice with a sheer drop below.

"Are you the same? I don't know who you are anymore, Ranulf. I came to Kingsclere expecting one Ranulf and found quite another. You seemed to be a typical courtier of Rufus's court, but you went to Rouen and were accepted as one of Curthose's cronies. Today I see you are thick as thieves with Henry, who seems as if he would snatch whatever his brothers have, if given half a chance. Will you go home and tell Rufus what both of his brothers are saying, then?"

"No," he said, the decisiveness of his tone surprising her. "No, I shall not go back and be a telltale to Rufus—or rather, I shall tell the king enough to satisfy him. But 'tis Henry who holds my allegiance."

"Why?"

The question seemed to surprise him by its directness, and he turned back to the narrow embrasure.

"We were raised together in his father's household," he began musingly, "but it's not simply because I know him best, or think he would reward any service best. I support him because he'd be the best king for England. He has none of Robert's foolishness or Rufus's vices, and he has the best brain of the three."

"I see. And the fact that he's the most ruthless of the three doesn't bother you?"

"You see much in a brief meeting," he muttered. "He comes by his ruthlessness honestly enough—he's the son of the Conqueror, who would have been set aside as a bastard if he'd shown the slightest weakness. And Henry will be nothing but a forgotten third son if he isn't as ruthless. And the kingdom will be the worse for it. Ruthless or not, Aldyth, he's English in a way—the only one of William's sons to be born in England. Does that influence your feelings toward him at all? Or would you rather resurrect some pathetic Saxon relic like Edgar the Aetheling for a king?"

"What should it matter how *I* feel about any of them?" she asked curiously, then was stopped by something she saw in the midnight eyes. "You wonder if I will betray you, Ranulf?"

He stood waiting, watching her.

"You actually think that I would tell your secrets, Ranulf?" she cried. "How little you must trust me, after all. And to whom do you think I would betray you, my lord?"

He raised a hand. "I know not where your loyalty lies, after all, Aldyth. You are English. Your brother has made no secret of the fact he despises all Normans, and—"

"And I have told him on every occasion that he is being foolish," Aldyth replied. "Oh, what do I care which Norman—or paynim sultan, for that matter—sits on the throne? They may all kill one another or not, these three sons of the Conqueror, and I shall not care, Ranulf. But that you could think I would betray you—yes, that I care about."

"I have hurt you," he said, coming forward with his hands extended to her. "I never meant to, Aldyth. 'Tis just that I have been playing a role for so long—even my mother and father did not know the truth. I did not want to assume anything...."

She whirled away from him, putting the bed between them. She did not trust herself at that moment not to give in to the urge to let him comfort her. And who knew where that might lead? "All right, you did not take my trust for granted. I will say it now—I would not ever stoop so low as to betray you, Ranulf. Your confidence is safe with me.''

"Thank you." He was about to say something more when below them a trio of short blasts upon a horn pierced the sudden quiet.

"There's the dinner horn, my lord. You should hurry and dress. The prince indicated you should not be late."

Aldyth, assuming she was to help serve the supper again and hoping no surly pages such as Fat Louis lay in wait for her in the count's castle, followed Ranulf into the hall. She took a moment to study his appearance and took pride in her part in it.

He wore a long robe of smoke gray velvet with silver Englishwork at the neck, all embroidery she had done. The fabric emphasized his powerfully muscled shoulders as he moved. An enamel-link belt rode low on his lean hips. Black hose revealed a length of sinewy legs before disappearing into soft, leather slippers—without the curled points that were popular at Rufus's court, she noted approvingly. He was easily the handsomest man there—even more so than Henry, who was certainly well-favored.

Ranulf was ushered above the salt, past the knights and half a dozen beautiful, splendidly dressed ladies to the high table and to a carved wooden chair to the right of Prince Henry. The place next to that was empty, also. Aldyth allowed herself a brief moment of longing, wishing she could shed her disguise and sit at his side, gorgeously arrayed, as his lady. But that was not to be, she reminded herself.

"Ah, Ranulf. Now we can sup. But first, I must tell you I was devastated on your behalf when I learned you had so generously given up your mistress—Vivienne, wasn't that her name—to the joys of wedded bliss. I would not have you bereft at my court in this festive time of year, my Ranulf.

Therefore I have a little reward for your service in my cause."

He snapped his fingers in the direction of a tapestry behind the dais.

What emerged from the alcove hidden behind the tapestry would have made Aldyth gasp if she hadn't practiced dissembling so much of late.

A woman lifted the heavy fabric and emerged from the shadows, gliding forward so smoothly that she seemed to float rather than walk to Ranulf's side.

"Lord Ranulf of Kingsclere, may I present the Lady Desiderata," intoned Prince Henry next to him. "Desiderata—it means 'to be desired,' of course. I'm certain you'll agree the name suits her admirably, *hein?*" The prince gave a low chuckle as he watched Ranulf stare at her.

Lady Desiderata was blessed with a spectacularly pale countenance that set off her fiery red cloud of hair to perfection. She parted full, lush lips in a seductive smile that revealed perfect, pearly teeth. Her eyes were topaz.

Cat's eyes, Aldyth thought, even as her heart sank. Ranulf would not be able to resist the invitation inherent in the woman's swaying hips. She was dressed in a *bliaut* of silver samite that might have been painted on her, so lovingly did it cling to every one of her considerable curves. 'Twas as if she had known that Ranulf would dress in gray and had chosen her silver gown to complement his choice.

"Lord Ranulf, I would welcome you to the Cotentin," she said. Her voice was low-pitched and throaty and caressed his name as she said it. "My lord has bid me see to your *every* need. I'm sure you'll be quite comfortable here."

Could Ranulf find nothing to say? Aldyth found her hands clenched around the platter of meat she carried as, all around them, Henry's knights whistled and catcalled.

Ranulf continued to stare up at the woman standing before him, his lean face impassive.

"I—I'm sure I shall," he said, which set off new hoots from the lower tables. Lady Desiderata continued to stand next to him, smiling her untroubled, secret smile.

"Well, don't just sit there, man! Have you been at my brother's court so long you've forgotten what to do? Invite the lady to sup with you!"

It was as if Ranulf came out of a deep trance then and got to his feet. "Certainly, my lord. 'Twas just that I could not believe my eyes. Lady Desiderata, would you honor me by your presence?" he asked, bowing and indicating the chair beside him. The woman inclined her head in gracious assent and slid into her seat.

A black curtain of misery dropped around Aldyth, numbing her fingers, and she dropped the platter full of roast capon.

It landed with a *thunk* on the rushes below. It was not a loud noise, but the resultant stampede of snarling, yapping hounds that rushed from their places beneath the table to partake of the unexpected bounty was a cacophony of noise that ensured that all eyes fell on her as she attempted to at least rescue the platter. She was so humiliated that she did not even look up to see if Ranulf noticed her *faux pas* or whether he was still entranced by the siren sitting next to him.

"Here, take these, you stupid boy," the seneschal hissed, having intercepted another platter of meat destined for the knights' table. "'Twill keep them busy for a time."

Those at the high table seemed unaware of her clumsiness. Presenting the platter, she was in time to hear Prince Henry say, "I chose well, did I not? I thought Desiderata would suit you."

It was well that she did not have a flagon of wine, for she would have been hard-pressed to know whom to pour it on, the smug, self-satisfied prince or the sleek cat who sat gazing lazily at Ranulf as if he were the next mouse she planned to devour—after playing with him for a suitable time, of course! But if Ranulf was willing to play the mouse for such a cat, he deserved to be devoured, Aldyth thought sourly.

Chapter Fifteen

The next morning, Ranulf slipped from his bedchamber quietly in order not to awaken Aldyth on her pallet. He was to go hawking with Henry. He went down to the hall but did not find his liege lord there, nor, to his relief, did he see the flame-haired courtesan, Desiderata. Upon hearing that Henry had broken his fast early and had left for the mews to prepare his falcon, Ranulf took some bread and watered wine and went out to the bailey without delay.

He found his horse saddled and being held by a stable-boy, while Henry, already mounted, controlled his restive stallion expertly with one hand and held his falcon on his other wrist.

"Good morrow, Ranulf! How do you like my latest treasure?"

The "treasure" was a gyrfalcon of startling white plumage with black tips. An ornate leather hood covered her head, while from her impressive talons thin leather jesses, trimmed with tiny golden bells, dangled.

"A handsome bird, is she not? I know I should not have her, as a mere count," Henry said, rolling his eyes drolly. "A peregrine is supposed to be my due—but I could not resist her."

"I can see why," Ranulf answered. "Yes, she's very beautiful." The privilege of watching such a prize falcon do what she had been trained for would more than make up for the lack of a bird on Ranulf's own arm.

The falcon twisted and turned her head and bated, flapping her wings in an agitated fashion at Ranulf's words.

"She does not know your voice as she does mine," Henry explained. "I trained her myself. Her name is Valkyrie, for I imported her from Norway. Hmm," he said, looking back at the door of the hall, "what can be keeping Desiderata? I told her to meet us here."

"The lady is accompanying us? How—how pleasant a prospect," Ranulf said, hoping his voice did not betray the lack of enthusiasm that he was still having trouble understanding himself. Lady Desiderata had left the hall with him last night and had lost little time in inviting him up to her solar. She had wine mulling on the brazier there, she said, which would surely help him sleep.

In the old days he would have gone without a moment's hesitation. He knew she had hopes his sleeping would be done in her arms. He was astonished to hear his own voice telling her he feared he was too weary to be good company and perhaps it would be best if he went to his own chamber. He did not add "alone." He did not have to.

What was wrong with him? he had wondered last night, and he wondered it still. Surely a woman such as Desiderata, who would expect nothing of him but some pleasant hours in her bed and then a few silver marks when he departed, was the ideal solution for the frustrated pangs of desire that he felt whenever he looked at Aldyth. Desiderata would be an entertaining, exciting bed partner. As much as her lush curves promised heaven, however, he could not bring himself to follow her to her room. When he thought of doing so he felt . . . nothing.

"Yes, I thought she would enjoy coming along," Prince Henry was saying. "She was certainly entranced by *you*." There seemed to be some veiled inquiry in the prince's tone.

"I cannot think why I should have impressed her," Ranulf replied dryly. "I fear I was dull as a stick last night after supper. Fatigued after our journey up the coast, I suppose."

"I told her that must be it," Henry replied, confirming Ranulf's suspicion that Desiderata had reported that he had not accepted her invitation last night. "The poor girl was questioning her charms when I spoke to her this morning."

Ranulf suppressed a surge of irritation. It was one thing to be offered a bedmate, another to be made to feel guilty because he had not taken advantage of what was offered. Doubtless Henry pressed the lady on him with the best of intentions, however, and it would be churlish to act ungrateful. He could not expect his liege to understand that he did not know his own heart right now. When Henry had last seen him, he would have cheerfully taken a comely, willing woman to bed within an hour of meeting her. But that was before Aldyth had come into his life again.

"I will make certain the lady knows that the lack was in myself last even and not in her," he replied carefully.

"My lord? You did not wake me this morning, and I awoke to find you gone," said a voice at his right knee, and Ranulf was surprised to look down and find Aldyth standing there.

"Ah, 'tis my sleepy page!" Ranulf said with forced joviality, while he studied the reproachful face staring up at his. "Think naught of it, lad, I knew you were tired. I fended for myself, as you see."

Henry could not see her because his horse was on the left side of Ranulf's, so she evidently felt it was safe to give him a saucy look. "My lord is too kind. You go a-hawking?"

"Yes," he said with a nod at the falcon resting regally on the prince's wrist. "You may do, uh, as you wish while I am gone, Edward. Perhaps you could select something for me to wear this even."

"Yes, Lord Ranulf." She looked wistful. "Have an enjoyable time, my lords."

Aldyth had turned on her heel and was about to leave when the prince called, "Oh, boy! Edward, isn't it?"

"Yes, my lord?"

"Go see if you can find Lady Desiderata. She was to join us here long ago. If she is not in the hall you will find her chamber at the top of the west tower. Hurry along, now! We're eager to be off."

"Yes, my lord." Aldyth bowed to Prince Henry, but the look she shot Ranulf before leaving to do as Henry bid was stormy as the winter sea.

"Possessive little lad, isn't he?" Henry commented, quirking a brow at Ranulf. "He doesn't like it that you dressed without his aid, does he?"

"Yes, he's inclined to forget his place unless I've beaten him recently," Ranulf said, making his voice careless. "He's become rather spoiled during our Norman travels—fancies himself more important than he ought because I left my other page in England and took him. And now that Urse has gone home, he's become completely intolerable. I shall have to knock him down a peg or two."

Henry nodded. "Very wise to nip that sort of mischief in the bud. A page who's gotten above himself will make a surly squire and an unreliable knight. Now, back to Desi—"

"Desi?"

"My nickname for the Lady Desiderata. I thought you should know my castle is something of a haven for comely young widows disinclined to the convent or *damoiselles* of

little dowry who've been unlucky enough to bear bastards
and be cast out by their families. Desiderata, however, belongs to neither of those categories. I happened to save her
from a forced marriage to an ugly old goat of a knight who
had seized her when she had unwisely run away from her
father's keep. In gratitude, she gave herself to me, and I've
kept her by me ever since. No, she and I are no longer lovers," he said, answering the unspoken concern in Ranulf's
eyes. "You know I like constant variety in women—but we
are friends. She will please you, Ranulf, not only because
you're a fine, handsome fellow but because she wants to
please me."

Ranulf couldn't help but be a little repelled by Henry's
casual admission that he kept a collection of women, much
like a sultan among the infidels, and that Desiderata had
mixed motives for her actions toward himself.

"I would take advantage of no woman because she owes
you the roof over her head."

"Nonsense. Desiderata would be the first to scoff at that
notion. She was no virgin when I took her. She's well cared
for here and allowed to give her talent in the bedchamber
free rein. She's a born courtesan, Ranulf. Sooner or later she
would have hung horns on any man who wed her. She
merely didn't desire the ugly old knight who hadn't even
tried to charm her before trying to rape her. He, uh, won't
be imposing himself on any other beauteous ladies," Henry
added with a grin. "Don't be such a monk, Ranulf. Take her
and enjoy her!"

Fortunately, Ranulf was saved from the necessity of a reply by the appearance of the lady in question.

Desiderata made a deliberate entrance, calling, "My
lords! Have I kept you waiting? I'm so sorry!" as she
walked toward them with slow, feline grace. She wore a
gown of scarlet velvet that should have clashed with the fiery

gold-corded braids draped over her bodice, but the combination served only to remind Ranulf of a flame.

A groom brought a dainty white palfrey out from the stables, but she ignored it for a moment, standing next to Ranulf's knee and gazing up at him with lazy amusement as she laid a hand caressingly on his leg.

"Did you rest well, my lord?"

He nodded, fighting the urge to escape her touch by causing his mount to slide away from her. "As did you, my lady, I can see." Now what was he to say? His eyes seemed to have a will of their own, for they left Desiderata and looked over her head to see if Aldyth stood watching them from the hall. There was no sign of her, however.

"Come on, Desi, mount your palfrey," called Henry impatiently. "Valkyrie's getting restless. You'll have time for seduction later!"

The lady pouted prettily but mounted her mare, making sure she gave Ranulf an enticing glimpse of one long white leg before she settled her skirts.

As they rode out, a face framed by short, chestnut brown curls disappeared from a window overlooking the bailey. The shutters were banged shut, but the sound was swallowed by the clattering of the three horses' hooves over the drawbridge.

When the three of them trooped back into the hall hours later, Ranulf saw Aldyth sitting by the fire, listlessly petting one of the prince's hounds.

"Good afternoon, Edward. I hope your morning passed well?" he said, studying the wan face.

Aldyth shrugged. "There was little for me to do, my lord." She looked meaningfully at Lady Desiderata behind him, who was accepting a cup of mulled wine from Prince Henry. "Did my lady have a pleasant ride?"

Her voice was perfectly neutral. Try as he would, Ranulf could detect no flicker of an eyelash, no change of tone to indicate a hint of sarcasm or double meaning in her words. "Oh, she doesn't care overmuch for hawking," he said noncommittally. "'Tis a magnificent falcon that my lord has, though. You should have seen her stoop to seize a heron that flew up in the marsh! She was like a bolt of lightning!" His hand pantomimed the impressive swiftness of Henry's winged huntress.

A smile found its way through her mask of indifference. "I can just imagine, my lord. I imagine you were wishing you had your own merlin from Kingsclere on your wrist." Her green eyes sparkled. "What was his name, Charlemagne?"

"You remember well. Yes, 'twas Charlemagne, and very good he was at taken coneys, but I fear he cannot compare with the prince's gyrfalcon."

"Bah! You men! So bloodthirsty, from boyhood on," purred Lady Desiderata, coming and taking Ranulf's arm and fluttering her lashes at him. "You love blood and gore and nothing softer and finer—"

"Like yourself, my lovely Desi?" finished Prince Henry, coming over to warm himself at the fire.

She preened. "Perhaps," she said with an attempt at an enigmatic smile, but Ranulf caught her watching under her long lashes for his reaction.

It had been easier when they were out hawking to banter politely and without meaning with the red-haired temptress while concentrating on the performance of Henry's falcon. Now the evening loomed up before him, long and fraught with peril as he attempted to evade the enticement he would once have found a delightful game.

Desiderata, however, was not about to wait until evening. After the midday meal she said, "My lord, would you not like a bath? Surely your muscles are aching and sore after our little expedition. I will have the lackeys bring up hot water, and I have some oil of sandalwood that you will find very pleasant . . . after I wash your back," she added with a wink.

"Oh, I couldn't put you to the trouble," he drawled. "You must have things you wish to do, my lady. If you would be so kind, order the hot water, but Edward can see to the rest, can't you, my boy?"

He was aware of Desiderata's suddenly narrowed eyes and Henry's expressively raised brow as Aldyth murmured a surprised, "If you wish, my lord."

On the way up the stairs, though, he realized he had caught himself in a trap. He could not let "Edward" assist him in his bath! The mere idea of her hands on any part of him was already sending the blood coursing to his groin— even just the thought of her seeing him naked. God's toenails, just one look at his erect manhood and she would not only know how much he wanted her, she would be reminded of the rapacious Turold and frightened beyond reason.

"You may go, Aldyth," he said after the servants bearing the oaken tub and hot water had come and gone. "I need no help."

"But, Ranulf—"

He paused in the act of pulling his shirt up and over his head.

"Would you like me to summon Lady Desiderata after all?"

"Nay, 'tis not necessary."

She gave a tentative smile. "Well then, I would be glad . . . that is, I am well used to assisting men in their baths. My father's guests of honor . . ."

Suddenly he hated the common custom of the lady of the household helping any gentleman guest with his bath. He hated the idea that Aldyth had had to do such a service, meaningless or not.

"I said it is *not* necessary. I don't need your help, and I certainly do not need Lady Desiderata, do you hear me?" He realized he was nearly shouting, and he lowered his voice before adding, "Now go somewhere and leave me in peace." He had a glimpse of her green eyes, very round, very moist, as she retreated from his chamber and his churlishness.

The candles burned low in Henry's chamber. Desiderata, her head propped on a cushion as she lay on an ornate Persian rug before the rug, snored softly, having long since despaired of Ranulf ceasing to talk politics with Henry.

Ranulf noted the fact with an inward sigh of relief. Talking late into the night with Prince Henry about the English kingdom and who would reign over it had been deliberate on his part. He only hoped she would not wake when he left the chamber; he had no desire to hurt the lady, whose only fault was that she was not Aldyth.

There was a silence after a burning log splintered and sent a shower of embers falling into the ashes below. Henry was proud of having the luxury of a chimney in his bedchamber, Ranulf knew. Chimneys were not known in England as yet; the smoke from the great open fires in the halls was supposed to escape through a louvered hole in the roof, but it did not always work, and braziers were still the only source of heat in bedchambers. Someday, Ranulf thought, he would remodel Kingsclere, and it would have chimneys like this.

"It appears the lovely Desiderata does not please you, my friend," Henry said suddenly, with a meaningful glance at the slumbering woman.

"No...I mean yes! That is to say, my prince, I do not know," Ranulf replied uneasily.

"Perhaps you have been frequenting the king's court for too long?" probed Henry with an ironic smile. "I know my royal brother has no use for women himself, and perhaps you—"

"There are some vices Rufus has that I do not," interrupted Ranulf stiffly.

"Easy, Ranulf! I do not mean to offend you," Henry said. "'Tis just that you seem rather distracted, and I thought mayhap—"

"You thought wrong, my lord," he heard himself snap. "Ah, pray forgive my sharpness. I...I am in love with someone else and...," Ranulf's voice trailed off as he wondered how to finish his sentence. He could not say, *And she is afraid of men and is posing as my page until her former betrothed can be dealt with.*

"You have a sweetheart back in England?" Henry was amused now. "I had no idea, Ranulf, forgive me. So the fiery darts of Cupid have pierced the heart of the notorious Lord Ranulf, eh? Who is she—someone you must love in secret? The wife of a powerful lord? No? By the rood, can you mean you have fallen prey to some innocent *damoiselle?*" He laughed heartily. "Ah, that's rich, my friend Ranulf!"

Ranulf was far from amused, but letting Henry think it was a lady back in England made Aldyth's secret safer.

"Well, I will press you no more about Desiderata, then. I have no current mistress myself. Mayhap I will rekindle the flame with Desi for a night or two—strictly to divert her from you, you understand? Am I not a good friend as well as your liege?" he asked with another chuckle.

Ranulf tried to direct Henry back to political subjects, the causes that had convinced Ranulf that Henry would be a much better, fairer king for England—his proposed legal reforms, his philosophy about the relationship between the Crown and the Church, for example. But Henry was feeling playful now and would not be led.

"Since you have shared the revelation that you are already smitten and do not care to celebrate the New Year in Desiderata's bed, how shall we pass the days?" he mused. "There remain but two days of the old year... Ah! I have it! I suppose you did not think of getting your sweetheart a New Year's gift before you left England? You purchased naught for her in Rouen?"

"I...no..." Actually, Ranulf had thought about the fact that he had no gift for Aldyth and regretted the lack. He had fantasized about the shimmering jewels he would love to adorn her with, but he told himself it was folly. She would accept naught from him, even if he had anything to give her.

"If the morrow is fair, we shall ride into Barfleur. There is a Jew who has a goldsmith's shop there—amazing for such a small town, but I have promised him he may go to England if and when I am king, and he has promised me the support of his brethren.

"And don't worry about Desi," the prince said smugly. "I'll purchase some shiny bauble that will distract her."

Chapter Sixteen

Try as she might, Aldyth could not understand him. The very thing that should have made Ranulf happy—the availability of an attractive woman of easy virtue—had made him crosser than ever, she mused on her pallet while Ranulf was dining with the prince and Desiderata.

Why was Ranulf acting so oddly? He had left the table in the courtesan's company on that first night in Prince Henry's castle. Why had he returned to his chamber so soon? He could hardly have had time to be intimate with Desiderata, even if they had dispensed with all the civilized preludes!

At the time, Aldyth had felt her heart had won a reprieve—but it was only that. He had just been postponing the inevitable, probably because he was too tired from the journey to woo the lady with his usual style. Doubtless they had already arranged an assignation on the morrow, though.

After Aldyth made that assumption, it had been especially galling that she should be the one ordered to go and fetch Lady Desiderata this morning. Resentfully she had visualized a hunting lodge or other such building where Henry would leave Ranulf and Desiderata alone together.

Aldyth's stomach had churned and her heart had ached the entire morning as she wandered from the bedchamber to the hall to the parapet and back to the hall again, oblivious to the castle's bright holiday decorations.

The threesome had come back in good spirits, but Aldyth could not detect any special closeness between Ranulf and Desiderata. Did that only mean they were more used to these games of passion, more skilled at dissembling? But why should Ranulf bother to hide his feelings? He had already indicated Aldyth was not worldly enough for him.

Then he had all but forbidden Desiderata to help him bathe. Aldyth was mystified by his behavior. Surely a bath was an enjoyable setting for a seduction, and yet Ranulf had acted as skittish as an elderly monk confronted by a succubus!

Could he possibly have thought he was too sweaty and dirty from the ride for a lady of Desiderata's daintiness? Aldyth was too cynical to believe the courtesan was any more fastidious than she was coy. And then he had been so testy about ordering *her* out of the room, as well.

She had seen the raised eyebrows of Prince Henry and Desiderata and the look they had exchanged. They were wondering if he was indifferent to women.

What a laughable thought! Aldyth had been at Winchester long enough to have heard that Ranulf was accounted a legendary lover by the ladies of the court. And she hadn't imagined that kiss in the barn at Kingsclere, or his reaction to that impulsive victory kiss outside the tavern in Honfleur. That had been the real Ranulf—passionate, fiery, certainly not made of the stuff of a successful celibate.

What of the times she had looked up to find him gazing at her, only to have him quickly look away? There had been an expression she could not read slipping from his features, but when he looked back, that urbane, languid mask was again in place.

Ranulf's behavior regarding the bath *had* been strange, but he had gone to take supper with the prince and Desiderata hours ago. Probably he and the courtesan had left Henry's company after a while and were even now carnally entwined on Desiderata's bed.

Surely there was no worse torment than imagining the man she loved making love to another woman.

Lady Vivienne had said, *I know the right woman exists for Ranulf somewhere.... You have an image of him as wicked, dissolute, lost to all that is good between a man and the one lady who is destined to be his. But that is not the truth of it, Aldyth....*

The words sounded unreal now. Ranulf's kindness to her had made the Norman lady idealistic about him, decided Aldyth. But Lady Vivienne had been wrong when she had hinted that Aldyth was that one "right lady" for Lord Ranulf of Kingsclere.

Earlier this evening Aldyth had stolen a look at herself in Ranulf's piece of silvered glass. Her hair had grown out but little. Her eyes looked enormous in the pale, wan face. How could a girl who looked like a peasant boy hope to compete with the charms of a woman such as Lady Desiderata?

Once Aldyth had decided to be realistic, she would have given anything to be able to return home to Sherborne immediately. Surely Turold had resigned himself to his loss and she would be safe. Perhaps he had even decided to marry Maud and make an honest woman of her.

Jésu, please let Ranulf be summoned home soon! She longed to end the torment of being with him while knowing he was not for her.

And then all at once she heard the creak of the door opening as he entered the chamber. Now that it was so late, she had not expected him to return tonight, but here he was.

Pulling the blanket up about her, she feigned sleep, but the flickering hour candle allowed her to study him covertly as he moved about the room. What had happened while he was gone? Had he bedded the courtesan? If so, what could have made him want to leave her bed before dawn? As he drew closer, pulling off his tunic, she could smell wine but no trace of the costly scent Lady Desiderata wore.

She gave up the agonizing questions for the secret pleasure of studying the masculine beauty of his body. As he pulled off his *sherte* and the woolen tunic below, she was treated to the sight of the candlelight dancing off the planes of his chest and shoulders. A small amount of curly hair narrowed to an arrow that pointed down past the flat belly. He turned his back to her, untying and pushing down his short braies, and she caught a tantalizing glimpse of small, tight buttocks above powerfully muscled thighs. This was not the body of a languid court popinjay but of a warrior.

He turned around again, as naked as God had made him, and she squeezed her eyes shut, but not before the image of his maleness had seared itself on her brain. She bit her lip.

"Aldyth?" he called softly, uncertainly.

Had he seen her looking at him? She willed herself to remain still, apparently relaxed, and made her breathing steady and even. There was silence, and a moment later the creak of the rope mattress as he lay down upon the bed.

As Aldyth was breaking her fast in the hall the next morning, she stole glances at Ranulf and Lady Desiderata, who sat next to him nibbling on a piece of manchet bread.

Ranulf seemed in a better mood this morning and smiled when the courtesan addressed him, but Aldyth could detect no change in the way he treated Desiderata. There were no long shared looks, no lingering touches, nothing that would indicate any change had taken place in their relationship last night.

She heard Ranulf and Prince Henry speaking of a ride into the nearby town of Barfleur this morning.

"Ah, and may I come along with you handsome gentlemen?" murmured Desiderata, looking appealingly at Ranulf. "Or do you wish it to be just you men, with the New Year so close upon us?"

How bold to hint about the gift giving that customarily took place on New Year's Day! Aldyth had to admire the woman's audacity, even if the thought of Ranulf giving Desiderata a gift made Aldyth grit her teeth.

Surprisingly, though, it was Prince Henry, not Ranulf, who replied. "Why certainly, my dearest lady, we wouldn't think of leaving you to languish in the hall on such a fair day. As a matter of fact, I haven't bought your gift yet, and I thought you might like to help select it at the Jew's shop, eh?"

Aldyth watched the courtesan preen at the prince's words, but she saw her studying Ranulf a moment later. Was Desiderata disappointed that it had not been Ranulf who had invited her to come along, or who had mentioned buying her a present?

Aldyth was taken completely by surprise when he spoke up a moment later. "Edward, how would you like to come along with us? You must have been bored with so little to do yesterday. Would you not enjoy an outing, too?"

Even as her heart surged with joy that she was being asked to join them, she saw Desiderata's eyes narrow.

"So solicitous of a mere page," she purred. "Is he not the noblest of lords, to be so kind to a *boy?*" The words were admiring, but the way she said them, with the merest inflection, implied something less than courteous—implied, moreover, that Ranulf might be something worse than the rogue he was reputed to be.

Aldyth bristled. How dare the courtesan imply that Ranulf was one of *those* men?

Ranulf merely raised an eyebrow and favored Desiderata with an opaque glance. "I'm certain Edward can make himself useful, perhaps by carrying your purchases? Won't you, Edward?"

All eyes were suddenly on her, so only Aldyth saw Ranulf's wink. "Oh, uh . . . aye, Lord Ranulf—that I will."

Desiderata had to be content with that. Henry, ignoring or unaware of the charged atmosphere, said, "Well then, let us be off. Desi, we'll wait only a few minutes for you, so if you wish to go, make haste."

Abram BenIsaac came outside his shop at the sound of their horses.

"You are welcome to my humble shop once again, my most revered prince. I thought I might be seeing you soon, now that the Christian New Year is upon us."

Prince Henry seemed pleased at the goldsmith's greeting. "Of course you knew you would see me, you cheeky rascal! Am I not your best customer?" he asked, slapping BenIsaac on the back of his fine, brocade-trimmed tunic.

"But of course you are, my prince. And I see you have brought another customer to me," the swarthy man said, indicating Ranulf with a respectful bow, "and a beauteous lady. You are here to select her a New Year's gift, yes?" He looked from Henry to Ranulf, as if unsure of which lord to address. "I have just the thing for the lady—a ruby necklace that will bring out the fire of her hair."

"Yes, I will be buying the lady a bauble," Henry said. "Now, are you going to let us stand out in the wind all day, or will you let us come inside?"

The day was remarkably mild for late December, but the goldsmith smiled obsequiously. "A thousand curses upon my head for my thoughtlessness, my lords, my lady. Of course, come in. I, Abram BenIsaac, would be honored by your presence."

"And you'll ritually disinfect the place when we leave, I know," Henry retorted dryly. "After you, my lady."

Desiderata swept in with disdainful hauteur as she passed the well-dressed goldsmith.

"Edward, hold the horses," commanded Ranulf, handing the reins of the other three mounts to Aldyth.

The palfreys had been given a good run on the way into the town of Barfleur and were content to stand, giving Aldyth no trouble. She studied the prosperous-looking stone front of the goldsmith's shop. There was a large window—with real glass, she noted, never having seen the costly substance except in churches and the residences of the highest nobility.

She took advantage of the window to peer into the shop. There were Desiderata and Prince Henry, peering into a carved wooden case that the Jew held before them. As she watched, BenIsaac held up a ring of gleaming gold set with a ruby as big as a man's thumbnail. Desiderata seized it, thrusting it on her finger and smiling coquettishly up at Henry, who studied it with narrow eyes before saying something to the goldsmith. BenIsaac must have named a price that was too high, for Henry put it back in the case, shaking his head.

Desiderata looked sulky, and Aldyth saw her sidle up to Ranulf, who was standing by himself, bent over another velvet-lined case on a table. She said something to him, leaning over to whisper in his ear.

As Aldyth continued to watch, he looked over at Desiderata, smiled politely, then went back to his perusal, holding up first one, then another golden necklace, some of simple design, others with intricate carving, still others with jewels interspersed between every few links.

Aldyth observed him curiously. For whom was he thinking of buying a New Year's gift if not for Desiderata? His mother, perhaps? But there was such an intensity about the way he studied each piece the goldsmith held up for his consideration, such a faraway look in his eyes, as if he contemplated the way in which the lady who was to receive the gift would look upon it. This could not be a gift intended for Lady Nichola of Kingsclere.

Perhaps her form cast a shadow through the window, or the very steadiness of her staring somehow made him aware that he was being spied upon, for he turned around and caught sight of Aldyth.

She tried to look unconcerned, smiling back at him, but he appeared fiercely displeased as he turned back to the jewelry, placing his back squarely to her in such a way that she could not see what he was looking for.

Well! And what was he being so secretive about, anyway? As if she cared whom he bought a New Year's gift for! Aldyth turned her attention instead to Henry and the courtesan.

Henry had evidently been shown and rejected several pieces of the goldsmith's art, for shiny golden cups, girdles, rings, bracelets and necklaces littered BenIsaac's tabletop. Desiderata avidly eyed each new piece held up, then looked stormy as it was rejected. She brightened as Henry held up another necklace of sapphires, which glittered blue fire even in the dim light.

But wait! While she had been regarding the byplay between Henry and Desiderata, she had missed Ranulf making his selection. Out of the corner of her eye, she saw BenIsaac handing something to Ranulf, which he put into a pouch on his sword belt. What had he bought?

Then the goldsmith said something to Henry, evidently naming an acceptable price, for the prince pulled out a purse and handed BenIsaac three silver marks. His purchase made, Henry fastened the necklace around Desiderata's neck.

Aldyth saw the goldsmith bowing with oily courtesy, calling out blessings and farewells as the three, their purchases made, headed for the door. She moved quickly away from the window and was unconcernedly stroking her piebald mount when they came outside.

Desiderata was still fingering her new necklace. "Thank you, my lord. I shall have to give you something very special for the New Year in return," she declared, batting her eyes at Henry.

"I shall look forward to it," promised the prince, giving her bottom a familiar pat as if Ranulf and his page were not even there.

Then the courtesan looked back over her shoulder at Ranulf. "Your sweetheart back in England is a lucky woman, too, my lord," she said sweetly, but her eyes were narrowed. She reminded Aldyth more than ever of a cat. "I'm sure she will adore your gift."

Ranulf's dark eyes darted to Aldyth, their expression unreadable, then back to Desiderata. "I hope so, my lady."

A sweetheart in England. Of course. Somehow hearing her suspicions put into words by Desiderata made Aldyth feel doubly miserable. Ranulf was in love with someone back in England, and that was why he had been immune to the courtesan's obvious charms.

He must love her very much, Aldyth thought, her heart feeling like a lump of frozen lead within her chest. There were not many men who could resist a temptress like Desiderata, even when his ladylove would never know he had indulged his desires. Who was she? Was she a lady of the court or some heiress that he planned to wed? How had he developed such a relationship without her hearing of it? Well, Lord Étienne and Lady Nichola will be relieved, she thought distractedly.

She managed to contain her tears until they were cantering along the coastal road back to Henry's castle and she could fall behind, unnoticed by the other three. Then she let them flow, hoping the wind from the Channel would blow them away before they reached their destination.

Perhaps Ranulf would want to stop on their journey home and give his New Year's gift to his beloved, thought Aldyth, picturing the misery of continuing her masquerade while Ranulf courted his sweetheart under her very eye. No! She would never accompany him on such an errand! She would run away from him as soon as they reached English soil again—nay, better yet, she would leave him right after New Year and find her own way back across the Channel....

Aldyth was so preoccupied with her woeful thoughts that she failed to hear the dog that had come running out from a farmhouse by the road to announce their passing. Yipping and nipping at Motley's heels because it was the hindmost of the four, the dog succeeded in frightening the normally placid cob. The horse reared, neighing in fright. Aldyth, caught unawares, was thrown backward off the piebald.

Her scream was cut off as she landed heavily on her back.

Chapter Seventeen

She couldn't breathe. The world tilted crazily around the clump of dead grass on which she lay. Black waves of unconsciousness lapped at her brain. This was dying, then. She opened her eyes and saw Ranulf bent over her, his lean face pale with alarm. It was well that the last sight she saw in the world should be him, the man she loved. Aldyth was content.

And then the air burned as it rushed back into her lungs. She blinked. Flexing her arms and legs experimentally caused a throbbing pain to announce itself in her left ankle.

"Aldyth!" he whispered. "Are you all right? Don't try to move! Thank God!"

The pain and relief that she was not dying after all made her want to cry, but she remembered that a boy would be expected not to give way to girlish tears. "I think so, my lord," she said, remembering to pitch her voice low to remind him that Desiderata was watching them from horseback just behind them. "I...just couldn't...get my breath...for a moment...and my ankle hurts. I think...'tis broken."

Immediately he moved to her foot and, with infinite care, removed her boot and inspected the ankle, cradling it on his

knee, probing carefully. She winced and could not suppress
a small whimper when he hit a tender spot on the outside of
her ankle.

"Aye, there! Ah, it hurts, my lord!"

"Yes, but I think 'tis only badly bruised. The bones underneath seem sound enough," he said, still eyeing her with
concern. "Do you think you can sit up?"

Just then Henry came trotting back, having recaptured
Aldyth's mount.

"Edward just got the wind knocked out of him, my
liege," Ranulf told him. "And sprained his ankle, it seems."

Henry nodded. "'Tis well that he landed on turf instead
of this cursed stony road. Are *you* all right, Ranulf? You're
pale as a ghost."

"I? I'm fine, my liege. I was just picturing having to tell
this pup's mother that he'd broken his neck in Normandy,
and I've no liking for hysterical women, I vow." His attempt to sound lazy and cynical fell short of the mark.

Aldyth saw Desiderata eyeing them very suspiciously.
"I . . . think I can stand, my lord, if you'll just help me a little." She found it hurt to put any weight on her leg, so she
leaned against Ranulf and tried to hobble back to her
blowing cob. "Can you just . . . give me a leg up? I think I can
ride—"

"Nonsense. You can't even stand on that foot. Nay, you'll
ride pillion with me back to the castle, and then you're going to bed with your foot propped up for the rest of the day.
Perhaps one of the wenches can prepare some sort of poultice—"

"*Such* a tender master," murmured Desiderata above
them. "He could not be more chivalrous to a *damoiselle*,"
she added, her words making the purring voice a snarl.

"Sheathe your claws, my lady," Henry told her, a trifle
curtly. "You should hardly be jealous of a page."

Aldyth didn't miss the angry flash of those feline eyes. If Desiderata were indeed a cat, she'd be hissing and spitting, she thought.

"Jealous? *I?* I have no reason to care how Lord Ranulf treats his precious page. I merely thought it touching, after all—"

"Enough!" the prince snapped. "I'll lead the cob."

"My lord, I really *do* think I can ride. You needn't—" Couldn't Ranulf see how his solicitude was angering the courtesan and making her suspicious of him? If he wanted to be convincing, Ranulf should be treating "Edward" with the same rough indifference most lords had toward their underlings.

"Be quiet, Edward. Don't be foolish. I have said you're riding pillion, and so you shall."

"'Tis you who are being foolish, my lord," she hissed at him from behind the cover of the horse. "You should be flirting with Desiderata, not—"

"Be quiet," Ranulf commanded, his face emotionless as he assisted Aldyth onto the back of his palfrey. He seemed determined to ignore both Desiderata's gibes and Aldyth's nervousness.

She tried to hold herself rigidly erect behind Ranulf so that she didn't come into contact with him, but it was necessary to lock her arms around his waist to hold on as the horse began to move.

"Lean against me or 'twill be an uncomfortable ride for you," he said over his shoulder.

She had no choice, even under the courtesan's gaze. The motion of the horse as it began to trot forced her to relax, her cheek touching his shoulders, her breasts rubbing against his back. Since she apparently had no other alternative, she allowed herself to enjoy the heavenly closeness as they made their way back to the castle.

At the castle, he helped her down from the palfrey's back. The ankle was throbbing in good earnest now, but since Desiderata was still present she thought it best to hobble up the twisting stone steps to Ranulf's chamber, using him as a crutch on her left side.

The first pair of steps was awkward, but she stubbornly set her teeth against the pain, determined to make it if only to escape that feline scrutiny.

"You make it needlessly difficult. Here, put your arms around my neck. I'm going to carry you," Ranulf told her.

"Nay, you must not, she's staring at us," Aldyth whispered urgently to him.

"Hush," he said in a low voice. "I care not." With that, he scooped her up, one hand under her legs, the other around her shoulders, and made his way up the stairs as if she weighed nothing at all.

As the staircase twisted around and they were lost to the sight of the woman below, Aldyth allowed herself to look into his face, which was almost on a level with hers. He was smiling slightly, and from this proximity she could see that his pupils were dilated in his dark, almost black eyes. His nostrils flared as their eyes met. He smelled of horse and sandalwood and maleness.

By the time they got to the top, she was trembling. Could he feel it? He pushed open the door with his foot and deposited her in a chair by the table.

"Thank you, Ranulf. I—I'll be all right now, if you will but send up one of the women with that poultice you mentioned. ..."

"I'm not leaving you till I'm certain you're all right."

What did he mean by that? Did he intend to undress her and examine her bone by bone?

"Nay, Ranulf, please. I'll be fine, truly. Lady Desiderata is already eyeing you oddly. She'll either think you prefer boys or she'll figure out I'm female!'' She closed her eyes to shut out the image of Ranulf coming closer, kneeling by her chair.

''What matters it what that trollop believes? Are you so tired of my company, Aldyth?''

The accumulated tension of maintaining her disguise and her long-suppressed desire for him, mingled with her present confusion at his sudden change of behavior, touched off an explosion.

''Damn you, my lord liar! I don't know who you are anymore! You acted as if you were one of Rufus's rogues, then I find out you're intriguing with Henry. And why aren't you pursuing Desiderata or one of Henry's other ladies-in-residence? I thought she was exactly the type of woman you—''

''To the devil with her! Why are *you* being such a shrew? God's toenails, wench! I thought you'd broken your neck out there!''

He was shouting at her!

''And what would it matter if I had? You made it very clear I wasn't... wicked enough for you. You only brought me along out of chivalry.''

''Is that what you think, you little fool? I'm tired of hiding the truth. I'll show you what I feel for you—and I promise you, Aldyth, it isn't chivalry.''

Rising on his knees, he seized her face between two none-too-gentle hands and took her mouth with his.

It was an angry kiss, full of force and hunger. The storm of his sudden passion broke upon her, claiming her with shattering intensity. ''I tried to leave you alone, Aldyth, for your good as well as mine,'' he said, keeping her face imprisoned between his hands so that she must look into the black depths of his eyes. ''I didn't want to expose you to the danger or let myself be distracted by loving you—''

"Distracted?" she repeated.

"Yes, distracted—by you as my wife, Aldyth! I dared not heed anything else until I was done with all this plotting. Oh, I was going to come for you, as soon as the right man wore the English crown. Realizing you might not have waited for me, you might have wed someone else, made me die each time I thought of you. Yes, what I'm doing is dangerous, and if Rufus discovers whose man I am, I could lose my head. And as my wife you could be made to suffer, as well. But God's toenails, I've already lost my head! I'll keep you safe somehow, Aldyth, but I can't live any longer without you—"

"Then do not be without me another moment, Ranulf," she told him hoarsely. "You great fool, why do you think I followed you to Normandy? I'd rather live with you, whatever the danger, than without you in the greatest safety."

He leaped to his feet. One hand dived under her thighs, the other behind her back, and she was being carried against his chest again, but only for a moment as he moved toward the velvet-hung bed.

She thought he would drop her there, like a conqueror's prize, but even in the throes of passion he had a care for her injured ankle and lowered her with infinite gentleness, careful not to let her foot hit the bedpost. He shrugged off his cloak, then pulled over his head his short outer tunic and the longer one underneath. He stood gazing at her for a moment, still clad in his *sherte* and *chausses*, his dark eyes sweeping over her from head to foot.

Aldyth felt a surge of regret for her page's clothing and shorn hair. This was not the way she had pictured this moment. Nay, she had imagined wearing some gauzy, lacy nightrail, her hair fanned out over the pillow or hanging over him like a shimmering curtain....

Evidently he agreed—about her garments, at least. "Aldyth," he growled, "you have spent too long a time in 'Edward's' clothes. I would see the woman underneath." He pulled the short pageboy's tunic with its silver unicorn emblem over her head, then her *sherte,* and frowned when he saw the band of cloth wound tightly around her chest.

"So that's how you made yourself look flat as a lad," he said with a chuckle. "I remembered your body feeling much more...*womanly* against me in that barn at Kingsclere."

Aldyth blushed, but it was the very thing she needed to hear to restore her damaged feminine self-confidence, enabling her to reach up and pull out the bone pin that held the binding in place—the bone pin that had pricked her side countless times during this masquerade—and, under his rapt gaze, unwind the cloth until her breasts fell free, soft and womanly.

"Is this...is this better, my lord?" she asked softly, feeling all female as she saw the heat in his eyes.

"Ah, yes. And one more thing will make it better still..." His breathing was ragged as he reached for the string that held her braies in place at her waist and pulled them off her, still remembering to ease them gently over her swollen ankle.

She lay exposed to his gaze and felt no shyness about it as she saw the admiration register in his face. The throbbing in her ankle and her boyish haircut were forgotten as she saw him reach to unfasten the tie at the neck of his shirt and pull it off, before turning his attention to the tie at his waist.

His hands shook and he swore softly as he strove to undo the knot his haste had caused. His impatience made her smile. Worldly, wicked Lord Ranulf, balked by a mere knot!

He was not to be put off, though. Reaching for the knife that had dangled from his girdle, he made short work of the cord.

"My lord, you make more toil for your long-suffering page," she mocked. "Poor Edward will have to find another string—" she stopped speaking as the linen slithered down over his hips and pooled at his feet, revealing his rampant staff.

"Edward is dead, at least in this room," he growled in a husky voice as he caught her gaze. "But we'll never mourn him, will we, Aldyth?" he asked as he lay down beside her and gathered her against him.

She shivered as she felt the hard, muscled length of his warrior's body touching every inch of hers. His maleness pulsed against her abdomen. For a moment, she was afraid. She had never known a man intimately, and he was built like a stallion, not a mere man. And yet he had not fallen on her like some ravening wolf, the way Turold had, intent only on breaching her virginity.

And then his lips touched hers, and she forgot her fear and felt only fire as his tongue stole inside her mouth, caressing hers. She felt his hand cupping her breast, stroking it with his thumb, until the nipple was as erect as his manhood. Her breast tingled at his touch, and yet it was the pit of her belly that felt aflame as he continued to circle the areola. Then his mouth left hers.

Aldyth felt abandoned and was about to beg him to kiss her again, when she felt his lips close about the breast he had been touching. The change, from his dry, firm thumb to the hot moistness of his mouth and tongue around her nipple, made her gasp and arch against him, calling his name.

His other hand, beneath her, splayed over her buttocks. Her corresponding relaxation against him a heartbeat later brought her squarely in contact with his hardness, and she moaned inarticulately, clutching at him as she felt it seeking, probing at her woman's entrance. She ached to feel his full length inside her.

"Soon, sweetheart, soon," he promised, "when you're ready..."

"Ranulf," she cried softly, *"please..."*

He rolled her onto her back, and his hand left the breast he had been holding up to his seeking mouth and stroked slowly over her taut abdomen, lower, lower...

She whimpered as he touched the silken triangle of curls at the juncture of her thighs, and he dipped his hand between her legs, parting her slightly, a finger sliding gently inside her. The shock of the gentle invasion made her go rigid.

He grinned wolfishly. "Ah yes, you're ready for me, my darling Aldyth, and so quickly. How wet you are, love, wet for *me*..." His voice, she noted with amazement, was not mocking but held an awed wonder that filled her with glowing heat. Perhaps she *was* woman enough for him, after all.

A second finger joined the first in its stroking, in and out, in and out, while his thumb did wonderful, magical things to the little bud of flesh just above them.

She would die, consumed in flames, if he did not take her soon—this very moment!

Somehow he read her mind, for he lowered his long, lean frame onto her then and his hand left her, replaced by the velvet-tipped hardness that throbbed just outside her opening.

"Now, Aldyth," he breathed, impaling her eyes with his midnight gaze, "I'm going to make you mine *now*..."

His hands burrowed under her hips and lifted her to him then, and his mouth covered hers, swallowing her soft cry of pain as he buried his shaft deep within her, and she left girlhood behind forever.

Chapter Eighteen

Their hearts thudded as he waited, poised above her, for the ripple of pain to subside. He kissed away the crystalline tear that trickled down her cheek, making her love him all the more.

"You have given me a gift, my sweet Aldyth," he whispered to her, "for no man has ever been where I am. Nor ever will be," he added, his voice husky. "And now I will give you a gift."

He began to move inside her, slowly at first, pulling and pushing the tingling nub of flesh just above his shaft. She pushed upward, tentatively at first, and was rewarded by such a great wave of ecstasy that she repeated the motion as he surged against her again.

"Yes, my love! Ah yes," he breathed into her neck. "More . . . take me deeper . . ."

Her hands tightened around his hips, pulling him deeper, deeper, and all the time he kept up a steadily spiraling rhythm that made her heart race and her lungs burn for air. She felt as if they were running a tormenting race, a race that neither would win unless they both won. But the things he was doing to her made her no longer able to think, only to feel . . .

To feel some approaching culmination that threatened to shatter her into tiny pieces. But he was relentless, pushing her closer and closer to that dangerous precipice.

She dug into him with her hands, holding on to him for dear life. And then suddenly it was as if there were not even a soft down mattress beneath her back, and she was launched into empty air.

She felt him thrust again, and then he was falling with her into the white-hot heat....

He was lying on his side, gazing intently at her when she returned to earth minutes—hours?—later and opened her eyes.

"Are you all right, sweetheart? I wasn't too rough with you?"

"Oh, Ranulf," she breathed, still taking it all in. "That one moment of pain was well worth what followed. I had no idea..." *If I had known, I would have given myself willingly to you that day in the stable,* she thought, but did not dare to voice the words aloud.

"What about your ankle? God's toenails, Aldyth, I'm a brute for forcing myself upon you when you've just fallen off your horse and come within a hairbreadth of breaking your neck—"

She had forgotten the injured ankle; it reminded her of its presence now with a faint throb, but she felt too wonderful to give it much heed. "Hush," she whispered, laying a finger over his well-chiseled lips. "My ankle is well enough, and you did nothing I did not want. We've already wasted so much time..."

He nodded, tracing the line of her chin, his dark eyes regretful. "'Tis true. I've already told you why I thought I should not let myself love you."

"Foolish man," she said fondly, allowing herself the joy of running a hand through the tousled, raven black hair.

"But I believed also that after Turold you were afraid of all men. I...I thought I would frighten you if I let you know how much I desired you."

She stared at him. "Ah, Ranulf, I could never be afraid of you! I've loved you since we were children."

"Even when I played the debauched rogue toward you in the stable, Aldyth? I was trying to frighten you away, did you know that? But I did not feign wanting you—saints, that was true enough!"

She kissed him softly. "I wanted you, too, even when you acted the rogue," she admitted. "You don't know how close you came to succeeding in tumbling me in the hay!"

"Too bad I didn't," he said with a grin. "We might have saved ourselves a lot of grief. You wouldn't have had to chop off your beautiful hair, for one thing," he said, fingering a lock that fell low over her eyes. "But, Aldyth, what about when you saw me mince into the hall that night at Kingsclere? Surely I disgusted you—confess!" he teased.

Aldyth rolled her eyes. "Verily, that *was* a shock. I could not believe how you had changed. Or so I thought."

"So they all thought," he said more soberly. "I've hated deceiving my father and mother, too, but unless all treated me as if I were radically, even disgustingly changed, Rufus might not have trusted me as much as he did."

"You were very convincing," she told him. Then, imitating the languid, drawling voice he had sometimes assumed, she mimicked him. "'Warin! This cloak has a speck of dust on it! Dust on my garments sickens me! Clean it immediately, boy!' Oh, Ranulf, I cannot wait to see their faces when we're able to tell them the truth at last."

"I hope it may be soon, just as I hope we may soon wed," he said, pulling her against his chest.

"Oh, Ranulf," she sighed rapturously, as if words could not express her joy.

He thought to doze a little, but the action brought her soft breast into contact with his chest, and then she stretched a shapely limb over his legs. He felt a stirring reaction in his groin, felt his staff start to swell in response. Nay, 'twas impossible. And too soon for her. She would be too sore. . . .

He rolled away from her, wincing inwardly as he glimpsed a streak of blood on her thighs.

"Ranulf—" Her arms reached out to him.

"Nay, I've just remembered something," he said, turning his back to her as he stood up, fighting for control, trying to will his pulsing manhood to cease its clamoring for more. "There's something I want to give you right now. It's early for a New Year's gift, I know, but I want to see how it looks."

Ranulf crossed the room to where he'd discarded his clothes when he had undressed and found the sword belt with the small pouch attached. Reaching inside, he brought out the necklace he had purchased at the goldsmith's shop just hours ago.

He watched the green eyes widen as he held out the intricately worked, gold link necklace with its pendant of jade carved in the shape of a rose.

"Ah, 'tis lovely, Ranulf," she breathed, fingering the jade rose. "I've never seen a stone of such a hue."

"'Tis from far-off Cathay, the Jew told me," he said. "I thought it the exact color of your eyes."

She shivered with delight as he fastened it about her neck. Ranulf tried not to look as the pendant settled between her soft breasts, whose tips looked as if they were roses, too.

Then Aldyth laughed. "It seems I resented a woman who doesn't exist." At his puzzled look, she explained. "When you went to the goldsmith's shop and it became obvious that whatever you bought—I couldn't see what it was—was not for Desiderata, I thought you had a lover back in England. Some highborn noble lady, I thought. Oh, Ranulf, I was so jealous!"

"Foolish wench," he said fondly. "I'll never give you cause not to trust me."

But suddenly she looked distressed. "But I have nothing to give you!" she wailed. "I had no money. How..."

Standing by her side of the bed, he kissed her forehead. "Shh. You have given me yourself, my dearest love. What greater gift can there be to a man from a maiden?"

But she was not ready to give up so easily. "I see that I could give you that gift again," she murmured, reaching a hand out daringly and stroking his staff, which had stubbornly refused to relax. Now, at her touch, it sprang fully to life.

He groaned as he felt her touch. "Cease that, you shameless wench! You need to rest now. We dare not make love again so soon, with you so recently a virgin."

She ignored him, grinning as that one part of him, at least, did not try to deny its delight in her attentions. He was rapidly losing his struggle to do what he knew he should.

"I would make up for lost time," she purred, all woman now.

He gave himself up to the inevitable. Lowering his long frame onto the bed, he lay down on his back, grinning up at her as she leaned over him on her extended arms.

"Very well, Aldyth, I will surrender to your insatiable demands. But I know a way we may make love that will allow you to take only as much of me as you are able."

"I want all of you," she told him frankly, her eyes glowing. "Now, show me, my loving lord, this wondrous way...."

He pulled her over him, reveling in the sight of her luscious breasts so near to his mouth. Her eyes closed in bliss as she positioned herself above him and guided him inside her.

"Now ride me, sweetheart...."

"Oh, Ranulf," she breathed as he reached up to cup one of the rosy-tipped globes. She moved forward tentatively, taking him deeper still, and he thought he would die of the pleasure. Never had any woman—

"My lord, when you didn't come back down I got worried, and I thought I had better bring up the poultice—" began a voice, and then a woman's shriek shattered their paradise.

Desiderata stood just inside the door, eyes bulging at the scene before her.

Aldyth looked up and caught sight of the intruder, then gave a muffled shriek of her own as she rolled off Ranulf and grabbed for the rumpled bed linens to cover herself.

So shocked that her mouth gaped open like a carp, the Norman courtesan dropped the jar she carried—right on her foot, an accident that only served to accelerate her fury.

"So *this* is why you won't even look at me, you deceiving *cochon!*" Desiderata cried, clutching at her foot. "Your little page was a girl all along! How you must all have been laughing at me—Henry, too! How pathetic I must have looked, throwing myself at you, when you already had a peasant wench to serve you in bed as well as at table. Liar! Scoundrel!" she shrilled, stooping to pick up the jar containing the poultice, which she then hurled at the pair on the bed. Aldyth ducked against Ranulf's shoulder, covering her head.

Desiderata's aim was abysmal, causing the jar to shatter on the corner of the bedside table, which in turn caused the fat candle atop it to fall on its side, dangerously near the bed curtain.

Heedless of his nudity, Ranulf reached out and righted the candle before it could do any harm. Then, trying to smother the rage he felt at this untimely breach of a very private moment, he said, "Stop screeching like a fishwife, Desiderata. This is none of your concern. Go away."

Beside him, Aldyth raised herself up on one elbow, still clutching the linen around her chest. "My lady, please. No one was laughing at you, on my honor. Prince Henry didn't know, either, I swear it. There were reasons I needed to travel in disguise—"

"On your honor! You swear! Don't you dare condescend to me, you draggle-tail slut with your serf boy's hair! I'll claw your eyes out, you trollop!"

"That's enough!" Ranulf roared, leaping from the bed to intercept the wild-eyed woman who was advancing, fingers curled into claws, toward Aldyth's side of the bed.

The sight of a very powerfully built, naked man standing between her and her goal was apparently enough to halt Desiderata's incipient charge. She backed up, but then she caught sight of the golden necklace gleaming around her rival's neck, its jade pendant nestled in the shadowy cleft between Aldyth's breasts.

Her eyes narrowed to slits and she hissed, "So that's who you bought it for, even as you lied to my lord about a sweetheart in England. So Henry doesn't know the truth, either. I wonder what he'll say, my fine Lord Ranulf, when he learns that you've deceived him? If you lied about that, he'll wonder what else you might have lied about, *hein?*"

She stormed out the door, slamming it behind her.

Ranulf turned back to Aldyth, only to find her gazing sorrowfully at him, her eyes gleaming with unshed tears.

"I should have stayed in England, as you wanted, Ranulf," she said with a heavy sigh. "Now I've ruined things for you, haven't I? Now the prince will distrust you and—"

"Hush right there," he told her gently. "We both made love, did we not? While 'tis not as I'd have willed it, I'd already begun to think we'd have to tell Henry, for I was damned if I was going to go back to this damnable masquerade again, at least not here. And no, I doubt very much my liege lord will suddenly decide I'm unworthy of his trust because of anything an angry harlot says."

"But, Ranulf—"

"Hush, I said. 'Tis I who should apologize for forgetting to lock the door so that Desiderata could intrude on us so easily, love, and then vent her spleen on you like that." He held her close, kissing the top of her head.

"You don't think Henry will be angry?" she asked, her green eyes searching his face for any hesitation.

"I'd stake my life on it," he promised her. "But I do think the sooner we go and face him, the better. There's no telling what that bitch may have accused either of us of doing. Did you by any chance happen to bring any women's clothes with you?"

Chapter Nineteen

Henry looked up from the scroll of vellum he'd been about to read when Ranulf, carrying Aldyth, knocked at the open door.

"Come in, come in, my lord. You're too late, however. Desiderata's already been here and tattled into my interested ear."

Ranulf set Aldyth down and knelt, lowering his head. By his side Aldyth did the same, feeling very much like a mouse whose tail was caught by the paw of a very large, hungry cat. The silence stretched on interminably, and she could feel the prince studying each of them in turn.

At last Ranulf got to his feet and assisted Aldyth to do likewise, though she was sure she looked the clumsy fool struggling up on one foot, with Ranulf helping to pull her. When he encouraged her to lean against him, though, she felt strength and reassurance flowing through him to her.

All is not lost, his touch told her. *We shall get through this.* Then he just stood there, neither rigidly at attention nor relaxed. She darted a glance at his face and saw that he was looking the inscrutable prince straight in the eye.

Suddenly Henry gave a hoot of laughter. "You were ever a proud cockerel and fearless as a lion."

"My liege?"

"Stop standing there like I'm going to order you to be flayed alive and give the wench a chair. It should be obvious, you black-a-vised knave, that she cannot keep standing on one foot like a heron."

But Ranulf made no move to assist her to the backless curved chair that faced Henry. "My liege, I would present Lady Aldyth, daughter of my father's castellan of Sherborne."

Aldyth made an awkward attempt at a curtsy, but the prince forestalled her with a hand. Rising, he brought the chair over behind her and murmured in perfect English, "Sit, please, my dear lady."

His switch from Norman French to English made her blink in astonishment.

"You are surprised to hear me speak the tongue of the English people whom I would rule someday. But why so? Of all the sons of the Conqueror, I am the only prince born in that foggy land."

"I—I speak French, your grace." She felt it necessary to remind him.

"Of course, I have already heard you do so," he told her, "but I wanted you to feel at ease."

She felt the force of his charm like a warm ocean wave. No wonder he had held her beloved's allegiance. But she reminded herself that this very charm had made Ranulf wary of trusting him with her identity.

He leaned back and studied her, his gaze as piercing as that of his gyrfalcon. "Of course..." he murmured, speaking to Ranulf. "How could I ever have been so blind? Oh, I thought her rather a delicate lad, to be sure, but how could I have missed those long eyelashes...that sweetly curved throat...." His gaze roved lower, causing Aldyth to blush, the heat spreading up from the neckline of her undergown. Her breasts still felt strange, released from their binding, and she could see that the prince's eyes lingered on them.

"My prince, I'm sure an explanation is necessary as to why I deceived you about Lady Aldyth's gender," Ranulf interposed from his position behind her chair.

Henry chuckled. "Not at all, my lord. I was beginning to worry about you actually, thinking my elder brother's...differences...might have rubbed off on you, while all the time you found it titillating, I'm sure, to have such a secret. By day, to the world, she was your page Edward, seeing to your comforts as any well-trained page boy would. At night, in the privacy of your bed—ahem! She saw to, shall we say, *other comforts?*"

Aldyth sensed Ranulf stiffening behind her. "Your grace, the lady has plighted her troth to me. We are to marry."

Henry looked nonplussed for only a moment, then backed away, hands raised, palms outward.

"So, my lord! Why don't you just come right out and say it— 'Take your lecherous eyes off the lady, for she is mine!' See how easy it is? Oh, and my congratulations to you both," he added with a grin.

"Thank you, your grace," said Ranulf, still sounding somewhat strained. "I know myself to be very fortunate that the lady honors me with her love."

"Indeed," Henry countered dryly. "You were going to tell me why you felt it necessary for such a winsome lady to accompany you dressed in the rude clothing of a page?"

Aldyth felt Ranulf had borne enough of the blame. "'Twas not entirely his idea, my lord. I fled to him—actually, to court—dressed as a boy in an effort to elude my betrothed."

"Your betrothed? You have two of them?" Henry questioned, amused. He sat back down. "Say on, dear lady. This gets better and better."

"I found out on the eve of my wedding that my betrothed, Turold of Swanlea, was a brutal man whom I could not marry. I fled him and came to court, where my brother Warin was a page to my lord."

"You then appealed to Lord Ranulf's chivalry to help you? You must have been known to one another, since your father is his father's vassal," the prince commented, making a tent of his fingers and regarding her over them.

"Not right away," she admitted, then blushed anew as she added, "we had quarreled the last time we had seen each other, before I became betrothed. I . . . I felt I should not reveal to Lord Ranulf who I was."

Henry clapped his hands together gleefully. "There's more here than you're telling me, I'll warrant. But keep your secrets. Tell me, though, my lady, how long did it take Ranulf to discover your sex? Did he see the truth with his own eyes, or did some spiteful wench have to tell him, as Desiderata did to me?"

"He saw it rather swiftly on his own, your grace," Aldyth said with a shy glance behind her at Ranulf. "He has a keen eye."

"As I do not, it seems."

"But I knew her, my liege," Ranulf put in from behind her, beginning to sound more relaxed now that no reprimand had come from Henry. "One does not forget the face of the lady one loves, even though she disguises it by butchering her tresses and affecting a gruff voice."

Ranulf's words warmed her, and she allowed herself to smile.

"And you took her with you to Rouen dressed that way?" Henry asked, clearly interested in the rest of the story.

"Yes, my liege. As I told you when I came, my squire and Lady Vivienne were with me then, but I did not tell you the lady was never actually my mistress. She was only posing as such. As for Aldyth and I, well, we did not... There were still misunderstandings between us, and I could not appear with two lemans, after all.''

''Why not?'' Henry asked baldly. ''I have, lots of times—even in the same bed at the same time. I recommend it, as a matter of fact. Oh, excuse me, my lady,'' he told Aldyth, looking genuinely ashamed. ''Forgive my wayward tongue. I forgot myself again.''

''But I have not your grace's endurance,'' retorted Ranulf, sparing Aldyth the necessity of a reply.

''Nonsense. But you're the wiser, I'm certain. And when did you clear up these...misunderstandings? I assume not on the road between Rouen and the Cotentin, since your lady was introduced to me as Edward.''

Ranulf cleared his throat, obviously at a loss.

''This afternoon, your grace,'' Aldyth said.

Henry broke into delighted laughter. ''So when Desiderata blundered into your, shall we say, moment of intimacy, that's what you were doing? Clearing up your misunderstandings?'' He slapped his thigh. ''My lord, she's delicious. In truth, I envy you.''

Aldyth felt her face grow as hot as the coals in the nearby brazier. The thought that the courtesan had apparently described the way she had been lying atop Ranulf, her breasts—aye, her whole body—bared while he buried himself in her, made her sick with embarrassment.

''Nay, dear lady, do not blush for what is good and natural—even magical—between a man and a woman. And I regret that spiteful bitch Desiderata ruined the moment for you, damn her red head. She'll never bother either of you again, I swear it. I'll keep her out of sight for the remainder of your time here, I promise. Please say you'll forgive me, Lady Aldyth?'' he pleaded, flashing her a smile so little-boy earnest she could not help but smile back.

"Very well, your grace." She could almost find it in her to forgive Desiderata, too, providing that Henry kept his promise and she did not have to see her. After all, the courtesan's spite had resulted from her frustrated desire for the same man Aldyth loved, and she found that very easy to understand.

"Yes, I do envy you, Lord Ranulf," the prince continued. "'Tis well that I must keep myself for a royal marriage or I might be tempted to reenact a certain episode of our youth. Remember Lisette, Ranulf? Yes, I see you do. Have you told your lady about her? Nay, you haven't, have you? Well, you will forgive my doing so, but it was long ago, after all, and I would have Lady Aldyth understand why her lord might not have been so eager to reveal her as a lady even to me, your liege lord."

Henry waited.

"Go on, my prince. I'm sure you won't be satisfied until you tell it," Ranulf said, but he was still smiling.

"Very well. Lisette was the daughter of a Norman sergeant at arms at Winchester, very buxom and beautiful with blond hair and eyes as blue as the Virgin's robe, but even at thirteen a born slut. She quite enchanted young Ranulf, who was growing up in the household with me, and he was blind to her, uh, shortcomings. He worshiped the very hem of her dress, did Ranulf, and he would bring her violets and honey cakes he'd filched from Cook and so forth—all for just a smile from those pouty lips, eh, Ranulf? He was just thirteen, too, and as handsome a boy as a wench could wish. I was twelve, and a selfish brat even then, right, Ranulf? Well, *I* wasn't blind to the way she looked at men, from the other men-at-arms clear down to the scullery lads. I knew what she was. But I'll never forget the look in Ranulf's eyes when he caught me tumbling her in the hayloft."

Henry paused, and his gaze left Aldyth to go to Ranulf's face.

"I hurt you terribly with my selfishness, didn't I, my lord? You never spoke to her again, but you never tasked me with it, either, as you might have. I was expecting you to beat me to a pulp, with no thought that I was a princeling and you were just a noble's son fostering in our household. You didn't do as you might have—but you remembered, didn't you? Knowing that I am still a self-centered scoundrel, my lord, and even though you trust me with your future, you didn't trust me around your lady, did you?"

Ranulf said nothing, and finally the prince smiled crookedly. "I can't say as I blame you. But hear me, Ranulf, you have nothing to fear of me regarding this lady who loves you and whom you love. I appreciate your loyalty too much to do something so reprehensible a second time—even assuming so good a lady would look at me twice with you in the room, which she would not."

"'Tis gracious of you to say so, my prince," Ranulf said with a solemn smile.

"'Tis only the truth. Now, since you intend all honor to this lady as your wife, may I assist you in wedding her? I can have my chaplain say the nuptial mass within the hour, or as soon as you say."

Aldyth gasped.

"I would wed her gladly this minute," began Ranulf, "but there is still the matter of Lady Aldyth's previous betrothal."

"Ah, yes, the Church can get sticky about such things, viewing a betrothal nigh good as a marriage. We'll just have to wait a little longer, that's all. I'll send word to my bishop to get working on it immediately. Now, I have a letter here I must read. Why don't you carry your bride-to-be back to your chamber until supper? I'll send up another poultice, I gather the first got dropped in the rushes when Desiderata blundered in. Only this time,'' he added with a wink, ''I'll make sure the wench knocks and waits for you to admit her.''

''Does he really have his own bishop?'' Aldyth asked Ranulf when they were out of earshot up the twisting stone steps.

''I wouldn't doubt it,'' he answered with a grin. ''If Henry only had more coin to go with his charm he could have a cardinal or even the Pope himself in his pocket. But mayhap he can help speed up the ending of your contract with Turold.''

''Aye, he *is* charming,'' she agreed, ''but a woman could never trust him out of her sight, I think. I'm glad you are as you are, my love.'' She looked into the lean, handsome face so close to her own as they reached the top of the stairs.

''And I'm glad we are back at our chamber and there are hours until the supper horn blows,'' he said, nuzzling her neck as he shouldered his way in. ''As soon as the servant comes, there are things I would do...things that will not be impeded by a poultice on your ankle.''

Chapter Twenty

Henry had apparently kept his promise, for Aldyth saw no sign of Desiderata when they went down to supper.

The prince bade Aldyth sit next to him on the dais and placed Ranulf on her other side. It was a dizzying change of state for her. Only last night she had been Edward, Ranulf's page, offering dishes on bended knee, and now she was sitting at the high table next to a prince of England, a man who might someday be king! Wouldn't her father and brothers be amazed?

Before the meal began, Henry reached under the table and brought out a wooden crutch, its arm piece padded by a piece of sheepskin.

"I had my carpenter make it—with a little help from the shepherd, of course. 'Twill spare Lord Ranulf's energy for other efforts," he told her with a wink.

Aldyth knew he was vastly pleased with the flush he so easily elicited in her with his double entendre, but she was nevertheless touched by his thoughtfulness. And he continued to exhibit that unfailing courtesy as supper went on, making sure she had the choicest bits of capon, venison and fish and that the wine cup she shared with Ranulf was never empty. He asked her about her family.

In spite of his charming conversation, though, Aldyth was always more acutely aware of the presence of Ranulf on her other side, his thigh brushing hers, his eyes meeting hers as their fingers touched on their shared wine cup. Her body tingled at the thought that soon they could return to the tower room in which they had experienced such sensual delights this afternoon, and that they would have all night to lie in each other's arms.

"The message I was reading was from my brother the duke," Henry said at the end of the meal. "It seems you're being summoned back to England, I'm sorry to say."

Ranulf's eyes, suddenly troubled, met Aldyth's, and she found herself reaching for his hand. *No! The king could not be ordering Ranulf to return, just as they'd found their happiness together!*

"Be easy, you two, you need not set out on the road on the morrow," Henry said. "But apparently Robert is under the impression you're in disfavor with the king. Is that so, Ranulf?"

Ranulf nodded. "All I said to Robert was that the king was displeased with me, and it was like turning a key in a lock. He accepted me right into the fold and gave me land. He trusts so easily, my lord."

Henry chuckled. "The more fool he. But poor Robert, he's worried about you. He thinks our brother is calling you home to your doom."

Ranulf looked troubled. "He was very gracious to me, my prince. No matter how this eventually comes out, I hope the duke will be all right."

Aldyth thought the prince seemed uncomfortable as he replied, "It's largely up to him, is it not? In any case, Robert makes mention that he didn't tell him you'd been visiting me, and he has already sent him a reply stating he'd asked you to stay until Epiphany, so there's no need for you to depart the Cotentin until after New Year's Day. Robert is expecting to see you back in Rouen before you leave. He'll want to know how you found me, which brother I'm currently favoring..." He waved a hand, amazingly cheerful about the lack of genuine trust that existed among the brothers. "So you'll have a bit of a honeymoon, at least, before you must return to England and my ruddy-faced royal brother."

"In any case, 'tis better that our journey home begin from Rouen rather than the Cotentin," Ranulf murmured, his brow furrowed in thought. "Ship captains can be bribed to tell from whence they sailed, and I haven't decided whether to mention to his grace the king about our little side visit here."

"Yes, you'll have to feel out the situation when you return to court," agreed Henry. "But in any case I am glad that both of you will be here to make merry on New Year's Day with me before you must go back."

The next two days passed in a passion-filled haze for Aldyth and Ranulf. They spent more time in bed than out of it, locked away in the sanctuary of the tower room, exploring the delights of each other's bodies and stretching the boundaries of ecstasy.

Aldyth had not guessed such joys existed. If she had, she was certain she would have let Ranulf make love to her long ago. And since she knew now that he had loved her even when he had been behaving so awfully at Kingsclere, she thought wistfully of all the heartache and difficulty they could have spared themselves if he *had* taken her upon the straw in some empty stall.

Ranulf was a skillful lover. How he'd honed that talent, she would rather not ponder. She was quickly learning the little tricks that made him tremble with desire for her, that made him instantly hard and ready to do the things that, in turn, had her panting and begging him to bring her to that shuddering explosion of heat. And she glowed when he told her he loved her and that there was no other woman to equal her.

They both glowed when they spoke shyly to each other of the babe that they might have already made together, though each secretly hoped that they would be able to wed before that child should make its appearance into the world.

"It's high time you two left the bedchamber," Henry gibed them when they came downstairs to his New Year's Day feast. "I'd be astonished if you both don't have bed-sores."

Would she ever be able to stifle the flush that the prince's bawdy jests caused?

"Ah, don't mind me, Lady Aldyth," Henry said. "I'm merely lonely, as I've discovered Desiderata left the castle yesterday morning in a fit of pique."

"She did, your grace? I'm sorry," Aldyth replied carefully. It was a lie. She was pleased that she need not fear encountering the courtesan anywhere in the castle on this, their last day here.

"Oh, don't give it a thought," the prince said with a breezy wave of his hand. "She'll miss me—and my largesse, no doubt, and she'll return, purring and smiling. Meanwhile, I would like to propose a toast to the year of Our Lord 1088. May we all gain what we want this year."

The toast was typical of the genial but self-centered prince, thought Aldyth as they raised their goblets.

"To peace and the good of England," Ranulf said.

"Indeed," seconded the prince with a wink.

To my beloved's safety, she thought to herself. *And to our happy marriage, as soon as possible. . . .*

Aldyth noted, though, that Henry wasted little time re-
gretting Desiderata's absence. After supper she passed him
in a shadowy corridor embracing one of the other "ladies"
who resided there, a petite blonde named Alinor.

Henry would have been surprised to know that even as
they feasted to welcome in the New Year, Desiderata was in
Barfleur, driving a bargain with the captain of a cog bound
across the Channel for England as soon as the winds and
weather allowed. The red-haired courtesan was pleased that
the captain agreed to take her for the price of her services in
bed until they should sail and for the first night they spent
in an English port. Giving away her body was easy enough,
and it meant she could keep the sapphire necklace against
future need. Henry had not actually given it to her, having
planned to bestow it with all ceremony on New Year's Day,
but she had seen where he had placed it and had taken it
with her when she left the castle early yesterday morn.

She would miss Henry, with his easy, generous ways and
comfortable hall, but she was still seething with rage at his
command to keep to her chambers until Lord Ranulf and
his boyish-looking, jade-eyed leman had departed.

There were other men where she was going, men of power
and fortune who would make life comfortable for her again.
But she was going to England to achieve something more
important, something sweeter. Something called revenge.

Chapter Twenty-One

"*A*dieu, *Noël*," sang Aldyth as they rode their hired horses northward from Portchester on the ninth of January.

Ranulf smiled at her as she sang the French Epiphany song. "Well, at the very least your French got a polishing while you were away. You no longer speak it with such a dreadfully thick English accent," he teased.

"Ewww, you mean I speek it like thees," Aldyth retorted, holding her nose so that her voice was very nasal, then swatted playfully at her lover. "Knave! You know I have spoken French as well as English from my cradle."

"You didn't speak it ill—for an Englishwoman, that is," he retorted, then caught her doubled-up fist before she could land a blow and kissed it. "I'm only teasing, love, you know that, don't you? Besides, sweetheart, you're utterly bewitching when you're indignant."

She pretended to pout. "The only reason *you* think I speak it better is because I've learned French love words," she accused with a sidelong glance that heated his blood.

"The pillow *is* the best place to perfect any tongue," he said with a grin. "And since we are only a few leagues from Beauworth, I'll be able to prove my contention tonight. But in the meantime, come here, wench. I'm certain it has been an hour since I kissed you last."

They reined their mounts close together, and his fingers held her face cupped so he could kiss her until she was breathless.

It would have been an odd sight, for Aldyth had resumed her disguise as Edward ever since they had left Henry's castle, in case they met men from either Robert's court or Rufus's. On this winter day, however, the road was deserted.

"Ah..." she breathed, her eyes still closed as their lips parted at last. "How soon can we reach Beauworth?"

He grinned. "Soon enough, sweetheart. If only 'twere high summer, I'd tie up our horses and make love to you in that beech coppice yonder."

She followed his pointing finger, then sighed. "I suppose we could come back when it *is* summer. Oh, Ranulf, will it always be like this?"

He knew she meant would they always be on fire for each other like this, so that the merest look or word from one would have them both hot with desire?

"It has been thus for me ever since you came back into my life," he said, ruefully shifting his position in the saddle. "It's only fair that you should have to suffer along with me at long last." God's toenails! He had made love to her in that inn at Portchester this very morn, and a single kiss had made him hard and ready again.

"Well, if we don't hurry along we shall have to be suffering together in some downsman's smelly hovel," she said, casting an eye on the lowering gray clouds above. "Those look like snow clouds."

They reached Beauworth just as the first flakes began to fall. A smaller castle than Kingsclere, of the basic motte-and-bailey style, it was held for Ranulf by a garrison of half a dozen knights captained by Sir René FitzGilbert, a square-jawed but affable Norman whose wife, Marie, served as its chatelaine.

Ranulf had told her he did not visit Beauworth often, even though it was but an hour from Winchester; nonetheless, the household always seemed to be expecting him. The same was true when Ranulf and Aldyth trotted into the bailey today. The hall was immaculate. Lady Marie had them sitting down to a tasty, well-cooked dinner within an hour of their arrival.

"You're very fortunate in both your castellan and his able wife," Aldyth remarked quietly, gazing around the hall as they devoured a savory pork pie.

"Marie swears she only cooks like this when her knee begins to ache, which is what tells her I'm coming," Ranulf told her loudly enough that Marie, who was hovering nearby, beamed beatifically at him. "I've never been able to catch her napping, but I suspect 'tis Sir René that keeps her on her toes."

"Ha! 'Tis quite the other way 'round, I do assure you, my lord," Marie asserted, jabbing her spouse jocularly with her elbow. "This great lazy hound would lie about the hall dicing all day if I allowed it."

"Nay, 'tis not so, wife," Sir René protested with mock outrage. "'Tis merely that I put up the whip I keep for you when my lord honors us with a visit." But it was clear from the affection mirrored in both faces that his words were only a jest.

While Aldyth had been bathing in the lord's chamber above the hall before dinner, Ranulf had explained to Sir René and his wife about Aldyth, especially as to why his beloved had arrived dressed as a boy, though she would be able to wear the proper clothes of a lady while she was at Beauworth.

"You think the king even has spies in the ports?" Sir René asked him.

"I think it's possible," Ranulf told him soberly. "Especially now that he suspects some of his nobles to be plotting to aid Duke Robert."

"Yes, we've heard the rumors," the castellan said with a sober nod. "'Tis natural we would, so close to Winchester as we are."

"Ah, the poor brave dear!" Marie said, focusing on Aldyth. "I've seen that she has but the one gown with her, my lord, but rest assured, there's good woolen cloth of my own spinning just waiting in the storeroom, and we'll soon remedy her lack."

"Thank you, Lady Marie. I knew I could depend on you. It may be a while before 'tis safe to take my lady home," Ranulf said.

But later, as they lay in each other's arms in the great bed in the lord's chamber, satisfied from their lovemaking, Ranulf and Aldyth almost quarreled.

"I do not understand why I cannot go to court with you—if I dressed as Edward, of course. Why must you leave me here while you go off to Winchester and London? I want to be with you, not here by myself."

"You won't be by yourself here with Lady Marie to look after you," Ranulf pointed out, maddening her with his patient tone. "'Tis not safe for you to come to court with me."

"It was safe before," Aldyth stubbornly insisted.

"For the short time you were there," he retorted. "Besides, at that time I thought you disliked me, so I could keep my hands off you, if not always my eyes. 'Twould not be so anymore, sweetheart. My face would give away the game in a trice."

He stroked his hands over her as if unable to control himself and laughed like a madman, which had Aldyth giggling for a moment.

"Please, love, just be patient awhile longer. I need to see how matters lie at court and to talk to your brother Warin. I sent him word as to when I'd be back, so he'll be waiting. I wonder if he's heard aught from Godric regarding you. Mayhap he'll even have news of Turold."

She considered his words. "And you'll try to send word to my father that I'm back in England and well?" She knew Ranulf had written her father earlier that she was with him, and Sir Nyle had written back that he was relieved she was safe with Lord Ranulf.

"If I can do it secretly. I don't want Godric getting wind of it unless perchance he's had a change of heart about Normans, at least the Norman who loves his sister."

Aldyth had to be content with that. She knew his reasons were sound, and she hated sounding like a petulant child, but she also hated the thought of any separation from him. They'd already lost so much time. But at least while she waited for him at Beauworth, she need not don a boy's clothes again or cut the hair that was finally beginning to grow, if only a little.

"I don't like being away from you, either, sweetheart," Ranulf told her. "I am going to begin, little by little, to edge out of the king's inner circle."

"Can you do that?"

"I think so, though 'twill have to be slow. I'll say my lord father is getting along in years and needs me more at Kingsclere. And I'll plead a need to pay more attention to Beauworth. I'll say Sir René is lax in his care of the keep if I'm not there often—an outrageous lie if there ever was one. Sir René needs supervision less than any castellan in the kingdom, except perhaps your good father. 'Twill give me

an excuse to get away every few days to come to you here.
'Tis but an hour's ride when we are in Winchester, though
'tis two days from London."

She must have still looked sad, for he told her he would
be unable to stay away and that his heart would be here.

Aldyth sighed and closed her eyes. If she must be parted
temporarily from her beloved, it might be very enjoyable to
spend her days stitching new gowns with Lady Marie and
learning how to make her delicious pork pies.

Desiderata was finding the shores of England strangely
inhospitable. She had set out from Dover on a flashy white
palfrey she bought with the sale of her sapphire necklace,
escorted by two burly Englishmen she hired to protect her
from brigands. Her destination was the royal court. She
couldn't wait to talk to King William Rufus and tell him
where Lord Ranulf's allegiance really lay. How she would
laugh when that damned arrogant lord had paid the price of
his treason. She would laugh right in his grieving leman's
face.

Her English escort spoke only halting French. She treated
the two men with a mixture of arrogance and flirtatious-
ness, and though she had not even asked their names, she
was contemplating rewarding them at the end of the journey by bedding both of them. They had such magnificent
physiques, after all, and so different, with their long blond
hair and shaggy mustaches, from Norman men.

Thirty miles outside of Dover, however, the two men exchanged a look, and the next thing Desiderata knew, she was
being dragged from her palfrey into a wooded area.

Ignoring her screeching, which soon changed from indignant to terrified in tone, they threw her to the ground and
then took what she had been planning to offer them at the

end of the journey. Not satisfied with her body, they also took both her palfrey and the remainder of her coins.

"This be what we think o' Norman whores," they said as they left her there.

She was found collapsed by the side of the road the next morning by a pair of traveling clerics and taken to a nearby convent. By nightfall she had a high fever and a congestion of the lungs and was talking out of her head. The nuns spent the next two months nursing the redheaded Norman woman back to health.

"It's come, sweetheart," Ranulf announced one day in late February, waving a rolled-up parchment in the air as he cantered inside the palisade. He was accompanied, as always when he visited, by her brother Warin, who was grinning as if he might burst.

"What has?" Aldyth inquired. The missive looked important, with its several wax seals dangling from scarlet ribbons.

From Ranulf's supremely pleased expression, she knew it wasn't bad news. He jumped off his horse and strode rapidly toward where she stood waiting at the entrance of the hall. Warin capered at his side.

"Come inside," she urged them, seeing the frost forming from their breath. "Whatever it is, 'twill be better by the fire."

"Sweetheart, I've ridden all the way from London, and I tell you this is wonderful news where we are!" He picked her up and began to whirl her about, as if Lady Marie and half the men-at-arms were not watching. "'Tis your freedom!"

"My freedom? Put me down!" she commanded him. "I cannot think when I'm dizzy!" But she returned his grin, caught up in his infectious excitement.

"Yes, your freedom. Henry's messenger managed to find me covertly in London. It's the official notification that your betrothal contract to Turold of Swanlea is nullified. You're free, sweetheart."

She took a deep breath and sagged against Ranulf in relief. It hardly seemed possible. Free! She was actually free of the shadow that had hovered over her for so long, robbing her of a portion of the joy she knew with Ranulf.

He went down on one knee. "Will you marry me, Aldyth? As soon as it can be arranged?"

"Hurrah!" shouted Warin. "Say yes, Aldyth!"

Aldyth made a motion to shush her little brother's exuberant yelling. She couldn't think. "But can you really marry me? What of the king? What would he say?"

"Yes, I can, but as for Rufus, I'm not sure. He's in a very uncertain temper these days, what with so many rumors of plots coming to his ears. He's not certain who to trust. But I would have you mine in all honor, Aldyth, before God and all men."

"Warin, go to the kitchen and see if Cook does not have some tarts for you."

"Aw, Aldyth . . ." Warin muttered, but he strode obediently out.

"Oh, Ranulf, I would wed you now, this minute," she said as soon as they were alone, "but I would not have you gain the king's wrath for it. Should we not wait until Prince Henry has the throne? In truth I feel your wife already—what difference would standing before the priest make?"

He held her close, smoothing her hair with his strong hands.

"And you are my wife," he told her, lifting her chin up so that she looked into the deep brown pools of his eyes. "But what if there was a child, sweetheart? What if there is a babe even now growing beneath your heart? I would not have him—or her—baseborn, Aldyth.''

She knew he was right. As yet she had not missed her fluxes, but they had only been intimate for a matter of weeks.

Aldyth took a deep breath. ''All right, we will marry, but secretly, here at Beauworth,'' she said. ''The priest here would be willing, would he not? Do you think 'twould be possible to have our parents here?''

''Yes, on both counts—Beauworth's priest will marry us and I'm sure we could get your father and my parents here. Oh, and Warin, too, of course. But as to Godric...I'm afraid my lord father reports he is not much changed in his dislike of all Normans. He does what my lord father bids him, but sullenly. I just don't believe we can trust him, sweetheart. I think it best that my father make some excuse for not bringing him when they come to visit so that he will not learn of our marriage until later.''

She sighed. ''I'm sure you're right, though it saddens me. Will Godric ever see the light, I wonder? If only he could see that you, at least, are everything good and noble and kind—''

He kissed her, shutting off her flow of praise. ''Ah, but you're prejudiced, my love. Very well, we shall marry just as soon as we can arrange to have our parents and Warin here as witnesses.''

Chapter Twenty-Two

By the next day, however, they knew they would not be able to send invitations to a wedding to Kingsclere and Sherborne for the time being. A messenger from the king arrived from London on a lathered horse at noon, bearing ill tidings for the lovers.

The king was summoning Ranulf and several other of his trusted nobles to join his household troops in reconnoitering southeast England, which seemed to be the hub of the rebellious nobles. Lord Ranulf was commanded to leave immediately.

They made preemptive strikes against rebel garrisons at Hastings, Dover and other key southeast towns, but word of the king's coming had leaked out and the rebels had gone to ground. The king's force captured none of the important rebels, such as Bishop Odo, the king's uncle, or Eustace, the Count of Boulogne, or the Earl of Montgomery's three sons. Robert had apparently remained safely in Rouen. Of Henry there was no word.

Ranulf wrote Prince Henry about what had been happening and inquired if his liege had any instructions for him. He sent the message in a secret pocket of his courier's saddle. Before going on to the Cotentin, however, the courier was instructed to deliver another secret letter to Aldyth, while a more innocuous missive was given openly to Sir René, in case any should question his errand.

Frustrated and furious, the king was not at all inclined to grant anyone leave, Ranulf wrote Aldyth. Rufus had ordered every noble present for the annual Easter crown-wearing to be held in London and drew his conclusions when he saw who was absent. Ranulf was sorry— "More than you can imagine, my darling, for my heart and body ache for yours," he wrote—but it would be impossible for him to come to her. Also at Easter, the king had begun summoning the levies owed him by his nobles, which meant Ranulf would have to begin drilling the men owed in knight service by his father as Earl of Kingsclere. He found it interesting, he added, that the king was busy recruiting as many loyal English to help his cause as possible.

Aldyth's eyes blurred with tears as she reread the middle part, where he admitted he longed for her as much as she did for him but could not come to her. She should never have let him leave without her, she thought. It had already been six weeks since they had been together, and there was no sign of when their separation would end, let alone when they could be married.

Clutching the parchment his hands had touched to her breast, Aldyth lay in their curtain-hung bed, lonely and miserable.

If only he *had* given her his babe to nurture within her body, she told herself, then she could have rested content at Beauworth until he could return to her. She would have spent her time serenely making tiny clothes for their child. But she had reliable evidence that she was not with child, and so she was restless and cross in his absence, longing for him with a hunger that she had not known was possible. Alone in her chamber, staring into the flickering flame of the hour candle, she began to make plans.

* * *

"I tell you, Turold, if I had not been there and heard it with my own ears, I would not have believed it, either!" Godric said as the two relaxed before the fire after a supper made by Turold's mother, Gundreda.

Godric had come to visit his friend at Swanlea, excited by the news he brought.

"But why should Rufus be asking for *our* help?" Turold asked, his tone skeptical. "He's never needed the English before, except as a captive population to gouge for taxes."

"He's never been faced with open rebellion before, and from some of the oldest families of Normandy. These rebels took sizable levies when they deserted to Duke Robert's cause. But even my lord of Kingsclere was surprised when the king offered the English tax relief and land in return to answering the call to arms. He's also promised to restore our forests and hunting rights and some of the laws abolished by the Conqueror. He's even hinted there'd be knighthoods for those who fight well." Godric shook his friend's shoulder to emphasize his point. "Think of the booty we could pick up along the way. Come with me, Turold. We'd be fools not to take advantage of the offer."

"You would fight for a Norman?" Turold asked, amazed at what he was hearing. "And what of Lord Étienne? You're squire to him, so are you not his to command, to send as part of his levy?"

"He says I may join as one of the king's Englishmen if I would be happier that way, and I mean to take advantage of his offer," Godric said.

Turold grunted, impressed. "'Tis right fair of him. And if I went . . . Fancy that, me a knight."

"I don't want ye t'go, Turold," came a sulky voice from the shadows near the rough-hewn table, but it was not his dour, ever present mother who spoke.

Maud came out of the shadows, her pregnancy beginning to strain the waistline of her worn, grease-spotted kirtle.

Turold raised a clenched fist and waved it at her. "What have ye to say about it, slattern? No woman tells me what to do," he growled.

"Not even the mother of yer babe? Don't ye want to see yer son born, Turold, my sweetling?"

It was all very well to have Maud so available when he felt like slaking his lust, but she annoyed him the rest of the time with her cloying affection and her incessant demands. Before Christmas, when he had returned from his fruitless search for the runaway Aldyth, she had informed him that she was pregnant. She demanded that he marry her, but when he explained he could not because he was still legally betrothed, she nagged until he agreed to wed her at least in the old Saxon way of handfasting.

He glared at her across the main room of the manor farmhouse. "There's plenty o' time before the brat will come, woman, and anyway, ye don't need me here for that," he retorted.

"Ye were pleased enow to be there for his beginnin'," she muttered, but Turold had turned back to Godric and they were again pondering the advantages of answering the Norman call to arms.

"But we'll have to see that the king lives up to his promises immediately after we've beaten his rebels for him," Turold told Godric. "You know how it is with the Normans. They have a short memory when it comes to gratitude."

"Aye. If that happens, then the English will already be gathered together in force, and we'll be near the coast. All we need to is drive the damned king and his minions into the sea."

Turold and Godric clasped hands, no longer just friends but comrades-at-arms.

Turold had not forgotten Maud, though he had pretended to while Godric remained. He'd be damned if he was going to let a mere wench get away with shaming him in front of another man or even his old mother. Later that night, when Gundreda was snoring on her pallet by the fire, he took the slovenly Maud by the hand and led her outside.

She had thought he meant them to go for a walk as a prelude to coupling in the woods somewhere, for the early spring night had been unusually mild. Once outside in the yard, however, he pushed her down on the midden heap and began to thrash her, not satisfied until she lay bruised and weeping on top of the sweepings from the barn.

Maud began bleeding an hour later and brought forth a tiny, dead babe before dawn.

She cried hysterically all morning, ignored by Turold, who was preparing to depart, and Gundreda, who was helping her son pack. Finally, at eventide, Maud arose, bathed the blood from her legs and consigned the dead infant to a shallow grave.

Then she smiled a secret smile, remembering the clerk who had come more than a fortnight ago bearing an important-looking message with official seals. It was a petty revenge, but now she was glad she hadn't told Turold about it. Illiterate, and jealous of anything that threatened her imagined ownership of Turold, Maud had feared the missive contained an offer from that cursed Aldyth of Sherborne to reconcile her differences with Turold.

Maud had burned the letter, unaware that it contained the news of the annulment of Turold's betrothal to her rival.

Two weeks after Easter, the king had assembled his royal expeditionary force and was hot to set out against Bishop

Odo, Robert's chief supporter in England and their mutual uncle. Odo had been raiding his own county of Kent, then returning to his headquarters in Rochester with the booty.

Though Rufus wanted to smash Rochester first, he had a cool head for strategy and told his nobles he felt he must guard his rear against attack. Accordingly, he would first take the main part of the army south against Gilbert FitzRichard at Tonbridge.

"But you, Robert FitzHaimo, and you, Ranulf—I would have you take a force against Rochester and see if you can bottle them up inside the castle against our coming. We hope to join you right speedily."

Ranulf and the other man bowed, then watched as the king mounted his horse and set his main army southward.

Ranulf sighed.

"I know you long to be in the thick of it, don't you, my lord?" asked Urse, sitting a horse nearby.

It was good to have his squire once again by his side. The giant Breton had joined him at the gathering of the levies in London.

Since their parting in Normandy, he had done what Ranulf had bidden him by marrying Lady Vivienne and setting up their household in a small rented house in London. He also reported proudly that he and his bride were already expecting their first child together, and that Aldyth's brother Warin was very disgruntled about having been left behind once again. Ranulf had been adamant about keeping the boy safe from the dangers of war. How would he be able to face Aldyth if aught befell her little brother? There would be other conflicts, when Warin was older.

"Yes," Ranulf admitted to Urse. "A part of me wants to go with Rufus. I doubt if our smaller force will be able to do much more than discourage the bishop's men from leaving their castle stronghold.''

But there were advantages to being separated from the king, Ranulf thought. If Henry chose this advantageous time to aid one of the brothers... But which one would he choose? If the answer was Duke Robert, Ranulf knew it was better for him to be away from the king, so he could join his liege lord more easily. He himself could not favor the duke, but Robert could be more easily overthrown afterward than Rufus.

Aloud he said, ''But I must confess, Urse, I'm also relieved to see that Godric and Turold remained with the main army.'' He had been startled to see that they were among the English recruits. Of all the unlikely men! ''There will be a time to try to make peace with Aldyth's brother Godric— provided he is willing—just as I plan to find time to thrash Turold within an inch of his life, but the middle of a war is not ideal for either endeavor,'' he finished dryly.

''I'll wager you pray that Turold won't become a casualty of the war before you lesson him,'' Urse said with a wink of his good eye.

Ranulf turned to his squire with a grim smile. ''You know, Urse, every time I think of what that knave tried to do to Aldyth, I imagine how satisfying it would be to kill him. 'Tis probably a good thing I shall have to wait.''

''I know what you mean, my lord. I would feel the same if any had offered harm to my lady.''

For a time, at least, Ranulf was glad he would not have to feel their eyes glinting daggers at him every time he passed. Neither man, it was clear, had forgotten that Aldyth had loved Ranulf, and neither man was totally satisfied that Ranulf was ignorant of her location.

He chuckled, and at Urse's inquiring look, he explained. ''I just keep thinking how enraged both Englishmen would be if they knew Aldyth waits for me, safe and sound at Beauworth.''

Urse started to laugh, then stared and pointed. "Are you sure, my lord?"

"What do you mean, am I sure? Of course I am. I..."

At that very moment, as if to mock his words, a small figure on a piebald cob came cantering across the field, heading straight for the army assembling to march southeast toward Rochester.

"It cannot be," he breathed. "I left her with Sir René and Lady Marie, with strict instructions to await me there." He had promised to send word of himself and of how the war was progressing so that she would know when to expect him home for their wedding. She was to write back, they had agreed, and to spend her time sewing the most beautiful of gowns to wear at their wedding. One way or the other, he intended to distinguish himself, so that whether Rufus remained on the throne or Henry had gained the crown, he would be free to marry Aldyth openly and with all honor.

They had been keeping their voices down so that FitzHaimo would not hear the conversation. "My lord," responded Urse softly, beginning to grin again, "when does she ever obey you when she does not want to?"

The rider *was* Aldyth, once again dressed as a page, grinning from ear to ear as she slowed the cob to a trot.

Thinking fast, Ranulf spoke to FitzHaimo. "I see my page has reached us," he said with a casualness he did not feel. "'Tis well. I had sent him home to Kingsclere with a letter for my father. It looks as if he's brought a reply."

Under his breath, he hissed to Urse, "I swear by the rood, 'Edward' will be back on the road for Beauworth, escorted by you and at least another soldier, within the hour." His jaw tightened. He was not about to let her expose herself to the danger of being with an army on the march.

"Yes, my lord," Urse said, but not as if he believed Ranulf.

Ranulf went to intercept her, conscious of FitzHaimo and Urse watching them.

"What are you doing here?" he demanded, unaware that his eyes were drinking in the sight of her the way a man trapped in the desert might stare at a clear blue pool. "God's toenails, Aldyth, you've cut your hair again!"

"'Twill grow again, when I let it," she said, not faltering in the face of his stern displeasure. "Admit it, you rejoice to see me," she teased, "in spite of the fact that that little muscle is jumping in your temple just as it always does when you're angry."

"I'm so pleased that I ought to blister your backside, my lady, and I would, too, if there were any place private enough to do it. You're going back to Beauworth, Aldyth."

"I am not. If you try to send me, I'll just return. Which is better, to keep me safe with you now or risk having me back on the roads?"

"How safe do you think you would be, living in a camp with rough men, with the possibility of attack by the rebels? And if that were not enough, Aldyth, you just missed running into Godric and Turold by an hour. There would have been the devil to pay if I'd had to fight them both for you."

"Godric was here? And T-Turold?" When she said the name of her former betrothed, she paled a little.

"Yes, they're with the king's English contingent, marching south to Tonbridge, but if all goes well for Rufus, eventually we shall all be one grand army together. What of your plan then, Aldyth? Can't you see why you must return to Beauworth and stay there?"

She had been waving hello to Urse but turned now back to Ranulf. "I won't leave you now that I'm here," she insisted, an almost mulish expression taking over her heart-shaped face. "You made Warin stay with Lady Vivienne, and I'm glad of that," she added quickly, "but now you have no one to cook your supper and tend to your clothes."

He snorted. "My squire can certainly do that," he said, nodding in Urse's direction.

She smiled maddeningly. "Not like *I* can."

He groaned inside. He could picture all too many things she could do for him that Urse could not!

"And you'd be without him near a fortnight if you send him to escort me back, as I can guess you'll wish to do. I will be your servant, and no one will guess—but I am *not* going tamely back to Beauworth like a witless fool."

"You were a witless fool to disobey me and come here," he growled, but he knew she had again defeated him. He had not the time to stay here by the roadside, arguing with her, and he believed she would do exactly what she said and keep attempting to return to him. Another time, her luck could run out and she might meet with some brigand who would not care if he attacked a wench or a lad. And the image of having her there beside him, even if it meant weeks of frustration because they could not be alone to make love, tantalized him.

"I suppose you'll promise to obey me perfectly after this is over and we are man and wife," he grumbled.

"Of course, my lord," she said meekly. But her eyes danced with joy.

Chapter Twenty-Three

"Good even, soldiers. May I sit down and share your fire? 'Tis a brisk night for late May, don't you think?" Desiderata asked the two men. They had been staring at the coneys turning on a spit as if the roasting meat contained all the answers to life. And so it did, mused Desiderata wryly to herself. It was very difficult to think much further than an empty stomach. She smiled winningly, hoping they would invite her to share their meal; if luck were really with her, they would have a few pennies to spend and would want what Desiderata was so talented at providing.

"Why, certainly," replied the blond one, while the brown-haired one just stared. "Come and share our humble supper, lovely one. 'Tis not often we get a visit from a fine Norman lady, is it?"

"Nay, it is not," said the other one, not exactly frowning, but not smiling, either. Desiderata was content. It was not necessary that both men lust after her—one was enough to get her a seat near the fire and a bit of roast meat to keep her going. If both men had found her equally irresistible, in fact, it might have led to one of the violent quarrels between men that sometimes got in the way of Desiderata's profession.

"Oh, you're *English*," she remarked, as if she were just discovering that fact and hadn't known it by their long, shaggy locks and bushy mustaches and the bands of engraved silver they wore on their upper arms. She made her voice breathy, knowing men found it enticing.

"Aye. I hope that does not disqualify us from your...uh, company?" the blond one said, patting the place next to him with a grin.

"Non, pas du tout. Not at all," she translated. "I have learned to speak the English very well since I have come to your land, and I find Englishmen very—how do you say it?—fair and generous and—dare I say it?—virile, my lords."

She could see her flattery was working. The blond Englishman was practically melting at her feet—except for his swelling cock, which she could see outlined against the fabric of his rough tunic.

"Best you know that I'm no lord, my lovely, just plain Turold of Swanlea, an English freeman. Now, Godric there—" he pointed to his comrade "—he's a squire and may be knighted someday, if you prefer that sort of man."

She found his honesty rather touching, but she would not be equally honest about herself. She would not tell him about the lung fever that had followed the robbery and rape by two other Englishmen, requiring an eight-week convalescence at a convent. Then, not only had she failed to gain an audience with King William Rufus so that she could denounce one of his lords as a traitor, but her efforts to ply her trade among the lords and knights in the king's train had met with disinterest at best. There were already plenty of harlots following the army, and the addition of a pretty redhaired Norman whore was not an occasion of great note.

"My name is Desiderata, sweet Turold, and *non,* I care naught about titles and such," she lied, stroking Turold's muscular arm. "I only care that a man is a man. And Turold of Swanlea, you look very much a man to me," she purred, marveling at how easy this was. Turold was practically drooling. But perhaps she had overplayed it. She was hungry, yet the heated gleam in his blue eyes made her wonder if he would manage to wait until after they supped to drag her off into the undergrowth.

"Mmm, does that not smell good?" she cooed, pointing to the meat the squire was turning on the spit. "I vow I would do almost anything for a bite of coney, dear Turold."

"Anything, Desiderata?"

"Anything, *after* we sup, Turold," she said, thinking she had better speak plainly.

"Very well, you shall have a bite of supper first, sweeting, and then...then I'll have a bite o' you, my Norman vixen." He chuckled, hugely pleased at his jest.

Later, as Desiderata lay against the stocky Englishman's chest under a yew tree, she had to admit that sex with Turold of Swanlea had been surprisingly pleasant. Not only had he given her a silver penny *before* taking her, thus preventing her having to nag for it later, the sturdy Englishman's braies had concealed the fact that he was built like a bull. She'd been thrilled to find he had the endurance of one, too, bringing her to a whimpering climax before he allowed himself to spill his seed within her. Most men didn't care whether the whore they'd bought experienced any pleasure or not.

Now he was drifting off into sleep, but she wanted to attach herself more firmly to him, and so she began to ask him about himself.

"Turold, you're a very handsome man, but your eyes hold great sadness," she said, running a fingernail across his muscular chest so that he roused enough to hear her. It was a wonderful thing to say to a man, a sentence that never failed to set them talking about their favorite subject—themselves. What man had not experienced some disappointment, and what man could fail to appreciate a woman who had noted their *tristesse*?

"That's true, Desi, and you're right clever to sense it, for I keep my feelings well hidden, as a man should," he said, cuddling her closer with one powerful arm while his fingers strayed onto her breast.

"That you do, but I could just feel life had not treated you justly," she purred, arching up against him like a cat confident that she will be petted.

"Aye, well, life has been fair enough, but there's a woman who cheated me," he told her, "of what was mine."

"And who was this evil woman?" Desiderata asked, thinking it was always a woman. "I hate her before you even tell me her name."

"She was my betrothed. We were to marry the next day, but she ran away, leaving me hurt and, worse yet, unable to wed another, for the contract still existed."

"This woman—you gave her no cause for her actions?" she asked, leaning on one elbow to look him in the eye. If Turold was a stingy man or a brutal one, she wanted to find out now, before she wasted any more time on him.

Turold looked abashed. "Perhaps I was a little…bold in my wooing, shall we say? But she ran from me without even giving me a chance to apologize."

Desiderata giggled. "Why, the silly, frightened virgin! Was she not brave enough to take the attentions of a real man? What a foolish wench, yes, and cruel, too, not to appreciate what a wonderful man you are," she said, right on cue.

"Aye, and what's worse, she left me for a devil of a Norman," he growled.

"You think Normans are devils?" she said, playing with him a little.

"I? Uh . . . nay, Desiderata. Nay, I don't feel that way about all Normans, of course," he said, so apologetically she almost giggled. "Have I not just shown you I worship you, my toothsome sweeting? 'Tis just that he stole my bride from me, the damned nithing!"

Desiderata had already learned that being called "nithing" was the worst of English vilifications. "But did you not accuse him, my mighty Turold, and fight him for your woman?"

"He was a lord and the son of an earl, and I could not prove that he had her concealed," Turold said grudgingly. "But I know he did. And then he was called to Normandy on a mission for the king, and I, of course, could not follow him there. I had a farm to care for, and an old mother, but I've kept an eye peeled for the bitch, lest she still be in England, hiding about her father's keep or somewhere . . ." His voice trailed off.

Desiderata's mind was racing. Could it be—

"What was the name of this Norman lord, darling? Tell me, and I will spit in his eye if we ever meet."

"Lord Ranulf of Kingsclere," he told her, and she gasped. "What is it, Desi? You sound as if you have already met the scoundrel, God rot him."

She laughed shortly. "I have met him, right enough. And you were perfectly right to suspect him, my clever Turold. Your runaway bride was indeed with him, the little slut."

"Aldyth? Aldyth was with him?" he said, staring up at her. "Where? How do you know?"

"I did not hear him call her by any name—any *woman's* name," she admitted, her mouth twisting at the bitter memory of her humiliating discovery in Lord Ranulf's bedchamber. "'Twas at Prince Henry's castle in the

Cotentin, where I used to live," she told him. "She was
posing as his page, and he called her 'Edward.' I thought it
a little odd for a handsome lord like him to be so kind and
considerate of a mere boy, even a delicate-faced one such as
this one. I even thought him—how do you say it—perverse? But no. All the time he was enjoying her favors, while
making us think she was merely his page."

"So Ranulf made you angry, too," Turold observed.

Had her jealousy been showing so obviously? She would
have to be more careful. Turold would not want to know
how Desiderata had craved the body of the darkly handsome Lord Ranulf.

"Nay, he was nothing to me, but I mislike deceit, and I
hate a traitor even more," she said righteously.

"A traitor? What do you mean, woman?" Turold's eyes
narrowed.

"Why, what do you think he was doing at Prince Henry's
castle? He was supposed to be visiting Duke Robert on a
spying mission for the king, and I suppose he might claim
he was doing the same thing by visiting Henry. But I was
awake when they thought I was asleep, and I heard Lord
Ranulf and the prince talking. Ranulf is the prince's man,
no matter how often he swears fealty to William Rufus. He
would help Henry gain England's crown at any cost."

Turold whistled. "So Ranulf of Kingsclere is not the languid, mincing peacock he affected to be, but a man playing
a role," he mused, "so that he could be in the king's circle
without suspicion. Do you know how important it is, what
you have just told me, Desiderata?"

She nodded. "But thus far I have not been able to gain the
king's ear to denounce Lord Ranulf. But neither have I seen
the *cochon* here, among the king's army," she said. "Where
is he?"

"He was ordered to take a contingent with FitzHaimo and surround Rochester until the main army can come against the rebels there. But now that we have taken Tonbridge and have captured the bishop here at Pevensey, it will not be long until we join the contingent at Rochester. And then... Ha! I cannot wait to see Lord Ranulf's face when we call him traitor to the king!"

Desiderata smiled back at him in the gathering darkness, imagining the man who had scorned her favors being executed. Would Rufus have him merely beheaded or tortured first, before he ended his miserable life?

Then she had a sudden thought. The king would listen more readily to Turold telling the tale, and then he would doubtless reward him for his loyalty. If she made her relationship with the Englishman permanent, she could live in comfort forever. But once Ranulf had paid the price of his treason and that damned Aldyth was available, the prize might slip from Desiderata's grasp.

"Turold...do you still want this Aldyth?" she asked, allowing an anxious note to creep into her voice.

"Nay, I'll not take the Norman scoundrel's leavings to wife," he growled. "But ye wouldn't grudge me the chance to make the bitch pay for what she did to me, would you, sweeting?" He caressed her and kissed her persuasively.

"*Non,*" she said, "I wouldn't mind, Turold. Promise me you'll hurt her very badly."

Chapter Twenty-Four

Godric froze as he heard Turold's promise of vengeance
against Aldyth. He had been sent to find his friend, for their
captain had summoned them to a meeting to discuss the
promised surrender of the Pevensey garrison on the morrow. Figuring Turold had been gone with the camp follower long enough to have sampled her wares thoroughly,
he had nevertheless intended to make plenty of noise as he
approached the trysting place out of basic courtesy. It might
have embarrassed the Norman woman to be caught with her
skirts up—at least by a man who hadn't crossed her palm
with a coin first.

But he had somehow managed to approach unheard, and
it was a good thing he had.

The lying knave! After Aldyth's disappearance and his
father's warning, Godric had questioned Turold closely as
to anything he might have done to make Aldyth unhappy.
Turold had always protested his innocence, saying only that
he suspected Aldyth had gone because she could not get over
her lust for her evil Norman lover. He had portrayed such a
convincing picture of the wronged suitor that Godric had
been willing to help him try to find Aldyth, even though it
meant challenging Lord Ranulf, his liege lord's son and heir.
Now, however, he had overheard Turold's admission that he

had done some "bold wooing," and he guessed the phrase to be Turold's euphemism for attempted rape.

How dared Turold threaten his sister with brutal retaliation for fleeing him? Godric clenched his hands into fists as he stood there, fighting the urge to leap into the clearing and bury his knife up to the hilt in the nithing's chest.

How wrong he had been, Godric realized, with a sickening sense of how he had failed to help his sister. *Aldyth knew she could not depend on you to come to her aid, you blind fool, and so she had done the only thing she could think of—she had run.*

And she had run to the very man Godric had wanted to spare her from, that licentious peacock, Lord Ranulf. If the Norman whore's words were true, Aldyth was still with Ranulf of Kingsclere. Had he already broken her heart? Would he abandon her somewhere, pregnant and miserable?

He could not, of course, do as he wished and attack Turold while his guard was down. Even if Godric's own moral code had allowed it, the king had made it very clear that fighting among the soldiers would not be tolerated. A minor offense would result in flogging for both parties, and murder would result in the ultimate penalty.

But he would have to make it clear that he would not be tolerant of any aggression against his sister. It was unfortunate, for he had enjoyed Turold's companionship, but he could no longer view the stocky farmer as a friend.

"Turold, what would you do if you were to find Aldyth, say, today?" Godric asked casually, several days later. It had been difficult to find an occasion to talk privately to Turold, for after that first meeting with Desiderata, he seemed firmly in thrall with the red-haired camp follower. She was at his side whenever Turold had no official duties, sharing their campfire and meager rations. Turold no longer shared the tent that he and Godric had rigged to shelter them from the weather's vagaries, apparently preferring to sleep elsewhere with his leman. But now, as they waited in front of the fortress at Pevensey, where the garrison was about to surrender to the king, Godric waited for Turold's answer.

Godric saw the flash of excitement in Turold's blue eyes. "Why do you ask? Have you seen her? Do you know where she is?"

"Nay...nay. I was just thinking about her, you know, and wondering," Godric claimed.

The face Turold turned to him now was blandly wistful. "What would I do? Why, Godric, I would welcome her with open arms, of course—if she would let me. Mayhap she would have learned the error of her ways by now. I would accept her with a humbly grateful heart and cherish her always as my wife."

Liar, thought Godric. As much as he despised him now, he was going to have to stick closer than a wet *sherte* to Turold so that he would be present if Turold ever found Lord Ranulf and Aldyth together.

But surely if his sister was still Lord Ranulf's mistress, he would not have brought her on the march. He would have secreted her somewhere safe, perhaps in that keep of his near Winchester—Beau something, wasn't it?

But would Turold wait to find them together, or was he bold enough to attack Ranulf when the two armies joined again? If so, should he, Godric, intervene?

Ranulf of Kingsclere was a Norman and therefore automatically an enemy of an English patriot. Moreover, he intended Aldyth only dishonor, was that not the truth?

Was it the truth? Godric pushed the helm with its jutting nasal off his forehead and rubbed his brow.

He had thought before that he had possessed the final truth—that the Normans were bad and he knew what was good for his sister—and look what had happened as a result. Could he have misjudged Lord Ranulf, just as he had been wrong about Turold of Swanlea?

Perhaps all Normans were not monsters. The earl, Ranulf's father, had always been fair to him, Godric realized now—perhaps more than fair in forgiving him for his youthful hotheadedness. And Godric had met good Normans on this campaign. Certainly all Englishmen were not all angels of light, either, as Turold's duplicity proved. When he met Ranulf of Kingsclere again, he would judge him through new eyes.

He would find out if Ranulf's intentions toward Aldyth were honorable and if Aldyth was happy with him. If she was, and if Ranulf dealt honorably with his sister, then Godric would give them his blessing.

"Thank you, Father, we're in your debt," Ranulf said as he and Aldyth rose from where they had knelt to receive the priest's blessing after he had wed them on the porch of Strood's small parish church. He handed the English cleric a purse.

"Thank *you*, my son," Father Lefwin said, acknowledging the donation. "I wish you all happiness and beautiful babes to bless your union."

Aldyth blushed. Could the priest possibly suspect that she was already with child? But no, the eyes in the beaming, cherubic face of the cleric seemed to hold nothing but genuine goodwill toward her and her Norman husband. Aldyth was also glad she had brought at least one gown and veil from Beauworth—even this kindly priest would have been shocked to know that under the concealing *couvre-chef* her hair was short as a boy's!

They bid the priest goodbye and strolled down the street to the small house Ranulf had rented. They had wanted to have a night together as husband and wife before rejoining FitzHaimo and the army division at nearby Rochester.

Her husband. Ranulf was now her husband in legal fact, though she had felt wedded to him ever since the Cotentin. But he had not been willing to wait any longer once she had shyly confessed that she had missed her fluxes—she who was normally as regular as the waxing and waning moon—and thought she might be carrying his child.

They would marry now, Ranulf had insisted. He was certain she was *enceinte* even if she was not, for her breasts had recently seemed fuller and more sensitive than before. Yes, they would marry without delay, even though it meant there would be no witnesses but the priest's housekeeper. It was now summer and this war against the rebellious Norman nobles showed no signs of being over soon, so he and Aldyth could not wait for a proper wedding at Beauworth, with family present.

He loved her, Ranulf told her, and he would not have his son or daughter born outside of wedlock or just barely inside it. They would just have to have another ceremony once they gained official permission from the king—if Rufus was even still on the throne at the end of this war.

But they had promised themselves they would not think of wars and plots on this all-too-brief wedding night, Aldyth reminded herself as they reached the rented house, their temporary sanctuary from the world.

As soon as they were inside, Ranulf took her into his arms. "Ah, sweetheart, you make a lovely bride," he told her after a kiss that had left her toes tingling and her breath hard to come by. His eyes echoed his admiration. "You are even lovelier, I believe, since you have been carrying my babe."

"Ah, Ranulf, you silver-tongued charmer, you've only known about him—or her—for a few days." But it was true that she had never felt better in her life. The babe had not, as yet, caused her to feel ill in the mornings, and perhaps she was one of the fortunate few who would not suffer any ill effects of being pregnant other than an increasing belly.

"Do you think Father Lefwin suspected, Ranulf? I mean, about the child?"

He kissed her forehead and chuckled. "No, sweetheart. After all, I can still span your waist with my hands!" He made a jest of struggling to do so, groaning so realistically that she giggled. "But I think that FitzHaimo may have guessed that 'Edward' should more properly be called 'Edwina,'" Ranulf added with a grin.

"Why?"

"I don't know. It might be my imagination, but I fancy he's been looking at me strangely of late. When I asked if he minded my being absent for a day, he smiled so oddly as he told me to go ahead, for even Rufus could not get the army to Rochester in a day's time now that Pevensey is about to fall. But I don't think we need worry about him even if he has guessed, sweetheart. FitzHaimo's a good man."

Aldyth sighed, sensing what he would say next. He did not disappoint her.

"But we both know Turold isn't a good man, Aldyth, and unless he's been unlucky enough to have been a casualty of the rebels, he's going to be coming with the king's army. Please, love, let me keep you safe here. I'm sure I can rent this house for as long as we need it. Please say you'll stay here so that I need not fear you encountering Turold when the armies come together again."

"My love, we promised ourselves we would not discuss anything beyond our love this night," Aldyth reminded him firmly. "I have said I would keep out of sight then, and I will. But for now, kiss me, Ranulf, and then I want you to

take me to bed and make love to me. The babe has not less-
ened my hunger for you, thank God."

On the sands of Pevensey Bay a celebration was being
held. The king's army was jubilant. Duke Robert's pirates
had been turned away by a blockading fleet from the Cinque
Ports. Robert of Mortain, the head of the garrison, had
made his submission and his soldiers had marched out and
surrendered. Even Bishop Odo had been captured and was
now the king's prisoner. Tomorrow they would march on
Rochester to quash the remainder of the rebellion.

Bonfires had been lit on the pebbly beach and the soldiers were feasting on roast oxen and fowls given them by a
grateful King William Rufus. Ale was flowing freely. The
camp followers, wearing their lightest kirtles because of the
warm mid-June weather, were dancing for the men. Every
now and then a soldier would pull one of them into the
shadows of the large black boulders that lined the beach.
She would emerge a few minutes later, her pocket heavier
with the coins the celebrating man-at-arms had paid her.
Yes, it would be a profitable night for the women who followed the army.

As she watched from one of the cliffs overlooking the bay,
Maud's eyes narrowed and her brow furrowed with concentration as she tried to identify Turold in the milling
throng below.

It had not been an easy thing to find Turold. She had
journeyed to faraway London town, only to learn that the
army had already left. She had traveled on to Tonbridge,
where the garrison had laughed at her and sent her on to
Pevensey. Her journey had been made easier when she had
stolen a clerk's donkey, an act for which she felt no guilt.
Was it not more fitting that she travel on the back of such a

beast as the Virgin had ridden? And now she had reached the bay and would soon be reunited with her husband.

Turold would be so glad to know his wife had finally found him. He would be overjoyed. His handsome face would break into a broad grin, and he would laugh triumphantly and run across the beach to scoop her into his embrace. Of course, he would be sorry to learn that she had lost the babe she had been carrying, but they would find someplace soft and private—not just a spot behind the rocks for a quick drunken coupling—and he would give her a new babe. And he would love and protect her forever after.

Maud gave a triumphant cackle of laughter as she thought she spotted Turold at last. A man with her lover's stocky build was sitting by one of the bonfires, gnawing on a hunk of roasted meat and watching the antics of a gyrating harlot.

Maud frowned. Well, it did him no harm to look, and as soon as she could descend to the beach and make herself known, he would not give the whore a second glance.

"Ah, my ravishing Desiderata, come sit in my lap," invited Turold, waving a half-eaten leg of capon at his leman. She had been doing what she claimed was a Moorish dance for him and the other men-at-arms lounging nearby, and she was flushed rosy from the fire and her exertions. The loose neckline of her gown revealed half of her breasts, and as she had gyrated, the other half had threatened to bob into view.

"Oh ho! I know why you want me to sit on your lap, my fine cockerel!" crowed Desiderata. "You have something for me that has naught to do with that capon leg you're offering as bait!"

"Aye, that I do, my lover. You bring out the best of me, I do swear." The other men guffawed, all but that damned Godric, who had been so gloomy of late. Well, Turold thought, he could ignore that sobersides. Tonight was a night for feasting and getting drunk and swiving anything female in reach, and Desiderata was definitely in reach. He thrust out his hand and grabbed one of her breasts and tweaked the nipple. With a squeal, Desiderata dropped into his lap and began to kiss him, accompanied by the cheers of his ale-fogged companions.

"Turold, would you like to continue our celebration somewhere more private? In our usual trysting place?" Desiderata had been guzzling ale with the rest, but she still considered herself a cut above the average camp follower and was not about to give herself to Turold in front of all his comrades. She was relieved when her lover, his responses slowed by drink, nodded at last. Like as not he'd fall asleep before he satisfied her, but that was all right. Earlier this evening he'd asked her to wed him, so she already had what she really wanted. And soon they'd obtain an audience with the king, she was sure of it.

"Follow me in a few minutes, all right, love? I'll be ready for you," she cooed, and headed up the track that led above the beach toward the grove of yews where they usually coupled.

Maud had witnessed the whole thing from a few yards away but had been unnoticed in the strolling crowd of soldiers and camp followers. Now she followed Desiderata, and when the harlot stopped in the grove and began to arrange a blanket under one of the trees, she stepped out of the concealing darkness.

"Who do you think you are, slut, to be stealing my husband?" she screeched, coming forward.

Desiderata stared at the wild-eyed harridan approaching her, hands clenched into claws, her hair standing out at the sides as if it had never known a comb.

"Who are you?" she retorted coolly, disliking the shattering of her jubilant mood. The woman must be some unfortunate lunatic disturbed by the noise. Perhaps if she gave her a penny or two she'd go away before Turold came.

"I'm Maud, Turold's wife, you trollop!" the crazed woman screamed, coming nearer.

"There must be some mistake," retorted Desiderata, truly annoyed now. "My man is no one's husband. He's soon to become mine, however."

"Turold of Swanlea is *mine*. He gave me a babe, only I lost it, and now I want another."

Desiderata stared at her. Well, perhaps this was one of Turold's former wenches. She could not judge him too harshly, after all—he was hardly her first man, either. She hoped he would be here in a moment and spare her having to deal with this pitiful wretch any longer.

"Well, perhaps he favored you once, but no more. He is mine. He wouldn't even look at the likes of you, you poor mad creature. Here's a penny. Get you gone, and buy yourself some food. Or go back down to the beach and they'll likely give you some ale. Yes, and give you another babe, too, if you offer yourself to enough of them."

Too late, Desiderata realized the danger of being arrogant while she was alone with this crazed woman. The madwoman had just pulled a wicked-looking dagger from under her cloak.

Desiderata looked wildly about her for a loose branch, anything that could be used as a weapon. She had left her eating dagger with Turold so that it wouldn't jab her while she was dancing.

Desiderata screamed as the madwoman charged.

He heard her calling his name while he was still climbing the steep path that led up from the beach. Then her voice was choked off and there was a horrible silence, followed by a bone-chilling, triumphant cackle. Turold began to run.

By the time he reached the grove, only seconds later, it was too late. A straggly-haired creature dressed in a tattered kirtle was dancing around Desiderata's corpse, holding aloft a bloodstained dagger and laughing dementedly.

"She said ye were hers, Turold! She said ye'd make no more babes on me but marry her and give them to her! She was wrong, Turold, wasn't she? I had to show her she was wrong!" she screeched.

"Maud?" he questioned, the fumes of the ale clearing from his brain as he stared, first at the capering madwoman, then at the body of his leman, whose throat had been slashed nearly from ear to ear. The blood still coursed from the wound, but Desiderata was motionless, her glazed eyes staring.

How could Maud be here? It was some fantastic nightmare. How could she have found him and killed his woman?

"I'll slay you, by God!" he roared, and launched himself at the apparition he had once known as Maud. But when insanity had robbed Maud of her reason, it had conferred speed and cleverness, and she easily eluded him. Her mad cackle taunted him as he lost her in the darkness.

Chapter Twenty-Five

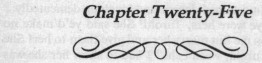

"If he's a prisoner, I'm the Pope," Urse commented as the royal army approached on a cloudy June afternoon.

Behind the jutting nasal of his helm, Ranulf peered through narrowed eyes at the bishop, arrayed in his gorgeous episcopal robes. Mounted on a white mule, Odo rode at the head of the troops beside the king, almost as if he and his nephew Rufus were cogenerals rather than prisoner and captor.

"If there are shackles, they're invisible ones," Ranulf agreed, watching as Bishop Odo made some remark to the king, then threw back his head and laughed.

"Aye. They look on the best of terms, do they not?" Urse said, then spat on the ground, disgusted. "That Odo, he's a sly one. Rufus would do well to forget he's his uncle, for he can't be trusted."

Ranulf nodded. While he waited for the king to come nearer to where he and FitzHaimo stood at the head of their smaller force, he studied the ranks of soldiers behind the king. Somewhere among the hundreds of Englishmen in their conical iron helmets and boiled-leather jerkins with sewn-on metal links marched Aldyth's former betrothed and her brother Godric.

He hoped time—and Aldyth's disappearance—had mellowed Godric's angry heart. Aldyth did not mention him, but Ranulf knew she would grieve if her relationship with her brother was not eventually mended.

He clenched his jaw at the thought of encountering Turold, however. Time and his love for Aldyth, which seemed to double every day, had *not* diminished his seething rage at the brute who had thought to force Aldyth to his will.

Aldyth had promised to keep to their tent as much as possible and to wear her hood and keep her head down whenever she had to venture forth. But it was June and increasingly hot, even with the cooling breezes off the Medway. Would she be able to keep her promise until he had the chance to confront Turold?

God's toenails, Ranulf thought, he should have used a husband's prerogative and ordered Aldyth to remain at the little house in nearby Strood that they had rented for their wedding night. Aldyth had claimed she would not obey such a command, but he thought she was bluffing.

Still, he had been reluctant to insist for two reasons. For one thing, he was loath to begin their marriage by acting the tyrannical husband. For another, he could not banish the niggling fear as to what would happen to Aldyth if some mischance befell him. How would she learn his fate? And what could happen to a woman alone if the rebels bottled up in Rochester broke out and fled south in the direction of Strood?

In any case it was no use to wonder. The die was cast. The army was about to become one again. Likely he and Turold would be too busy besieging Rochester Castle with the rest of the combined army to carry on private quarrels.

He could still wonder, however, what Prince Henry was doing. There had been no communication from his liege lord. Was Henry even now moving to take advantage of England's unrest? Why had he sent his loyal vassal no word, and left him to fret in uncertainty?

The king and his prisoner, the bishop, were now before them. Ranulf and FitzHaimo dismounted and knelt.

"My lords, you have done well," the king told them. "We are well pleased with your efforts in keeping the rebels contained while we obtained the surrender of the Pevensey garrison." Rufus smiled before he went on. "And now we would have you do one other service. His excellency my uncle has agreed to help negotiate the surrender of Rochester Castle. You and four others are to escort him, under cover of a white flag of parley, into the castle."

At his side, Bishop Odo smirked, the expression making his eyes disappear into slits in his fleshy face. Ranulf felt the same repulsion one would experience upon encountering a deadly adder in his bed.

FitzHaimo seemed to be having trouble clearing his throat. Ranulf knew it would be up to him.

"Your grace, forgive my blunt speech, but was your uncle the bishop not recently one of these rebels?" Ranulf asked, feeling the eggshells under his feet.

Rufus's normally ruddy face reddened even more.

"I agree, your grace," FitzHaimo chimed in, to Ranulf's relief. "If I may speak plainly, too, what is to stop him from rejoining his comrades within the walls?"

Odo pouted, but his eyes mocked them. "They do not believe in my repentance, nephew."

Rufus's face was obdurate, his eyes as stormy as the lowering sky. "Our uncle has made his submission, and we are well satisfied. He has been entrusted with this mission of peace." His eyes dared either man to dispute his will.

There was, of course, no further argument to be made.

"Let me be one of the four, I beg your grace," said a voice from among the mounted men immediately behind the king.

Ranulf recognized Perrin of Petersfield, the beardless young squire who had been at the king's side since last fall. He was wearing gold spurs, Ranulf noted. So Rufus had not been able to resist bringing his youthful protégé on campaign and had knighted him to give him an ostensible role. Ranulf steeled his features to remain impassive.

"Oh ho! So you would win glory, would you, Perrin? Well, why not? Certainly you may be one of my uncle's honor guard. You shall bear the white standard. That means we need call but one more. Hugh of Avranches, will you join them?"

The Earl of Chester inclined his head, but not before Ranulf saw the hastily smothered sneer at Sir Perrin's inclusion. If there is trouble, the look said, there will be but three of us.

"Leave your swords and shield here. You are to go in unarmed, as a demonstration of our goodwill," the king announced.

Ranulf felt the blood drain from his face. Had Rufus gone mad? Why not put the noose around their necks, as well?

"Surely your grace jests," Hugh of Avranches said flatly as the ranking noble.

"My lord, don't be an old woman! You have the might of England behind you—the rebels aren't fools!" Rufus said with a regal gesture. "*Eh bien,* no time like the present." Someone handed Perrin the white banner of parley. "Go forth, messengers of the king's peace. They are expecting you."

Ranulf gritted his teeth as he and the others handed over their weapons. He remounted his destrier, hoping Aldyth was not watching. He could see Odo trying to hide his smugness—why couldn't the king?

The king's army was perhaps three hundred yards from the walls of Rochester Castle. The five "messengers of the king's peace" had ridden two-thirds of that distance when the drawbridge was lowered and a party of a dozen knights, all armed to the teeth, trotted out.

FitzHaimo muttered something, his tone uneasy.

"They're but a welcoming party," Odo assured them, but just then the rebels drew their swords and spurred their horses forward.

FitzHaimo cursed and tried to grab the bishop's reins. He was thwarted by the mace Odo pulled out from his capacious sleeve.

Furious, Ranulf was just about to shout the Kingsclere war cry and seize Odo or die in the attempt when Hugh of Avranches cried, "No! There are too many of them, and we are unarmed! Do not fight, and we may yet be ransomed! Let them take us!"

He was right. They were surrounded. Only Perrin of Petersfield, who had been riding behind Ranulf, was too stupid to listen.

Dropping the white banner and pulling a dagger from his belt, he set spurs to his horse and charged, screaming, straight at the oncoming force.

"You idiot!" shouted Ranulf, spurring his own mount. He was able to draw alongside the king's favorite and, with desperate strength, yank the youth right out of the saddle and onto his own galloping war-horse. He threw the youth across the pommel like a sack of meal, holding on to the panicked, struggling Perrin with both hands.

"Shut up and be still!" snapped Ranulf as the king's favorite yelled a protest. "Or better yet, pray we may yet get out of this without broken heads."

He kneed his destrier, and months of careful training paid off as the huge beast swerved to the left, wheeling away from the leveled swords of the "welcoming party."

Ranulf used his own spurs, and the great stallion redoubled his speed, carrying his increased burden away from the enemy. But one of the rebel knights had guessed his intention and was moving to intercept them, his sword raised.

Without his shield, Ranulf was powerless to fend off the blow; he could only use his knees. His destrier swerved again, and the sword that had been meant to slash across his right arm was deflected to his thigh.

Ranulf felt the sword's edge like the bite of a dragon and swore even as the rebel raised his sword and edged closer to strike again. Then the wound went mercifully numb, though he could feel the warm rush of blood beneath his hauberk—and he shouted his family battle cry, "For God and Kingsclere!"

The destrier responded, baring his teeth and screaming defiance. The other horse was beside him, not in front of him, so he could only lunge at the attacker's stallion shoulder to shoulder, but it was enough. The other horse was knocked off his stride, allowing Ranulf's mount to escape and carry them back to safety.

The king and his entourage crowded around Ranulf's blowing destrier as Ranulf reined him to a halt. The king himself assisted the trembling Perrin down from his helpless position across Ranulf's saddle, while one of his nobles steadied Ranulf as he dismounted.

"Thank God you were able to rescue him!" Ranulf heard the king say, as if from a great distance. "Perrin, you're unharmed?"

The still-quivering young knight answered in the affirmative.

"Th-that was the b-bravest act of heroism I have ever seen, Ranulf!" Rufus praised, stammering and forgetting the royal "we" in his agitation. "I'm very grateful you were able to save young Perrin from the consequences of his own foolishness. I'll see you well rewarded, I promise you. Perrin, what possessed you to act so suicidally when you were outnumbered? Did you think I'd get you canonized for that piece of lunacy? By the Face, I'd rather have you alive, boy!"

"B-bishop Odo—" Ranulf began, then closed his eyes as a wave of dizziness swept over him. It had begun to sprinkle, and he concentrated on the cool, refreshing drops of rain falling on his face.

"Is safely back with his fellow conspirators behind the walls of Rochester Castle, along with their two new hostages, FitzHaimo and Hugh of Avranches. No doubt they'd guffawing over my royal stupidity. Go ahead, my lord, this is your perfect opportunity to say I told you so."

As much as he would have liked to say it, the buzzing in his head was growing too loud as the blood continued to ooze wetly down his leg from the wound in his thigh.

"Your grace, I..." Ranulf began, and then collapsed into Urse's arms at the same time as the rain began to fall in sheets.

Aldyth had seen it all. With the attention of the whole army on the drama being enacted before the walls of Rochester Castle, she had been steadily edging out of the tent into the throng of men-at-arms. None of them paid any attention to the slender boy threading his way through the ranks. The rain beginning to fall gave her the perfect excuse to pull her hood over her head, concealing most of her face.

She had been halfway toward the front of the ranks when Ranulf had mounted and begun to ride with the other four men, including one in the robes of a bishop whom she guessed was the notorious Odo, toward the castle walls.

She wanted to scream, *No! Can't you see it's a trap?* But she knew he could not have heard her, and it probably would not have stopped him anyway. Men! Why must they do such obviously foolish things in the name of bravery!

And then her hands had tightened into fists as she had spied the armed party thundering out of Rochester Castle, their swords raised. They clearly outnumbered the king's emissaries. Aldyth put her hands up to her mouth to stifle the screams as she saw one of the knights attempt to charge the enemy, Ranulf's move to intercept him and then his heroic fight to rescue the foolhardy knight.

A moan of anguish escaped from Aldyth as she glimpsed the enemy's sword descending and striking Ranulf's leg, but the sound was buried in the rising roar of rage from hundreds of soldiers all around her. She continued to watch, lips murmuring in prayer, for terrifying seconds as Ranulf on his war-horse fought to win free of his pursuer.

The army was not ordered to attack—the whole event had happened too quickly. The drawbridge was down only long enough to allow the bishop, the dozen rebels and their two new hostages to clatter back over it, and then Rochester Castle was again shut up tight.

Aldyth saw none of that. Her eyes were trained upon her beloved Ranulf as his human burden was taken from him and he staggered from his horse, only to fall a moment later in a boneless heap before the king.

Her screams as she dashed forward, heedless of her surroundings, rose over the murmuring of the men-at-arms as they awaited further orders.

"Ranulf! Ranulf!" Oh, Jésu, was his wound mortal? Was he dead?

It took her an agonizingly long time—in reality only seconds—to reach her lover's side in the downpour, but by that time the men about the king were trying to help Urse with his fallen lord.

"Al—Edward," Urse cried, sighting Aldyth. "No—don't come near— You...you shouldn't see him now—" he warned, but she ignored him.

"Here, what's this? Lord Ranulf's page? Easy, lad, easy," someone was saying, but then one of the nobles had pulled off Ranulf's helmet, pushing back his hair, so midnight black in contrast to the pallid, bloodless face. Someone else stepped back after having pushed Ranulf's hauberk up away from the wound, and she saw the widening stain spreading over the lower edge of his arming tunic.

Aldyth screamed again and, eluding an attempt to grab her, threw herself at Ranulf's body, sobbing, her fingers diving for his chest to see if he still lived.

The heavy metal links made it difficult to be sure his heart was still beating, but she thought his chest rose slightly under her cheek. Her hand flew to his neck, and yes, there was a thrumming against her fingers just at the angle between the neck and the jaw. But 'twas so feeble and quick! And still the crimson stain spread at his thigh.

"Oh, please! Can't you see he's bleeding to death? Help him, in God's mercy!" she screamed, then hardly knowing what she did, she kissed him, wondering dazedly if it would be the last time she did so while he lived.

"Send my physician to my tent!" bellowed Rufus at her side. "Here, you men! Carry him thence! No, you wait here," he said, fingers fastening like an iron vise around her wrist when she would have followed as Ranulf was being borne away.

Frozen with the realization that she was discovered, she allowed herself to be stopped.

"Look at me," the king's voice commanded.

Aldyth quaked inwardly as she lifted her chin, her eyes seeing first the springy, ginger-colored hair thinning at the top, then the high-colored complexion and, lastly, the penetrating gaze of Rufus's slightly bulging hazel orbs.

"'Tis a maid and not a boy," he said softly, cupping her chin and turning it first this way and then that, rubbing her cheeks with one callused thumb, feeling the softness of her skin through the dirt she always smudged on her face. "'Tis a maid!" he repeated to the nobles thronging around him. "Lord Ranulf's little page boy is a maid, not a boy—fancy that!" He looked at her with increasing intensity. "Well, say something, girl. You are female, are you not, by the Face of Lucca?"

"Aye," she sobbed, her tears washed away by the rain. "Aye, your grace, I am female."

"Who are you? Why did our Ranulf have you with him? He called you Edward, or something like that, did he not? Why would he do such a thing? This casts our Ranulf in a wholly different light, does it not?" he said musingly to the recently rescued Perrin, who still stood near.

Should she tell the truth? Would it be better or worse for Ranulf if she admitted that she not only was not a boy but wife to Ranulf?

"Your grace, Lord Ranulf meant to perform no deception toward you but only, in his chivalry, to aid me," she began.

There was the sound of a scuffling behind them, and suddenly a voice she had hoped never to hear again said, "Your grace, I believe I can tell you what you wish to know. My king, she is Aldyth of Sherborne, and my runaway betrothed."

Chapter Twenty-Six

Aldyth stared, aghast, at the rain-drenched man-at-arms who stood before her. There was an evil gleam of triumph in his pale blue eyes. "No..." she moaned. *No! Not here, not now, when Ranulf is bleeding, maybe dying!*

The king whirled around, surprisingly swift for a man of his barrel-chested bulk, and studied the dripping soldier. "And who in the devil are you, knave?"

Turold swallowed before answering. "Turold of Swanlea, your grace, and one of your most loyal of English subjects." He shut his mouth temporarily as Rufus held up an impatient hand. "And this is my woman—that is to say, my betrothed—who has run away from my generosity and kindness and treacherously fornicated with that evil demon that was just carried away..."

"Be careful, you babbling English magpie. You speak of a Norman noble and one of my most trusted lords," Rufus warned him sternly.

Turold paled, then went on. "But your grace does not know—"

"Your grace, I regret to interrupt, but a messenger has come from the rebel garrison," Beaumont said, his voice raised to carry over Turold's. "He would speak to you immediately as to their demands regarding the hostages."

Rufus peered at the mounted man through the downpour. "Oh, he would, would he? They dare to make demands when they have the might of England before their walls?"

"But, your grace—" began Turold.

"I have no more time for talk of runaway women and accusations about my lords. If he cuckolded you, you probably deserved it!" Rufus said with a derisive snort, and began to turn away.

"But there's treason, your grace!" Turold blurted out desperately.

Rufus's head jerked around, throwing droplets of rain from his ginger locks. "Treason? I would not toss that charge lightly, fellow."

"I...I do not, your grace," Turold said, but he trembled and licked his lips.

Rufus looked back at Beaumont, who indicated the mounted messenger carrying the same white banner Perrin had earlier dropped. He sighed.

"I will hear your claims, Turold of Swanlea, on the morrow at the hour of sext. Your charges may not matter to Lord Ranulf, you know—he may be mortally wounded from the look of it. And if he dies, I don't give a damn whose woman this is," he added with a sour look at Aldyth, and stalked off.

"Until then, Aldyth, you're coming with me," Turold announced, and reached for her.

"Nay!" she cried, backing up and shrinking away from his extended hand. "I must go to my lord. Leave me alone, Turold. You have no more right to tell me what to do."

"Come here, you willful wench, or it will be the worse for you," threatened Turold, advancing on her.

"Leave my sister alone, Turold," said another voice behind her.

"Godric!" Her mouth dropped open as she turned around and beheld her brother standing there, the rain running in rivulets down his shaggy golden hair. He held his arms open and she ran to them. "Oh, Godric!" she breathed, knowing somehow from the swift smile he gave her that he could be trusted to help her.

After that quick smile, though, his expression grew hard and cold as he turned his attention back to Turold. "Nay, you shall not touch her, not now. She will stay with me until your audience with the king tomorrow, and then we shall see."

"Stand aside, Godric. She's my betrothed. You know I have the right," blustered Turold, shaking his fist at Godric.

Would her brother surrender her to Turold's supposed claim? "Godric, I'm not—he's not—" she stammered. Her eyes flew from one man's angry face to the other.

Godric's hand went meaningfully to the *scamasax,* the short, one-edged sword at his hip. "I have said she will be with me until your audience with the king, Turold," he repeated, and Aldyth saw that his eyes held Turold's until the other man looked down.

"Very well, then. Until tomorrow," Turold snarled, glaring at Aldyth. "But after I tell Rufus what I know, her lover will die if he hasn't already, and she will be but one of the things the king gives me out of gratitude." He strode off, leaving Aldyth shivering.

He had called her a *thing.* That was all she was to him— less than a dog that must be brought to heel. Holy Mary, his boasts made it sound as though he had learned about Ranulf's secret loyalty to Prince Henry! How was that possible?

But she had to forget about Turold and his threats, at least for the moment. Ranulf was critically, perhaps even mortally wounded. She must go to him.

Her eyes stinging with tears, she raised her head from within the comforting circle of her brother's arms. "Godric, I must be with Ranulf. I must know...please, there will be time for explanations later, but now I must know if he lives!"

Her brother met her gaze, his own eyes troubled, but he seemed to sense her desperate need. "All right, sister. I will go with you."

She took off at a run, and he followed.

Moments later they were within the king's tent, where an aged, white-bearded man was bent over Ranulf's still form. Urse stood by, his brow furrowed with worry. She caught a glimpse of Ranulf's face, so pale it was the color of the sheet on which he lay.

"Does he...is he..." She could not form the words.

"He lives, but barely," the king's physician said. "Who are you?"

She glanced at Godric, then avoided his gaze as she answered, "I am Lord Ranulf's wife."

She could feel her brother's start of surprise but ignored it. "Will he..."

The physician was studying her boyish clothes and short hair but evidently decided it was none of his concern, for he merely answered her incomplete question. "Will he live? I don't know, for 'tis in God's hands now, but I have cauterized the wound and he is no longer hemorrhaging." He nodded at the iron rod that lay on the ground at his feet. She had an instant image of the physician heating it in the campfire outside the tent, then carrying it in, its end glowing white-hot, and touching it to her beloved's flesh. Now she realized what she had smelled when she had entered the tent—the odor of burned human flesh.

She swayed in Godric's protective embrace.

"Aye, 'tis fortunate he was insensible at the time, for the agony would have been terrible, but he would have bled to death else," the physician told her bluntly. "Now only time will tell. He will need to be kept warm and fed liquids as soon as he wakes enough to swallow. I will leave a vial of tincture of poppy with you, young woman, for the pain, but you must take care only to let him have a drop or two every few hours. Too much could be fatal."

Aldyth nodded soberly. She would be strong for Ranulf. She must.

Afternoon faded into evening without Aldyth noticing the change. She sat by Ranulf's pallet, her eyes never leaving his face, her hand going every so often to his chest to make sure he still breathed. His chest rose so slightly...

And then, still unconscious, he began to groan. He was not yet awake enough to be safely given the poppy juice. As tears slipped silently down her cheeks, she grasped his hand in hers, willing him to live, praying to God and whatever saint might be listening to relieve his pain.

Godric and Urse tried to get her to take some supper, but she waved it away. She was not hungry. How could she eat, while her beloved hurt so?

It was perhaps midnight before he woke enough to be given the poppy juice, and she managed to drip some precious drops of water down his throat before he slept. His eyes had opened and he had blinked at her, his gaze unfocused. She wasn't sure he knew her.

Two hours later, his forehead was as hot as the brazier Urse had lit within the tent. Now she used the water to bathe his forehead and then his entire body, weeping as she saw the ugly burn where the wound had been cauterized. The physician had left an unguent for the burn with directions to reapply it at intervals. He had also left a jar filled with a distillation of willow bark for the fever he predicted would come, and this she gave him, drop by drop, when he stirred again.

Finally, toward dawn, beads of sweat broke out on Ranulf's forehead and he slept, soundly and peacefully. Was it her imagination, or was his pallor reduced ever so slightly?

Urse went outside, his eyes suspiciously moist, and did not return for several minutes.

Godric, who had been dozing, woke then and joined her at Ranulf's side.

"He looks better, Aldyth," he told her.

She sagged against her brother's chest, tears of relief and weariness streaking down her cheeks. She was not imagining it. He *was* better. He was going to live!

But for how long, after Turold spoke to the king? She shuddered.

"Don't worry, Aldyth. I won't let you fall into Turold's hands, no matter what happens," Godric said, mistaking her thoughts.

"Oh, Godric," she sighed. "Turold's eyes are so cruel. How could I have ever thought I could wed him and be happy?"

"We were both deceived, Aldyth. I never guessed. I have much to regret, sister. You did not feel you could come to me, and you were right—I would not have believed he was so evil then. Not only that, but I helped him hunt you." He shook his head. "Can you ever find it in your heart to forgive me?"

"Of course," she told him, and hugged him, savoring the feeling of strength that seemed to flow from his massive chest into her body. He had filled out since she had last seen him. He had been a slender, rebellious youth. Now he was a man.

"Godric," she began, reluctant to shatter the feeling of closeness, but he must know the truth. "We were both mistaken about Ranulf, too."

She felt him stiffen slightly, but he kept his arms around her.

"He is a good man, Godric, even if he is a Norman. You can believe that, can't you? You're fighting for the king. Surely you have learned there are good Normans." Aldyth edged out of his embrace. She needed to see his face, to see his reaction to her words. She looked up at her brother, willing him to believe her.

At last he nodded warily. "Aye."

"The way he has been acting in recent months, Godric— it was all a pose. Part of an elaborate ruse. 'Twas not him— 'twas but a part he was playing."

"Why?"

There it was, the question she had been dreading. "I . . . I cannot tell you, Godric. 'Tis not my secret to tell."

"You had better tell me, sister, if you want me to believe in his goodness. I must know the truth—all of it, do you hear? You can trust me, sister. The secret will not leave my lips, but I *must know*. Why was it necessary for him to dress like a peacock and act the languid lordling?"

She saw the stubborn set of Godric's jaw. When he looked like that, heaven and earth could not change his mind.

She arose and quietly walked over to lift the tent flap. She went out into the cool dawn air, seeing that the sentries were still in place in front and behind the tent, but they were dozing. They looked Norman, not English. Good—they would probably not understand her since she was speaking in English. Most Normans did not deign to learn the conquered Englishman's tongue.

Even so, she dropped her voice to a whisper when she returned to Godric's side and began to tell him about Ranulf's loyalty to Prince Henry.

"Bah, who knows if any one of these Normans is better than the other?" he said when she had finished.

"But what about you? Aren't you fighting on behalf of one of them?"

"Aye, and taking the king's silver for it," he said, a cynical gleam in his eye. "But I do not believe Duke Robert would be good for England—he's too much the puppet of the Norman nobles."

She nodded and told him of her impressions of the court at Rouen. Then she contrasted Henry with Robert.

"I cannot say *I* am certain Henry would be a better king than Rufus, Godric, but I know Ranulf believes it."

"Well, if our king continues unwed, all Henry will have to do is wait. He's younger, and the way the king lives... 'Twill be child's play for Henry to wrest the throne from Robert someday, assuming Robert ever gets to the throne."

She was thoughtful. "Perhaps you're right. But, Godric, is that what Turold is going to tell the king about Ranulf? How could he know?"

"I don't know...unless mayhap that Norman whore told him something of it."

"A N-Norman whore spoke to Turold? Who was she? Do you remember her name?"

"Desiderata. A fanciful name for a slut, is it not?" he said with a sardonic quirk to his brow. "She'd been in Normandy until recently, she claimed."

"Aye," Aldyth said, lowering her head as a sickening sense of doom came over her. "She came from Henry's castle. She must have heard them talking. When Ranulf would not fall for her wiles, she left, but Henry thought she would return when she got over her anger." Her shoulders sagged. "Instead, she came here for revenge, it seems."

"They were lovers, Turold and Desiderata. I think the trollop thought he was going to wed her. But she's dead now," Godric told her flatly.

She listened, horrified, as Godric told her about Maud appearing suddenly in Pevensey and cutting Desiderata's throat.

"I gather your former tirewoman has gone mad as a rabid wolf and saw the Norman wench as a rival for Turold's affections," he added.

"So that's how Turold knows," she breathed. "Oh, Godric, he'll tell the king, and Rufus will order Ranulf executed!" She shoved her clenched hands against her face in order to keep from screaming. "Godric, I must go to Turold and tell him I'll come back to him if only he will keep silent—"

He shook his head. "It's too late for that. You forget, he's already mentioned treason in connection with Ranulf. And besides, Aldyth, did you not say you were Ranulf's wife?"

She nodded, her eyes blurred with tears. "Aye, we were married at Strood. I . . . I'm carrying his child, Godric. We would have wed before, but the king . . . Ranulf would not hear of waiting, though, once he knew . . ." She began to sob with fresh terror.

"Do not fear, little sister," Godric said, tousling her short brown locks reassuringly, "I'll not let Ranulf make a widow of you."

"But what will you do?" she asked, studying the resolute face.

"Whatever I must."

Chapter Twenty-Seven

Someone was shaking her. "My lady..."

Urse was bending over her, his florid face solemn.

Her eyes flew open and she saw the king's physician standing beyond Urse. Was it possible that she had slept? Had she actually fallen asleep when it was so important to nurse Ranulf?

The physician saw her eyes fly to Ranulf's reclining form but held a finger to his lips. "Do not fear, Lady Aldyth, he lives. He is sleeping and will continue to do so if we are quiet. 'Tis best that he does. I spoke with your brother earlier this morn— he watched over your lord husband while you slept. You were exhausted, he said—and no wonder." He looked back at his patient. "I have seen his wound, my lady, and though 'tis angry red at the edges, it appears to be healing well. I believe he will make a full recovery."

"Thank Our Lord and his Mother," Aldyth said devoutly.

"Amen to that, but no doubt your devoted care made the difference—and my cauterizing, of course," the physician added with a wink. Then his face turned serious again. "My lady, the sun nears its zenith. The king has bidden me to summon you to the hearing. He waits in yon grove of oaks with his assembled nobles to hear Ranulf's accuser... and you, of course.''

She was unable to believe it was so late, but when she opened the tent flap, the sun was indeed high in the sky. Its brilliance seemed redoubled, as if to make up for the day before.

"But... Ranulf..." she murmured, looking back at her slumbering husband. "Would the king hear testimony against a man without his being there to defend himself?"

The physician looked uncomfortable. "My lady, I know little of this matter, but I understand the time was set for noon. Undoubtedly if what his grace hears disturbs him, he will wait to hear Ranulf's side... before passing sentence."

Behind her, Urse began an angry muttering, but she paid no heed. "Before passing sentence..." she echoed, her heart thudding against her breast. "Sir, I understand. I will be there as quickly as I can suitably array myself."

The physician bowed and left them.

"My lady, I will go to the king. I will make him see that he must wait," Urse said.

She held up a peremptory hand. "No Urse, I must do it. Now step outside while I change," she said finally, and the giant obeyed.

She flew to the basin and splashed some water onto her face. Sometime during the evening, Godric had brought her belongings, and now she pulled out the mulberry-colored gown she had worn at her wedding. As she slipped it over her head and laced the side fastenings, then arranged the veil to hide her shorn locks, she hoped that she would appear Lord Ranulf's virtuous wife.

Where was Godric? What had his cryptic promise at dawn meant, that he would do whatever he must? Perhaps he had gone to try to persuade his former friend to change his testimony, or better yet, to disappear altogether before the hearing began. 'Twould do no good, she thought sadly. Turold would not change his mind.

Well, 'twas up to her. Was there a way she could save his life—without putting her soul in eternal jeopardy by lying?

When she left the tent, Urse fell in step beside her. "You should stay with your master," she told him.

Urse's face was stubbornly set. "He will sleep," he told her. "But he would want me to stand by you."

"Aldyth of Sherborne, we are pleased to see you dressed as a woman today," King William Rufus said with a wry twist of his mouth. Using a camp chair as an informal throne, he was flanked by his loyal nobles and the Archbishop of Canterbury. All of them stared at her curiously.

"Yes, your grace," she said meekly, her eyes downcast.

"We are here to give ear to the charges made by one Turold of Swanlea, an English freedman who says he is your betrothed husband, against Lord Ranulf of Kingsclere, with whom you have been, shall we say, in close association?" He gave a short bark of laughter, which the nobles at his side and behind him echoed politely.

Godric sat, hidden by the thick summer greenery, high in a tree just to the left of where the king sat. He was careful to do nothing to give away his presence. He had been lucky to discover in advance where the hearing was to take place, and luckier still to be able to take up his position before anyone came. He was glad to see Lord Ranulf's squire standing sturdily beside Aldyth.

Earlier, Godric had been unable to catch Turold alone, for the stocky farmer had been careful to surround himself with other soldiers. Godric had already realized the uselessness of trying to dissuade Turold from testifying, however. Godric had a more permanent solution in mind, and if it meant sacrificing himself to save Lord Ranulf and Aldyth, then that was just atonement for his failings toward his sister.

He was no great archer, preferring to take his chances in hand-to-hand fighting with his *scramasax*, but he had an Englishman's competence at bringing down game for the table. Turold would be a stationary target, and at this distance Godric could scarcely miss. He would see what Turold was going to say and be ready to put an arrow through his heart before he could endanger Aldyth and her beloved Norman. Leaning against the trunk of the tree, he held an arrow ready to be nocked into the bowstring and waited.

"We shall hear the charge of lesser interest to us first," Rufus announced. "Did you in fact, Lady Aldyth, desert this man, to whom you were betrothed in a legal ceremony by the Church, and run off with our Lord Ranulf when he journeyed at our command to Normandy?"

"I did, your grace." Her voice trembled, but it was clearly audible, Godric noted with pride.

"And why did you do such a thing, woman? Yon Turold seems a goodly man, strong and reasonably fair, and English like yourself," Rufus pointed out, then waited.

"I . . . I discovered he was a brute, your grace, on the eve of our wedding. I could not marry such a man."

"It's true, Your Grace. She came to us bruised and beaten," Urse asserted, but the king ignored him.

"A brute? Are you ignorant of the fact that a man is the head of a woman, that she is to be in subjection to him? So the Church teaches, I am told. Is that not right, Archbishop Lanfranc?" Rufus inquired.

The aged, austere man who was England's spiritual head nodded.

"What say you to that, Aldyth of Sherborne?"

She lifted her head. "It is the Church's teaching, but Turold of Swanlea had made a leman of my own tirewoman, and when I objected, he attempted to 'discipline' me by a method the Church would not sanction, I believe—he tried to rape me."

A buzz went through the crowd of witnesses.

"Turold, is that true?"

Turold smirked. "I may have shown my affection a trifle, uh, *forcefully,* your grace, but 'twas naught like rape. I was merely trying to demonstrate how faithful and attentive a husband I would be in future."

"Liar!" Aldyth cried.

"We would remind you both you have sworn on the holy relics to tell the truth," Rufus said. "And so, woman, you say he tried to violate you, and when you had eluded him, you fled to the side of Lord Ranulf, whom, I am told, was known to you since childhood?"

Godric listened as Aldyth repeated the story as she had told it to him, how she had fled to Winchester, merely seeking her younger brother's help, but had ended up traveling to Normandy with Ranulf when Turold had come looking for her.

"And there you began to share his bed?" Rufus inquired.

Urse bristled, but what could the squire do?

Godric hated the way some of the nobles began to leer at his sister, obviously seeing her now as a different sort of woman. If it were not for the more important target he had in mind...

Two other pairs of eyes watched the proceedings anxiously. One pair belonged to Ranulf, who had awakened in the tent in time to hear the last portion of the physician and Aldyth's conversation. He had struggled to dress himself, becoming near faint with the effort it took to drag himself from his tent to the edge of the crowd. As yet the king and Aldyth had not taken note of him.

Another pair of eyes belonged to one who had everything to lose if the king gave Aldyth back to Turold.

Aldyth's color rose at the king's accusation, but she nodded. "Yes, we became lovers, your grace. I... I have loved him since we were children together, and I am not ashamed."

Turold went purple with rage. "Do you hear the bold strumpet, your grace? She admits her sin with her own mouth!"

"Yes, and I marvel that you would have her back," Rufus said ironically, and behind him his barons and knights guffawed.

"She is mine, your grace, and I want her. I will know how to lesson her onto the path of virtue," Turold insisted stubbornly.

"Nay, I am no longer his, for Lord Ranulf had the betrothal annulled," Aldyth said proudly, holding out the rolled parchment document that she had been clutching at her side for the king's inspection.

"An annulment? 'Tis not possible! I heard of no such thing!" shouted Turold. He would have lunged for the document, but Urse prevented him.

Rufus handed it without a word to Lanfranc, who peered at it closely. "'Tis just as she said, your grace," he stated after a moment. "'Tis signed by the Bishop of Rouen."

The buzzing rose again while Turold went white, then purple with rage.

Godric waited to see if Aldyth would add that she and Ranulf were married, thus saving her good name. He knew it was dangerous that they had not gotten the king's permission. Aldyth was silent, however, allowing them to think her merely Ranulf's mistress. How brave she was.

"Aye, perhaps she has a writ from some bishop, purchased by her lover, no doubt, but you'll give her back to me after you hear what I have to tell you about your precious Lord Ranulf, your grace," shouted Turold. He stopped, staring over his right shoulder, but a tree branch blocked Godric's view of what Turold saw.

"And here he is, just in time to hear his death warrant!" Turold crowed, pointing.

Godric saw Aldyth whirl around and gasp, "Ranulf!" Heedless of her audience, she dashed in the direction that Godric had pointed and returned, slowly, a moment later, her arm around Ranulf's waist, helping to support him.

Godric whistled soundlessly through his teeth. The man had been at death's door but hours ago, and yet now he had managed to stagger the short distance from the king's tent to his trial. 'Twas an amazing feat of strength and will. No wonder Aldyth loved him.

"Good morrow, my lord," the king said, acknowledging Ranulf. "Should you be up from your sickbed?"

Godric's eyes caught a flash of movement at the edge of his field of vision. A woman, ill-dressed and poorly groomed, was edging forward through the throng of English soldiers. One of the camp followers probably, trying to interest one of the men into leaving the spectacle before him and engaging in a more private spectacle with her. Godric doubted she'd get any customers—at least not until the trial was decided. His eyes went back to the scene below.

"Probably not, your grace," Ranulf said, the effort to remain upright—even with Aldyth's and Urse's help—obviously costing him greatly, "but I would hear the lies this whoreson is about to speak, that I may counter them with the truth."

"Very well, my lord. You will swear to tell the truth on the holy relics." When Ranulf had done so, the king gestured at Turold. "Turold of Swanlea, say on."

Just then the woman Godric had glimpsed at some distance came beneath the tree, her movements furtive as she drew closer to Turold. But one of the archbishop's clerks noticed.

"Here now, woman," he said, going out to intercept her. "You have no business here at this time—"

Maud ignored him, keeping her eyes on the man she had loved to the point of madness. "She shall not have him! Turold is mine!" she screeched, her dagger held high and glinting in the sun for the space of a heartbeat.

Aldyth screamed. There were shouts from several of the men, and a bellowed warning from Urse.

Urse lunged for Maud. Ranulf leaped at her, too, but the madwoman was too quick. Before anyone could intervene, before Turold could realize that he, not Aldyth, was in danger, Maud plunged the blade into his back.

Turold's eyes bulged and he tried to turn and fight off his attacker, but it was already too late. Maud cackled insanely as she twisted the knife.

Blood spurted from Turold's mouth. There was a horrible gurgling sound, and he pitched forward.

The clerk approached and touched a hand to Turold's neck. He straightened after a moment. "He is dead."

Godric sagged against the stout trunk of the oak, weak with relief. Turold had been silenced.

All was quiet in the oak grove except for Maud's pitiful sobbing as she crumpled in a heap by the dead man. It was as if she finally realized what she had done. At an order from the king, two stout men-at-arms bound her and led her away.

The king turned back to Ranulf.

"'Twould seem your accuser is dead, my lord," he said with an upraised brow, as calm as if he saw murder done every day.

"Aye, your grace."

"Yesterday, when he came forward to claim the woman beside you, he hinted of treason," murmured the king, "but I had not then the time to hear him."

Ranulf took a deep breath. "It seems he paid a heavy price for his lies, your grace, even if he never got to voice them."

The king watched him, unblinking. Godric, in his perch in the tree, held his breath.

Then he heard the king chuckle. "Yes, you could say that, my lord. But you still have much to explain, Lord Ranulf. What of this Aldyth of Sherborne at your side? She has told us how you saved her from her brutal pursuer. How chivalrous, Lord Ranulf. But how energetic of you. Once we believed you were more interested in the latest fashion or a fine horse than in going to great trouble to win one of the fairer sex."

Ranulf grinned and shrugged with a trace of his old, drawling languidness. "What can I say, your grace? I am caught at last by a pair of jade green eyes." He put a proprietary arm about Aldyth's shoulders, pulling her closer. "Your grace, I would have this woman to wife, with your royal permission."

Rufus appeared to consider, rubbing his bewhiskered chin. "I'll have to think about it, my lord. This campaign against the rebels has been a sore drain on the royal treasury, and there may be those of my nobles who would be able to pay more for her. Beaumont, for example. Wouldn't you, my lord of Beaumont?"

Beaumont leered at Aldyth, his eyes lingering at her quivering breast.

"Aye, your grace. I'd be a fortunate man to...*have* her," he said with a wink, leaving it ambiguous as to whether he meant with or without marriage.

Ranulf's hand went to the spot where the hilt of his sword should have been, but he was unarmed. Godric saw a muscle in his temple working as he fought for control.

"No matter how much ready coin any of your nobles have, they did not save the life of your *squire* yesterday," Ranulf said, with ironic emphasis on Perrin of Petersfield's supposed role. "You promised me a boon, your grace, and I would dare to claim it."

The king threw back his head and laughed at his vassal's daring. "Very well, my lord. I am a man of my word, and so you shall have her to wife. And I think I shall not need to question your loyalty again, shall I?"

"No, your grace," Ranulf answered, but he was looking deeply into Aldyth's eyes.

A week later, when Ranulf was recovered enough to walk with only a little stiffness in his gait, they were married— *again,* thought Aldyth with amusement—in front of the king.

Now, as she lay in their second marriage bed, basking in the glow of satisfaction after Ranulf had just made love to her, he arose and brought out a letter.

"I was not lying when I told Rufus he would never have cause to doubt me," he told Aldyth, sitting on the side of the bed and holding out the parchment scroll.

She recognized the seal of Prince Henry and read the letter aloud.

"To my vassal Ranulf of Kingsclere, greetings. I would not have you ignorant, my lord, of the plans regarding the throne of England, even though these plans, it seems, must be consigned to the misty future. I know you have been poised to assist me, should I have judged the time to be right to take the throne that we agree should be mine, but I have studied the situation from across the Channel and must conclude that the time is not right. My elder brother Rufus has gained the support of the English people and they have rallied to his standard in a way I would not have thought possible.

"I see little chance of success with the mood of the people being as it is, and much to lose by too precipitous action. But time is on my side, my lord. With my royal brother's lack of inclination toward marriage and Duke Robert's lack of steady, effective effort, I shall eventually be England's king, if God wills it. And then I shall not forget your loyalty, Lord Ranulf. But I would not have you put your life in jeopardy for me until that time, Ranulf, or have you delay indefinitely experiencing those things that would make you blessed and content. I speak specifically of the winsome Lady Aldyth, who is much too good for you, you know. Marry her speedily, Ranulf, and give her babes, or by the rood, I shall think about doing so.

Henry, Count of Avranches and the Cotentin, and perhaps someday King of England and Duke of Normandy.

She stared at the letter, especially at its audacious ending, and then looked up at her bare-chested husband.

"He is a rogue, is he not?" Ranulf said with a bittersweet smile. "That missive came by courier only this morn, but I'd already decided much the same on my own, when Henry failed to come after I'd stood ready to help him for months," he told her, running a hand through her bedruffled hair. "I will no longer put my trust in princes,

Aldyth. What a fool I was to do so, when they follow no law but their own. Though I will be pleased if Henry is our king one day, no matter who sits the throne, I intend to stay as far from court as I am allowed. You are all that matters to me, Aldyth, you and our babe.''

She caught his hand and kissed it, then pulled him down beside her. ''Ah Ranulf....'' She would be sure to make it worth his while.

* * * * *

Author Note

The ruse by which Bishop Odo rejoined the rebels behind the walls of Rochester Castle is historical fact, but they were not triumphant long. The garrison, discouraged by the summer heat, disease, swarms of flies and, above all, the lack of help from Duke Robert in Normandy, surrendered sometime in July. Their lives were spared, and they were allowed to leave with their horses and arms.

The revolt was ended soon after that. William Rufus also put down a baronial revolt in 1095.

William II, popularly called Rufus, was not England's best king, but he was probably not her worst, either. While he was irreligious and stubborn and did not provide England with an heir, he did build the magnificent Westminster Hall.

His brother Henry was, indeed, king eventually, but he had to wait eleven years, until 1100. Rufus died in a hunting accident in the New Forest while out with Henry and one Walter Tyrrel. There were whispers that it was no accident, especially after Tyrrel fled and Henry departed immediately for Winchester, seized the royal treasury and had himself crowned king. Only after he was safely crowned did he see to having Rufus's body decently buried. Duke Robert, on his way back from a crusade, returned to find his younger brother firmly on the throne.

Henry paid him a pension for six years and then defeated him in the battle of Tinchebrai. He thus gained his brother's dukedom of Normandy and kept his brother a prisoner for the last twenty-eight years of his life.

In spite of his ruthlessness, Henry had been looked upon as a great king. Called the "Lion of Justice" for his stern but fair laws, he preferred arbitration to battle. There were no baronial rebellions during Henry's reign, for Henry left no doubt as to who was king.

He married the great-niece of the English King Edward the Confessor, Edith, whom he called Matilda. They had a daughter, Matilda, and a son, William, who would have been the heir, but he drowned in the "White Ship" disaster. Henry's wife had died, too, so the aged Henry married again in hopes of an heir, but he died before Queen Adelicia could conceive. He made his headstrong daughter, Matilda, heir to his throne, but his choice was not popular and she had to contest the throne with a cousin, Stephen of Blois. Stephen seized the throne and ruled from 1135-54, but Matilda's son, Henry II, succeeded him by the terms of their treaty while Matilda still lived.